THE
AI
ANALYST

Vinnie Mirchandani
and Kimberly McDonald Baker

For information about this title, contact the publisher:
Deal Architect, Inc.
www.dealarchitect.typepad.com
vm@dealarchitect.com
+1-813-884-4908

ISBN: 979-8-9916413-1-9 (softcover)
979-8-9916413-0-2 (eBook)

Printed in the United States of America
Cover and Interior Design: 1106 Design
Editing: Mark Baven and Margaret Newman

Disclaimer

This story is a work of fiction. References to real people, events, physical establishments, organizations, and locations are utilized only to provide an illusion of authenticity and are used fictitiously. All other characters and incidents portrayed in this book are fictitious and are not to be construed as real.

Table of Contents

Dedications

To my biggest fan, my beloved husband and best friend, Brinton E. Baker. Thank you for decades of nurturing love. And to my beautiful and brilliant daughters, Heather M. Parshall and Emily E. Rancatore, whom I love beyond what words can convey.
        –Kimberly McDonald Baker

To Rita and Thomas, eight years ago I dedicated a book urging you to adopt your own R2D2 and 3CPO as you blaze trails. This is another book on the possibilities of AI and automation, and I hope you dream even bigger. It is the best time ever to be alive—make the most of it!

To the Tampa Bay area. You have been a wonderful home to our family and business for 35 years and I am pleased to share glimpses of your beauty and hospitality in the book. It should show readers that Hurricanes Helene and Milton may have dealt body blows but will not dent your spirit. Keep on inspiring!
        –Vinnie Mirchandani

Prologue

~~→

A Small yet Influential Club

Wall Street loves the "Magnificent Seven" technology stocks—Alphabet, Amazon, Apple, Meta Platforms, Microsoft, Nvidia, and Tesla. In fact, they might make up a significant part of your own investment portfolio. And for good reason: during the decade ending December 2023, these stocks' cumulative market capitalization increased more than tenfold. Their growth has been so meteoric that it has eclipsed that of even long-established, healthy technology companies like Accenture, Oracle, Salesforce, and SAP. Not that they always head north—over 5 trading days in July 2024, their collective market cap fell $1.3 trillion!

Putting Wall Street valuations aside, the Mag 7's total revenues account for only about a quarter of what the world—corporations, governments, consumers—spends on information technology. So there's still room for companies like IBM (a century old), Snowflake (a decade old), Mistral AI (barely a year old)—and thousands of other vendors. Plus, technology is now the driving force for growth in economies like China, with companies such as Alibaba, and in India, with Tata Consultancy and many others.

No wonder there is an insatiable demand for information about technology markets: tech investors check out vendor trajectories, product buyers look for a negotiation edge with vendors—and vendors seek competitive intelligence about each other. Filling this crucial demand is a small club of technology analysts. Wall Street has sell-side analysts, hedge funds have buy-side analysts, corporate buyers look for advice from industry analysts, and vendors turn to market-sizing analysts.

Analysts and their activities are highly varied. They consult, write books, present at conferences, show up on TV, and provide expert testimony in lawsuits. They travel the globe, and speak the jargon of many industries. Boutique firms and individual bloggers have led an explosion in analysis formats including videos, podcasts, tweets, and Instagram galleries.

Most analysts stick to a specialty throughout their careers. But some, like Patrick Brennan of Oxford Research, break the mold and are polymaths. He is, for now, an analyst on AI and automation, but in addition, the research labs he runs have helped law enforcement investigate and crack several crimes. His niche skills allowed him to be embedded in the investigation of the disappearance of Barry Roman, billionaire CEO of Polestar Software.

Sound like a stretch? Few outsiders know exactly what technology analysts do, only that their impact is critical.

This is a story of their world.

Section A
The Disappearance

1

AWOL

Monday am PST

In East Palo Alto, CA, multiple phone lines were ringing in Barry Roman's corner office suite. The morning sunshine streamed in the east-facing windows, but his antique mahogany desk was positioned so that the sun didn't wash out the computer monitor which displayed his jammed schedule for the day. Barry would brag that his office—which was replete with politically correct reclaimed mahogany paneling—embodied the best feng shui design principles to harmonize his energy with the surrounding environment.

Alisha Wood, Barry's tall, lively executive assistant, let the calls go to voicemail. She was busy speaking with Polestar's Chief Counsel, Maria Albright. Maria was petite, but she made up for her lack of height in brains and spunk. She was known for her bright-colored jackets with dark trousers.

Alisha told Maria: "This is not like Barry. He would never miss an earnings call like this, despite all the crap he pulls. He would never do anything to damage the Polestar name or its valuation."

Maria agreed. "He has definitely pulled some shit but this is very unlike him."

Alisha told her what she knew. "Promptly at 8:30 am, I called Barry's phone but it went into voicemail, which is now full. Then I called George, his head of home security, who told me Barry was not at home last night. He completed a long business call to India and left the house in the late evening with one of his regular security guys, Phillippe. He told the security guard at the gate that he would spend the night at Tiffany's. Phillippe was driving the black Lexus sports car."

Alisha got distracted for a second. "You know, I actually got to ride in that car for a few minutes around the parking lot with Barry. He wanted to show off. The seats are made of this incredible cashmere-soft leather and I loved the smell. It's a very limited edition so there should be no difficulty spotting it. Barry told me that Phillippe referred to the car as a sex machine and thought driving it was better than sex. Barry had snarked at him: 'Oh yeah, let's compare our experiences.' You know those two have a great relationship with Barry constantly teasing Phillippe for the excess weight he carries with his two l's and p's."

Maria interjected, "Boys and their toys."

Refocusing her attention, Alisha continued, "I then called Cocoon, the new security company and they told me that they also can't reach Phillippe. Call goes straight into voicemail. Same with Barry. They're tracking the phones. I've called the aircraft management company and I'm waiting for a callback. Also, I've told his direct reports that Barry is out sick."

"Finally, I couldn't put it off any longer." Alisha paused, and admitted she had grudgingly called Tiffany Griffin, Barry's girlfriend. "Oh my God, can you imagine how that went? She's so insecure that when she heard Barry hadn't been at home last night and also wasn't with Elizabeth, she kind of lost it. She demanded to know if I knew of other possible romantic interests. I've spoken with Tiffany a few times and it's just plain embarrassing to field her calls. However, now we know he was not with either of them."

There was a pause, and Maria observed, "I bet he's gone off on one of his jaunts, just like before. The last time this happened, he'd flown his jet to Hawaii."

Alisha corrected her. "No, the last time was when he flew to Anchorage because he wanted to watch bald eagles and catch salmon. Hawaii was the time before Alaska."

"Alaska . . . that reminds me—please try his satellite phone." Maria waited while Alisha punched in the number.

"No answer. Let me see," she said, and pulled up the satellite phone account profile on her computer. "No inbound or outbound calls for over a week."

Maria sighed in exasperation. "It's just too much. I'm so tired of his bullshit. But every time he's taken off before, we got a call by dinnertime letting us know he's fine. And each time I told him that his antics can damage our stock price—and the Board could even decide to replace him as CEO. He always just laughs and says it won't happen again."

Alisha nodded in agreement. "Okay, but each time he's gone off the grid he's reenergized when he returns, and is a sweetheart to deal with for at least a few weeks. In fact, he'd usually come back with new product ideas, and when we announced these new products, the stock price would go up."

Her cell phone rang. "Oh, the aircraft management firm is returning my call. We'll find out where he's been flying." She tapped her phone screen and said, "This is Alisha Wood."

Maria watched Alisha's expression change from annoyance to surprise, and then she ended the call. Maria raised her eyebrows to indicate, "Well?"

"His jet's in the hangar. They haven't heard from him for over a week," Alisha reported.

"Oh shit! This has never happened before," Maria said.

The phone rang again. Seeing the call was from Cocoon, Alisha put it on speakerphone. "This is Terry Osborne, CEO of Cocoon, calling to let you know that we are still unable to reach Phillippe. We're reaching out to his wife to see if she's heard anything. Also, we're checking with the other guards in Barry's detail. The sheriff has been told Barry is missing but will keep it quiet while they look for his car. Of course, the hope is that they find the car—and thus Barry. Will call you back when we have news."

Alisha thanked him and the phone went dead.

■ ■ ■

Just prior to calling Alisha, Terry had dialed Carrie Respeto, San Mateo County Sheriff. Over the years, he had come to trust her and knew she could be discreet, if needed.

8

He explained, "Barry Roman is not answering his phone and neither is the security guard. Barry has a history of running this kind of stunt. The Chairman of Polestar is a little alarmed but has decided to not let anyone know, so that Barry can return and no one would be the wiser. It would be devastating for Polestar stock if it became known he's missing."

Sheriff Respeto knew of Barry Roman and his multi-billion-dollar lifestyle. She also knew he and his wife were incredible at raising money for charity, but had not met them personally.

Terry explained, "Late yesterday evening, they left his mansion and traveled in a black Lexus LFA Nürburgring Edition sports car. Could you please issue a BOLO—'Be on the lookout'—for the car? We can send a picture of the model with its distinctive triple tailpipe, license plate number, and VIN. This Lexus model is extremely rare, so maybe it'll be easy to find. We hope that when you find the car, you'll find Barry."

Sheriff Respeto agreed to keep quiet about Barry while the police looked for the car. She ended the call with, "Terry, you owe me one."

■　■　■

There was silence for a moment, and Maria reported, "OK, the security company has contacted the police, and we are at least getting their help finding the car. There is nothing more I can do here so let me touch base with Clive. He must be feeling stressed before the earnings call. I'll let you know what I learn. Meanwhile, don't tell anyone anything other than Barry's out sick." She left the office suite to the sound of phones still ringing.

After Maria left, Alisha got herself a coffee and sat back down but was unable to put her mind on her work. She just let the phones ring and looked east out of the window in Barry's office, across the Ravenswood Open Space Preserve and the sparkling waters of San Francisco Bay. She watched commercial jets on final approach northward into the San Francisco SFO airport. Looking through the southern-facing window at the far side of the room, she watched a single-engine plane take off from the Palo Alto airport. The sky over southern San Francisco Bay was always busy with other planes from San Jose, San Carlos, Oakland, and other airports and Barry enjoyed plane watching as he sat, lost in thought. *"Where are you this time, Barry?"* Alisha asked aloud to his empty leather chair.

She felt agitated as she thought of the years she had worked for Barry and what a truly amazing person he was. She thought how the Eagles could have been thinking of Barry when they sang "Take It to the Limit."

Barry had an amazing memory, which included being able to remember song lyrics and movie trivia, and he would likely reel off the rest of that song unless you interrupted him. Actually, Barry would prefer Led Zeppelin's words as his calling card: "I am a traveler of both time and space to be where I have been."

Alisha would tease him about his taste in music—"The '70s called the switchboard looking for you." And Barry would say, "Tell that to my son who bangs on his drum kit ferociously like John Bonham. YouTube is a great teacher. Or tries to sing and synch with the drumbeat, like Don Henley." He would talk about concerts at Polestar events with Coldplay and Lady Gaga, and say, "I would love to get Taylor Swift and Luke Combs. We can't afford Taylor—yet—and most of our team is too young to appreciate the genius of 'Fast Car'."

Alisha, who shared Barry's love of music and very much hoped they could afford Taylor Swift one day, was reflecting on details of his life. You can't work for someone for years and not know all the important stuff. Barry hailed from Boynton Beach, FL, where his dad was a fireman, his mom a teacher. He was pushed hard to do well in school and to excel at all kinds of extracurricular activities like athletics, chess, music, and auto mechanics. He turned out to be a child prodigy with an interest in all kinds of machines and gadgets. He may not have been born to wealth, but at 55 years, he was still a good-looking, six-foot male, quite competent at swimming, and played an excellent game of golf. The gods had also blessed him with charisma, which both got him into trouble and out of it. He told her how he always said "yes" to his parents and then did what he wanted. She got to see this first hand in his handling of Polestar's Board of Directors. He often would say "yes" to their demands and then do what he wanted. So far, his ideas had worked and grown the company. All was forgiven.

Alisha knew she worked for a man who was both a legend in the business world and a walking encyclopedia. He also had remarkable stamina—needed only four hours of sleep, was immune to jet lag, and stayed reasonably fit, though he had shown early signs of enjoying the good life—gourmet meals, fine wine . . . and a roving eye when it came to the other sex.

He was a generous boss and while she worked long hours, he paid her very well and had helped pay off her student loans.

He was going through a nasty divorce with Elizabeth. Alisha was in awe of the amount of personal stress he was able to handle, along with the demands of being an AI CEO. Not for her. She liked her life uncomplicated.

However, she had to acknowledge that she hated to deal with his "love interests," like the call with Tiffany this morning. What is the correct protocol for dealing with a girlfriend, when your boss is not yet divorced?

As she reverted to fretting, Alisha found herself repeating, *"I'm overreacting. I'm overreacting,"* like a mantra. *"It's just Barry being Barry."* This gave way to a familiar surge of anger as she thought of all the times she had worried about Barry, and she thought, *"I'm going to kill him when I see him. I'm not his mother and he needs to start behaving."* She felt better being angry than anxious, as anxiety made her feel powerless. Better the anger as it gave her the necessary energy to cope with the day.

Alisha turned her attention to Barry's schedule and called Alejandro Lopez, catching him just in time before he came up for Barry's biweekly hair trim. Alejandro ran the hair salon in the same building, which was very convenient for male employees. He was also popular with mothers—on Saturdays, Alejandro would serve up mohawks, fades, spikes, and countless other styles which delighted young boys.

Alisha told him: "Sorry for the late notice, but I need to reschedule."

Alejandro said, "no problem." He was used to Barry's chaotic schedule, and was eternally grateful to him for the thriving business at the salon.

She calmed enough to call a couple of colleagues and casually ask if they had heard from Barry. Neither had. She continued repeating, *"It's just Barry being Barry."* She would have loved to call her longtime colleague and friend, Patrick Brennan, but remembered Maria's admonition about not calling anyone outside the company.

■ ■ ■

Patrick, meanwhile, was 3,000 miles away, in St. Petersburg, a city on a bay that also faces west, this one in Florida. He had once been a protégé of Barry's, had worked at Polestar for five years, and still considered Barry a friend and a mentor. Patrick was in his early 30s, stood a lean 6'2", and looked much more tanned since he had moved to Florida—which only masked his intensity.

He was hosting an Oxford Research offsite event. The meetings were planned for the Mesa Hall at the James Museum of Western Art in St. Pete. Oxford was headquartered in Cambridge, MA, and Patrick had joined the firm after he left Polestar. He now headed the Industry Applications group and had helped plan a coming-out party for the company's new Research and Executive Briefing Center, a short walk away overlooking the stunning mile-long waterfront. Guests would stay at the historic Vinoy Hotel, which, along with the world-famous Dali Museum, bookended the waterfront.

His wife, Maya Advani, Chief of Staff to CEO Tucker Newberry, had conducted a location analysis across four West Florida cities, and St. Pete had easily won. Maya had also helped plan the logistics and agenda for the offsite.

Patrick felt lucky to be working at the same company as his wife. As he told people who asked, "We never run out of things to talk about." Maya had kept her birth name. When introductions were made, it was always Patrick Brennan and Maya Advani. She found people often forgot that they were, in fact, married. Single men constantly hit on her, as she looked like a ravishing 5'10" Bollywood beauty. Maya was US-born, but her parents were Indian immigrants. Once she started speaking, it was obvious that she had a high IQ. As an adult, such acuity meant she took no prisoners in her business meetings. Maya had interned for Tucker for a couple of summers while at Brown University, then joined full-time and quickly worked her way up to Chief of Staff.

Oxford's analyst group was renowned for its "Golden Circle"—a bullseye positioning tool for vendors, gauged on their position within a market segment. The concentric circle in the dead center was the one every vendor coveted. Each microscopic move from one circle to the next or within a circle was eagerly awaited by vendors every six months. Vendors had a love-hate relationship with market analysts—they extensively quoted Oxford when a Golden Circle was generous to them. Conversely, they often called and bitched to Oxford's CEO, Tucker, and pleaded for him to fire one analyst or another. Among analysts, it was considered a badge of honor to earn such a request.

Today—Day Zero—was set aside for fun. Guests had a choice of three recreational activities: Golf at the PGA-class Copperhead course at the Innisbrook Resort. Time on the beach at the Don CeSar, another historic hotel on the other side of town. Or a guided tour of the Dali Museum with an immersive digital experience at the new Dali Alive dome.

Tucker played host on the golf course, Maya at the beach on the Gulf, and Patrick was assigned to the guests who chose Dali.

■ ■ ■

At Polestar, Maria walked into the office of Chairman Clive Grisham, and asked CFO Bill Swanson to join them. They were updated on the search and the hope the police would find the car. While they were all concerned, they needed to focus on the immediate matter of the upcoming earnings call.

Maria said, "We have to assume Barry will be AWOL for the earnings call today. Bill, I assume this will be a piece of cake. No earnings surprises, no major announcements. Clive, please do a quick, warm welcome as the new Chairman and let Bill do the heavy lifting and most of the Q&A.

"We technically cannot say Barry is out sick or whatever. The usual rules apply about informing the SEC and the exchanges before public disclosure. So let's not go there. Tell the moderator to screen any questions about Barry."

"By the way, is Patrick invited?" Maria asked, hoping the answer was no. Patrick would very likely ask about the absent CEO, and had an uncanny knack of knowing everything that went on at Polestar even though he had left the company several years before.

All three looked at each other knowingly. They knew Patrick referred to Patrick Thomas Edward Brennan of Oxford Research, who in his own way was probably as brilliant as Barry. Patrick was of Irish extraction, and was proud of it. His bio included a bachelor's degree from MIT, a Masters in Engineering from Stanford with a focus on robotics, and a wide variety of internships, while a student. These three knew Barry had recognized Patrick's abilities from the beginning and immediately hired him on first meeting at a Stanford alumni event.

Bill had watched Patrick's rapid rise in the company, leading to him being put in charge of the automation group, where he had greatly contributed to Polestar's growth.

Bill said, "You know Clive, Polestar owes a lot to Patrick. We would never be where we are today without his help. I know that Barry himself gives Patrick a lot of credit for the company's success."

"Yes, Bill," Clive retorted, "but not today. We don't want Patrick finding out that we don't know where Barry is."

Bill replied, "As you know, anyone can sign up for the earnings teleconference but only a few are allowed to ask questions. If Patrick slips in a question, I'll humor him and say he used up his quota at the Analyst Summit last month."

■ ■ ■

Elizabeth, Barry's wife, had a morning visit from Terry. He was invited into a sitting room that would not be out of place in an *Architectural Digest* spread. Terry could not help admiring how the room framed her beauty. He knew she was likely in her mid-40s, but must have had some very good facial work, as she did not look a day above 30. Despite no makeup and her blond hair rather messily gathered in a ponytail, he thought she looked stunning. Terry let her know that only the sheriff knew Barry was missing. She had earlier been informed by George, head of their house security, that Barry and the security guard Phillippe were missing.

"Let me see if I understand this situation correctly," Elizabeth said. "No one knows where Barry spent last night. He and Phillippe are missing. The police are looking for Barry's car. This is being kept quiet for today in the hope he will turn up and no one will know the truth. But tomorrow, if he doesn't show up, then the investors will need to be informed. Yes?"

"Correct," Terry nodded. After he left, Elizabeth decided not to tell her children, so they went off to school.

2

How Do You Solve a Problem Like Barry?

Monday pm PST

The transcript of the PLST earnings call showed it was routine, even boring. However, boring calls often have an unintended consequence—they lead to a trail of snarky text messages among Wall Street analysts and others in the field. And Grisham's "William Buckley upper class" accent became the latest object of their snark.

Charles Morgan of Sheldon Freres, a NYC bank, shot off three successive text messages. He used to be even quicker on his Blackberry, which he still missed after a slew of iPhones. Charles was a much younger brother to the legendary Robert "Captain" Morgan who in the '90s carried a pager with an easy-to-dial number: 1-800-CAPTAIN. Clients would call him at all hours to get the latest on Oracle, Peoplesoft, and other hot stocks of that era.

One text was to the head of Polestar Investor Relations: "Where's Barry?"

That was ignored.

Another went to a banking colleague: "How many single malts would wash off this dude's accent and reveal a Southern drawl?"

The answer came back instantly: "Bubba probably drinks straight bourbon."

The third was to Patrick: "Man, you know everyone at Polestar. Where have they been hiding this bloke, Clive?" This, too, was ignored. Patrick wasn't on the call.

■ ■ ■

Maria, back in her office, now gave some thought to the next day if Barry still hadn't surfaced. *"It's a miracle there were no leaks today. There has to be an official announcement from the company tomorrow, and perhaps a stop to trading activity on the stock."*

In her anxiety, she found herself chewing her nails. Everything at Polestar revolved around Barry. She admired how he had come from a modest background, and had scored a scholarship to Embry-Riddle Aeronautical University, then transferred to the University of Florida where his social skills blossomed at a fraternity, and earned an MBA at Stanford. The "Legend That Is Barry" started at Stanford, where he teamed up with a couple of geeks at the engineering school and cofounded a software startup when the technology market was transitioning away from mainframes in the '90s. It was even more fortunate that his fellow cofounders were bought out cheaply at the very beginning, before they achieved any great success.

He had vision and while most technology companies liked to stay in the platform-and-tools market, Barry also expanded into applications (despite many naysayers), particularly those for vertical industry markets. Maria had often heard him tell Wall Street analysts that while these verticals are relatively smaller markets, they are sticky. "My customers are guaranteed cash flow for at least 20 years," he would say. She and many others recognized that this was a central insight helping to fuel his meteoric career in technology.

So, what do you do with a maverick who is so inspiring and yet so exasperating? *"Watch yourself,"* she scolded, as she thought of those who probably blurted out the words inspired by a famous namesake song, "How do you solve a problem like Maria?" Putting on her jacket, Maria decided it was time to go home. She felt like she had been run over by a truck.

■ ■ ■

Patrick had hoped he could slip away back to Oxford's office and tweak slides for the offsite. Or perhaps dial in to the Polestar earnings call. He didn't get to do either. Instead, he met up with his guests at the Dali Museum where they were getting a private tour which Maya had arranged. It was an "adults only" tour which covered aspects of Dali's life that would not be suitable for young ears. For example, the guide delved into some of the sexual symbolism found in Dali's art, which was quite fascinating to all. Patrick admitted to his guests that he would not be comfortable having a Dali in his house. He found many of the pictures unsettling and while he enjoyed the tour, he was happy to leave the art in a museum. He also pondered on the artist's self-definition as "the most paradoxical, eccentric, and concentric person in the world." This technology-savvy group loved the multisensory experience at the dome with projections on the ceiling, the walls, and the floors. Many admired the museum's structure, which featured over a thousand pieces of glass designed to withstand hurricanes, and an artistic rendition of a spiral staircase to nowhere. No wonder the building itself was called the Enigma.

■ ■ ■

Maya hosted 15 of the offsite guests who picked the beach option. Her bronze beauty and her tall, slender frame really stood out in a bathing suit. She had arranged day pool and spa passes at the Don CeSar, the century-old "Pink Palace" on the Gulf. Guests enjoyed the pools, the white sands, and the azure sea. Some hung out at the tiki bar, and others went jet skiing.

During her scouting visits as part of the Florida location search, Maya had negotiated a group rate for Oxford with the general manager at the Vinoy. When first negotiating with the manager, she had jokingly asked, "How about $7 a night?" In the '70s, when the hotel (along with the city) had hit rock bottom, rooms could be had at that trivial rate—a far cry from the $25 it commanded in 1925. And far less than the additional $150 you would pay if you stayed with a pet these days. The manager explained to Maya the extensive renovations and rebranding she had overseen over the last few years. Maya committed to 500 nights over the next year, and got a sweet deal that included suites for the Oxford execs. All the offsite guests stayed there. No pets were invited!

■ ■ ■

After the golf, the beach, and the Dali, the guests got changed in their rooms at the Vinoy and proceeded to dinner. The group included all the analysts and research staff, as well as six client executives—three from vendors (including Polestar) and three from user organizations. These executives each sat at the head of a table and chatted with Oxford folks about their IT projects and market intelligence needs. There was lots of chatter about Generative AI in particular though most shortened it to GenAI.

After dinner, Tucker kicked off the proceedings. He had founded Oxford Research almost 30 years ago and had watched it grow to its present dominating position of helping IT professionals making technology decisions. He was in his early 60s, with a full head of silver hair and a build some would call wiry. In his youth, he had been a marathon runner. Even now, he could play 18 holes of golf, no matter how hot the weather. The Florida sun had not bothered him today and he was ready for a full evening of entertaining his guests. He announced that the theme for the offsite was "Back to the Future." Tonight would focus on the past, and the next morning would emphasize the present. After a breakfast panel with the six customer executives, the rest of the offsite would consist of presentations and breakouts about the future.

After those introductory remarks, Patrick and Martha Weingarten, the longtime head of research, hosted Tucker in a fireside chat. He and Martha informally reminisced about the dawn of the analyst industry in the '70s and its maturation in the '80s.

Tucker described how customers back then did not really understand the power of data processing, as IT was called back then. He described how a group of strategy consulting firms—Arthur D. Little, Index, Nolan Norton, and others—had focused on the economics of technology and how it could bring corporations operational efficiencies. Business school professors started to highlight the opportunity to use technology for competitive advantage. The business model for these consulting firms was project-based—putting in long days at the client's site, crunching lots of numbers, and presenting hundreds of slides. "Boy, did we have executive access!" Tucker exclaimed. "I spent many weekends working with CEOs of the largest corporations in the world—often at their beach houses."

Martha then explained how analyst firms like IDC and Dataquest focused more on market sizes and shares, which particularly interested vendors. Others, like Forrester and Gartner, served more of a corporate buyer market.

She explained how the analyst model, in contrast to management consultants, was more of a blended publishing and advisory model. It wasn't unusual for an analyst to handle

1,000 client calls a year where they were asked about a piece of technology or outsourcing service. Some overachievers could brag they did 2,000 calls per annum. With so many data points, the analysts had their finger on the pulse of the market. They could also speak credibly to vendors about market trends.

And analysts were encouraged to be provocative. Martha said, "I have mentored a number of analysts throughout my career. Good analysts have two qualities—they are both curious and skeptical. If you don't have those traits in the fast-changing technology world, then go get another job." One of her favorite expressions, even today, was "Sacred cows make the best hamburgers." She described how she once tore apart a vendor presentation: "You are allowed to be stupid or lazy, but not both." She said she had a third expectation of vendors, which she would share at her dinner table in the coming evening.

Tucker and Martha discussed the Gartner IPO in 1993 that literally made hundreds of analysts, overnight millionaires. It led to a glowing *New York Times* article, from which Martha read a quote: "Gartner may well be the richest publishing house in the world—a 'mini-Microsoft' in its field."

Patrick had been worried that the audience would be bored with this walk down memory lane. Then he saw that even the youngest analysts were listening closely. Few of them knew much about the history and evolution of the technology analyst profession.

Martha said, "But that was decades ago. If you put today's enterprise applications on a grid of industries and countries, Gartner today barely covers 25 percent. And they

24

have nowhere near the access they once enjoyed to the technology buyer. They make vendors fill out long surveys for their Magic Quadrants (their equivalent of Oxford's Golden Circle). Vendors, in turn, use a cottage industry of 'analyst relations' advisers who coach them how to game their responses. It's become formulaic—and analysts still cling to application categories which have been around for decades."

Tucker summarized, "So we need to catch up to the velocity of change in business, not just technology. Clients don't want to merely read our research and talk to us on Zoom calls. They want customized advice. They still want it in bite-sized chunks, not long projects. But they want us to present it coherently. Nothing annoys them more than being handed off from one analyst to another. They have complex problems and they want us to respond accordingly.

"We also need to recognize that there are other critical markets we should be analyzing. The Russian invasion of Ukraine showed us we will be dependent on hydrocarbons for a long time. How do we use fossil fuels while neutering their emissions? We should be able to talk authoritatively about carbon capture and storage, and about the total cost of ownership of electric vehicles. Honestly, if I was starting my career today, I would join an energy research firm. Or a healthcare research firm. In the US, nearly a quarter of our GDP is spent on our health and yet our outcomes are miserable.

"Or look at how the world is changing. So many emerging countries are becoming the 'new world.' They're growing much quicker than the US, EU, China, and Japan. We have an opportunity to help multinationals rebalance their global portfolios and help customers in those fast-growing economies.

I don't want to steal his thunder, but Patrick will talk more about these new horizons tomorrow.

"Don't get me wrong. IT, especially AI, will keep us busy for a long time. But it was such an invigorating time that Martha and I experienced in the '80s and '90s. There's no reason we cannot recreate that excitement again, in a variety of new directions. The technology world today feels like it did back then."

■ ■ ■

Clive sat at his desk, having finished his first Polestar earnings call as Chairman. He wondered if he had signed up to babysit Barry. It's one thing to sit on the Board, but that's totally different from trying to control the uncontrollable.

Clive admired what Barry had done with Polestar. How could he not? Polestar was an exciting company that had developed an ecosystem of robotics, drones, sensors, and now AI solutions. He had liked being on the Board but now as Chairman, he was already starting to have his doubts.

He knew the Board had essentially forced him on Barry. Actually, Polestar's rapid growth and going public had done so. It had attracted several large investors, who pushed for representation on the Board. Barry treated the Directors as he had his parents. He'd say "yes" to most of them, and then go do his own thing. It helped that he and Elizabeth, together, owned a controlling portion of company stock.

The investors pushed for a strong Chairman to both mentor and monitor Barry. Barry had made an impassioned presentation to the Board: "I welcome a strong Chairman,

I really do. But please make sure he isn't so "woke" that he confuses our company's mission. Too many companies have gotten sucked into the Diversity, Equity, and Inclusion (DEI) noise and forgotten about their core customer demographic. You can have black, white, brown, gay, trans, and whatever else employees. Our mission is to make each of them a superworker. Tell our Chairman to stay out of DEI politics."

Clive agreed with Barry's DEI position, at least to begin with, but started to put other guardrails around the CEO. It started with a new security detail. They hired Cocoon, the new executive security firm which had specific guidelines and instructions—take different routes every day, use decoys, report unplanned stops or even rerouting requested by Barry. However, they did not count on Barry's charm and how he chose two of the bodyguards as his preferred drivers. They did not always follow Cocoon's policies.

Clive also told Barry to hire a pilot and not fly on his own. That prompted Barry to complain to a couple of directors about Clive's "schoolmarm" ways and ask if there would soon be a curfew. One of the directors counseled him: "We're spending on you only a fraction of what BlackRock spends on Fink's security and Tesla on Elon's. Imagine how stifling you'd find that." Barry responded simply, "I miss startup world."

Relieved that the earnings call had been uneventful, Clive hunched his shoulders and thought about the tension over Barry's expense reports. His expenses were legendary, especially when you heard the anecdotes which accompanied them. Like the time when Barry took a group to a fancy restaurant and passed around a box of Cuban cigars. He had bought it for the equivalent of $3,000 and slipped them through US Customs. The maître d' noticed, and politely whispered in Barry's ear: "Not while you are in here, please." As dessert and port were being served, the maître d' noticed Barry smoking his cigar. He ran to the table and this time, not so discreetly, screamed at Barry: "Not in my house!" Barry quietly asked him to look around. Every table had someone holding a cigar, as Barry had given the box to one of his staff to pass around.

Clive prided himself on always being polite and rarely using profanity. It offended him that Barry could be rude and crude with his sales team, and quote the Leonardo DiCaprio character from *The Wolf of Wall Street*: "I've been a rich man, and I've been a poor man. And I choose rich every fucking time." And the Alec Baldwin character in *Glengarry Glen Ross*: "First prize is a Cadillac El Dorado. Anyone wanna see second prize? Second prize is a set of steak knives. Third prize is you're fired."

But Barry would also remind his staff what a privilege it was to deal with Polestar customers. His motto was, "Keep Wall Street happy, but make it extremely easy for our customers to do business with us." Barry would never fail to point out to his sales team how easy he had made it for retailers to contract their warehouse bots. "Not everyone is an Amazon and needs large distribution centers. We saw a growth in smaller warehouses located close to customer demand. I told Swanson to offer our bots as-a-service, and deliver as few as five as a start. Then seasonally we would deliver five or 10 or 15 more bots, as their customer demand spiked. Customers loved this flexibility, and it was one of our most successful product introductions." Clive also knew that one Christmas, Barry had sent each of his salespeople a tree ornament embossed with a well-known quote attributed to Gandhi: "A customer is the most important visitor on our premises. He is not dependent on us. We are dependent on him. He is not an interruption on our work. He is the purpose of it. He is not an outsider to our business. He is a part of it. We are not doing him a favor by serving him. He is doing us a favor by giving us an opportunity to do so."

How do you solve a puzzle like Barry? Clive hummed under his breath.

■ ■ ■

Meanwhile, not far from the Oxford offsite, Tony Batista and Jimmy Mancuso were catching up. Tony was a procurement executive at Sheldon Freres, a Polestar customer, in a different department than the analyst, Charles. His dinner companion was his childhood friend, Jimmy. The two had grown up as neighbors and young hoods in New Jersey. Tony had cleaned up and gone into corporate life, and Jimmy had moved to Tampa, where he was into real estate but rumored to still have mob connections. Their childhood friendship had endured over a common passion for baseball and steaks. They would meet at least twice a year at NY Yankees and Tampa Bay Rays games and combine those with meals at Lugers and Berns, respectively. Berns was reputed to have the largest wine list in the world. In the past, this list used to be tethered to each table, as it had become a collector's item for patrons. Tony tried his darnedest to get Jimmy to try out New York's culinary bounty, but Lugers it was, without fail.

"You're not your usual self," Jimmy remarked.

"I'm about to take a big haircut on my annual bonus thanks to this asshole in California," Tony said.

"Tell me about it."

"Do you buy generic drugs?"

"Of course I do—who doesn't?"

"When drug patents expire," Tony explained, "a new set of pharma companies take the formula and make them much cheaper. That doesn't happen in software, even after decades. Our bank proactively went to what is called a third-party maintenance provider for support of a very old software product which is hardly getting any improvements. Saved our company 50 percent for two years. Then Barry, the CEO of the software company, sued the provider. My CFO says they can't include the savings in the bonus calculation till the lawsuit is settled. Shit, that could take three fucking years! I ain't waiting!

"And last year, this bastard from Polestar—that's the company—invoked an inflation clause on a few key products they'd acquired and jacked up our prices by 15 percent. Wiped out all my other IT savings. As you know, my bonus depends on the savings I deliver, and Polestar is one of those companies where I never appear to show any savings."

Tony stopped and smiled. "But we may have caught the SOB with his hands in our cookie jar. We think they are illegally using our banking data to train their AI machines. So, at the moment, our attorneys are very quietly looking into it. The plan is that the settlement we're after will require them to retroactively match the third-party maintenance pricing, and lower the inflation uptick."

"How long will your negotiations take?" Jimmy asked. "A while."

Jimmy snapped. "What the fuck happened to you? Think back to when we were young. Would you have let someone stiff you three times in a row? This is your boy's future he is stealing. You know I'm *il padrino* to the young man."

Jimmy was spiritual Godfather to Tony's son, Michael, who had been born with a lifetime disability. He knew that Tony's wife, Connie, was frequently in therapy as she still blamed herself for her son's state. Worse, Tony was always financially stressed with the enormous cost of care, including frequent modifications to their house as Michael grew. He was continuously challenged to contribute to a fund meant to support Michael once he and his wife passed. At their regular meetings, Jimmy would pass him a large envelope filled with notes. Tony would just hand them to his wife.

One time, Tony could not find his jacket as he went through security at the airport. When he found it, he noticed the envelope had been opened. He counted the notes: there were ninety-five $100 bills. Somebody must have helped themselves to the rest, he figured. Perhaps someone who needed cash for Lugers where they did not take cards?

Tony thought to himself: *"Glad I'm not flying overseas. It would not have looked good for a bank executive to be flying with $10,000 in undeclared cash."*

As a senior bank executive, Tony really should have asked the questions: "Why does Jimmy carry so much cash around all the time? What kind of business is he in?"

Ignorance, in this case, was bliss.

Jimmy's next comments prompted more concern.

"Allow me to send one of my young delivery boys to pay your hotshot CEO a visit. Paulie is a cool kid. Pretty smooth. He handles some of my troublemaker tenants. You'll relate to him—he's also a techie. My IT manager, in fact."

Tony burst out laughing. "Jimmy, we're not talking about your Microsoft Office and Norton Antivirus scale here."

Jimmy responded, "OK, big shot. Leave it to me. I'll keep you out of it. We'll deliver him a message—very professionally."

Tony insisted, "No thanks! Please stay out of it. Seriously."

■ ■ ■

For the rest of the day, everyone at Polestar in the know about Barry's disappearance kept silent, hoping each phone call would reveal he had been found. The security company had no news. The police had no news. Barry's disappearance had not yet made the news. That was the only good thing to say about the day.

Tuesday would be worse. Far worse.

3

Who Exactly Is This Patrick Fella?

~~→

Tuesday am PST

Lenny Jr. sat on top of the picnic table at his campsite, smoking his first cigarette of the day and listening to bird-song at Uvas Canyon County Park on the northwest side of Morgan Hill, CA. His backpacking tent and sleeping bag were packed up and waiting on the ground next to him. Sunrise peered through the trees surrounding him. A blue-and-gray California scrub-jay sat on a branch nearby—Lenny's only company in the campground on this early Tuesday morning.

"You look like you're in a Detroit Lions uniform, bird," Lenny said to it. "Today is my 91st day of sobriety, and I'm telling you, just for today, I'm not gonna drink." The bird looked at Lenny, and tilted its head while the man continued. "I'm gonna drive to Redding today, and get there in time to hit the barber. You want to come along for the ride?"

He lit a fresh cigarette from the stub in his mouth. A gust of wind disturbed the bird and it flew away. "Story of my life, bird!" Lenny muttered, tossing the cigarette stub on the ground.

He fought off tears. *"Can't believe Dad's really gone. Thank God we don't have to pay to bury him, though. Uncle Sam's final token for ruining his life in Vietnam,"* he thought. *"But I'm not going to cry over that sorry son of a bitch,"* he silently instructed himself.

His sister had emailed him photos of the Northern California Veterans Cemetery. It was nicely kept, with rows of gravestones evenly spaced and marble walls with precisely cut niche markers. Big Leonard had already been cremated and the family would gather to put his urn in one of those niches tomorrow.

Aching for a drink to help numb the sorrow that at times felt overwhelming, Lenny took a final drag on his second cigarette, dropped it to the ground and absentmindedly stepped on it. He then carried his gear to the campground parking lot and packed it in the back of an old Jeep Wrangler that hadn't seen a car wash in some time. A stream of dust trailed behind the Jeep for a brief moment until it dispersed in the gusty wind, as Lenny made his way toward Highway 101 northbound.

Lost in grief and memories, and envisioning the honor guard ceremony Big Leonard would receive the next day, Lenny reached Redding in six hours. By then the fire in Uvas Canyon park had spread north of the campground, jumped the Uvas-Carnero creek and was trespassing into the Upper Uvas Creek Open Space Preserve, with its fire fuel as far as the eye could see.

. . .

Alisha exited the secure elevator to the CEO suite, where Maria was waiting for her. They had spoken a couple of times during the previous evening but there had been no news of Barry. Alisha felt exhausted as she had not slept well. Maria also looked tired.

"I saw your meeting request for a 7:30 am C-level meeting, but I don't think we gave catering enough notice to bring in breakfast," Alisha said.

"Sit down," Maria said, closing and locking the outer office doors, and then closing the inner doors for sound protection. Alisha sat on one of the sofas in the reception area. "I received a call from the San Mateo County Sheriff. They found Barry's car in a ravine off Woodside Road, with his dead bodyguard. No sign of Barry. The Sheriff has called the FBI."

"Holy shit," Alisha said. She thought she might faint. It was good that she had sat down. Maria, looking rather pale herself, continued. "There's not much information at the moment and they'll give us the details as soon as they can. The Chairman already knows and will be here in a moment. They are also sending someone to inform Elizabeth."

Alisha started to shiver, and said, "Yesterday, I was so convinced that he would eventually show up that I wanted to kill him for causing all this fuss and being so reckless. Also, even this morning, I was concerned that we didn't have time to order breakfast. Now who cares?"

Once Alisha regained her composure, Maria counseled her. "The only thing you are authorized to say to anyone is 'No comment.' We're following the manual to the letter," she said, handing Alisha a Crisis Management Plan binder. "In a few minutes I'll explain more, in the meeting."

"Wow, just wow" Alisha muttered, wondering if she was awake or having a terrible dream. She stood up and went to her desk in the waiting room of Barry's office, set down her tote bag, and looked through the open door to see his desk exactly as she left it the day before. Alisha imagined Barry, with bloody injuries and amnesia, wandering around the hilly terrain of Woodside, looking for help. *"How can this be real? That man is surely larger than life. God, please help him,"* she thought.

■ ■ ■

Elizabeth had the police visit her shortly after 7:00 am that morning. She appeared in her dressing gown to the officers, a man and a woman. They had her sit down and explained that Barry's car had been found in a ravine. The security guard was dead and there was no sign of Barry. The police were organizing a search and the FBI had been alerted. At this time, they had no more information for her. Elizabeth's shock froze her face into what the police officers interpreted as a cold and uncaring expression.

The female police officer leaned over and gently asked if she had anyone she could call for support. Elizabeth told the officers about her best friends Emily Rancatore and Theresa

Clark, then quickly called them and received assurances that they would be over soon. The police left when they saw she had supportive staff in the house and that her friends were on the way. She refused their help in breaking the news to her children.

What to do about the kids? Julian, 15 years old and Jennifer, turning 13 were both ready for school. Jennifer was demanding he turn down his music which she said sounded like "cats wailing." He was about to respond in kind when Elizabeth called them into the room. She explained that their dad was missing. They immediately came over to her and sat with her on either side. It all went very quiet. Max, the lab, came by and leapt on Julian. Elizabeth, her arms around all three of them, thought of how wonderful it would be to see Barry walk in and complete the family. She had to admit, it was never the same without him.

Elizabeth told them: "You don't need to go to school. I'll call the school to settle the matter. The police are doing everything possible to find your dad. Please don't discuss your dad being missing with anyone outside the three of us. Polestar needs to make an official announcement before you can share news with friends. I have Emily and Theresa coming over, so I have support. There's no need to worry about me. We just have to wait for the police to give us further news."

Julian and Jennifer headed off to breakfast, to be followed with video games. For once, Elizabeth felt very grateful for those time-wasters. Even Max could not compete for the kids' attention.

Emily and Theresa arrived within the hour, and thus began the long wait.

．．．

This momentous day was a sharp contrast to the evening, a month earlier, when the chandeliers in Elizabeth's dressing room reflected off the three-sided full—length mirror that showcased Emily. Seated at her antique dressing table, Elizabeth wore a peach silk bathrobe as she finished curling her hair in preparation for the Save Breasts, Save Lives charity fundraiser. Elizabeth had vowed never to bring in professional hair and makeup stylists again, after previously hired stylists had sold photos and information about her to gossip blogs.

At $10,000 per ticket, the gala was one of the most expensive fundraisers in Silicon Valley, and the proceeds funded breast cancer research, primarily at the University of Michigan, Elizabeth's alma mater. As Chair of the foundation hosting the fundraiser, Elizabeth was intent on maintaining her usual role at the event. Barry loved this party and refused to step back from his traditional co-speaker position when Elizabeth had asked. So, acrimonious divorce filing or not, Mr. and Mrs. Barry Roman would take the stage together.

"We're running late, let me finish your eyes, Betsey," said Theresa, the third of the 'triple trouble trio' from their college days in the Zeta Tau Alpha house at UM. "Betsey" was the nickname only Elizabeth's husband and two best friends were allowed to use. With over two decades of shared history, Theresa, Emily, and Elizabeth knew everything about each other and were as dependable and loyal as the best family members. They had attended fraternity tailgate parties every Saturday during football season in Ann Arbor, were bridesmaids in each other's weddings, and knew they could safely vent among themselves without any fear that secrets wouldn't be kept. And until Barry took up with Tiffany and moved into the new estate that had originally been planned as a family home, their husbands—Phil Rancatore, Marc Clark, and Barry Roman—had always enjoyed each other's company.

While Elizabeth looked into the makeup mirror and blinked her freshly applied lashes, Emily said, "If you had a date for this year's gala, it might make Barry think."

"I don't care what Barry does. I'm not going to show my kids that it's okay to date while you're married." Turning to her friends, Elizabeth asked, "What kind of man does this? Flaunts his girlfriend at the charity event he and his wife founded, when he's not divorced yet! Subjects his wife and children to embarrassing public scrutiny and humiliation!" Elizabeth's voice was getting louder, the "eleven" lines between her eyebrows showing.

"When Barry had those flings in the past, he was discreet. The kids never knew, even though I did. But now he's parading around town with that woman, with no conscience, or concern for our children!

"You know what it's like, every time I see tears in my kids' eyes, or they try to pretend their day at school was fine but then I hear that both of them are being taunted by their little shit classmates? It's like being stabbed between the ribs and into my heart." Elizabeth sprayed hairspray over her hair for what seemed like a full minute.

Pausing for a few seconds to let the hairspray settle, Emily reached out and gently squeezed Elizabeth's hand, her eyes soft with empathy.

39

Trying to lighten the mood in the room, Theresa starting singing along to the college-era music playing in the background.

Elizabeth slipped on a cream-colored silk satin dress, Grecian style, with a deep V neckline, exposing her cleavage while also looking classically elegant. "I love this dress," she said. But in contrast to the smooth cream silk, Elizabeth's skin was flushed, her jaw tight, her expression still angry.

"It would be so much easier on us if Barry just died," Elizabeth stated in a suddenly quiet voice. She twirled in front of the mirror in the satin dress and admired herself. "If he just crashed his plane. Or a Great White ate him while he was surfing off Maverick's. Or if he had a heart attack while fucking his whore—that would be justice."

With her lips pressed into a line, Theresa raised her eyebrows at Emily, and spoke calmly, still trying to derail the thought train Elizabeth was on. "Sweetheart, you don't mean that. It's the betrayal speaking. Wishing him dead won't erase your hurt."

"I wish he would just die, vanish from our lives so we wouldn't have to go through this agony."

"Doesn't everyone who's going through a divorce think that?" Emily interjected, trying to allay Elizabeth's dark mood, while she and Theresa looked alarmed. "How are you going to stand on a stage with him and deliver a speech tonight? I think you should call your therapist."

"Seriously, Betsey, you sound like a psycho," Theresa agreed.

Elizabeth smiled and said, "Ah, but I look like an angel in this dress."

The three women stood looking at each other for a moment.

A knock on the bedroom door was a welcome interruption. "Come in," Elizabeth called out, and Malosi, her 6'4" Tongan bodyguard, opened the door. "It's almost six; how long until we leave?" he asked.

"Fifteen minutes, gorgeous," replied Theresa with a wink.

Thirty minutes later, adorned in the $20,000 cream silk evening gown and two million dollars of jewelry, Elizabeth was sitting in the back of a VPAM 6 level armored limousine, with Malosi in the front seat next to Steve, the driver. Elizabeth had trusted Steve and Malosi with her life and, more important, her children's lives, for many years.

Elizabeth especially enjoyed Malosi's sense of humor. He always knew when she was tense and, unlike many bodyguards who were seen and not heard, he'd interject a smart-ass comment at unexpected but perfect moments. Holding her favorite diamond necklace away from her chest, she amused herself by admiring the colors that reflected in the stones and the sparkle they spread around the limousine interior.

Emily and Theresa were seated across from Elizabeth. Emily was crooning along to Ed Sheeran's sultry voice: singing "The shape of you" while Theresa poured three glasses of Cristal champagne.

The song brought back memories. Elizabeth realized she was wearing lipstick, which she used to apply just before leaving the limousine. She remembered how Barry frequently liked to put up the limo's solid black divider and get very friendly on the way to events. The challenge had always been not messing up her hair and makeup, and ensuring her dress was fully zipped before stepping out of the car. Steve never told them that the divider didn't muffle noise as much as they thought it did.

Now, looking out the windows, Elizabeth felt very alone as she noticed the rolling hills of vegetation were straw-yellow on both sides of I-280. As the car merged onto I-92 westbound toward Half Moon Bay, Elizabeth said, "Guys, let's open the windows for a bit. I want to smell the Eucalyptus trees after we pass the reservoir. I need that breath of serenity."

"That's okay," Malosi said to Steve, who rolled down the back windows.

"So refreshing!" Elizabeth said after inhaling the gorgeous aroma of the tall trees with their long, thin, pointed leaves, silvery trunks, and peeling bark.

"They're an invasive species and a fire hazard," Malosi interjected, and Elizabeth rolled her eyes.

"Buzz kill," Theresa retorted, raising her champagne glass toward him in a mock toast.

On Miramontes Point Road, Half Moon Bay police officers checked IDs and gala tickets of everyone in each car that passed South Maple Avenue. Anyone not on the official event guest list was ordered to turn around using the small parking lot reserved for access to the California Coastal Trail. The trail was closed for the day, with armed security patrolling the trails and beach south and north of the resort.

A half-dozen residents of the Cañada Cove Mobile Home Park, a community for senior citizens with a long waitlist for lots, sat in folding lawn chairs at the park's entrance on Cañada Cove Avenue, watching the parade of limousines and high-end cars pass them on Miramontes Point Road. "Our taxes are paying to protect these rich assholes," said long-time resident and former history teacher Alan Jacobson, in between sips of canned Budweiser. "But who do we complain to? No one listens to poor folks like us."

"Poor?" replied retired social worker Sarah Skylar. "People who can afford to pay $1,400 a month just for a lot rental are not poor. Anyplace else and we'd be solidly middle class! This park has been here since that whole Ocean Colony sub was a farm, and decades before that Ritz-Carlton was even a dream. That hotel ruined the down-to-earth culture of Half Moon Bay."

Inside an unbadged Mercedes-Maybach inching along Miramontes Point Road on its way to the Ritz, invisible behind blackened windows, two couples were discussing the seniors gathered across the street in Canada Cove. "Can you imagine living in a tin can on cinder blocks, with nothing better to do than watch the one-percenters drive by, wishing for a glimpse of one of us? I couldn't do it. I'd have to kill myself."

Meanwhile the occupants of Elizabeth's limousine had traveled south on CA-1, and turned right on Fairway Drive, into the gated Ocean Colony neighborhood, to avoid Miramontes Point Road entirely. Today the subdivision's gate was manned by multiple security guards. Steve opened his window and presented a document. "Elizabeth Roman, for the breast cancer event," he said. A security guard raised his hand over his head to signal another security guard inside the gate. The limo proceeded on Fairway Drive until its end at the parking deck of the Ritz-Carlton Half Moon Bay.

Elizabeth's cell phone rang. "Twenty minutes now, Mrs. Roman," said the voice of Dr. Peter Sparano, the foundation director. Escorted by Malosi, Elizabeth emerged from the car and entered the staff entrance to the hotel, followed by her girlfriends.

In the ballroom on the ground floor of the hotel, guests were enjoying appetizers and taking advantage of the top-shelf bar. Photographers stood just inside each entrance, snapping couples as they arrived. A video camera was focused on the stage, which was decorated to the theme of "Wish Upon a Star." A large, lighted crystal star hung over center stage, with smaller stars suspended throughout the room, their internal LED lights shining through the crystal to bounce a rainbow of colors off walls, tables, and guests' jewelry. The volume of conversation was very loud, evidence that most in the room had consumed a few drinks already.

"Good evening, ladies and gentlemen, please take your seats." Speakers broadcast the banquet manager's voice above the din in the ballroom.

Emily and Theresa walked down the hall to the main elevator bank, while Elizabeth and her bodyguard took the service elevator to the ballroom level. When the service elevator door opened, a security guard nodded and led the way to a door behind the stage. Elizabeth walked through the door, saw her estranged husband with his usual bodyguard, and took a shaky breath. She still thought Barry was gorgeous, and she saw his eyes scanning her from head to foot.

"You look good enough to eat," they said to each other at the same time, continuing a decade-long inside joke that they had repeated every time they prepared to take a stage together. In spite of herself, Elizabeth laughed, relaxing; genuine smiles spread across both of their faces. Barry straightened the diamond necklace glimmering above Elizabeth's cleavage, then leaned in and whispered suggestively in her ear, surprising her.

The two bodyguards looked at each other but kept their expressions blank.

Behind the stage's black draping, a sound technician handed a wireless microphone to Elizabeth, who carefully clipped it to the neckline of her dress and tucked the small, accompanying box into a hidden pocket in the skirt's side seam, while Barry fastened his own microphone. For lesser mortals, the sound technicians would help clip on the microphones, but the Romans' bodyguards never let sound technicians touch them.

"Shall I kick it off now?" Dr. Sparano asked gently. Elizabeth nodded. As the director took the stage, Elizabeth rotated her shoulders while she waited, inhaling Barry's familiar after-shave, until she heard "Please join me in welcoming the foundation cofounders, Chairwoman Elizabeth Roman and Barry Roman!"

As the applause sounded, Barry placed his hand on Elizabeth's elbow and they walked through the overlapped black curtains and proceeded downstage. After several seconds, the room grew quiet.

Elizabeth began by welcoming the attendees. "Good evening and thank you for joining us at the seventh annual Save Breasts, Save Lives gala. Tonight, we gather as a united front in the battle against breast cancer—a cause that, over the past seven years, has been significantly propelled forward by your generosity. To date, we have raised an astounding $75 million, a testament to what we can achieve when we channel our resources and commitment toward a common goal. Barry and I established this foundation because this disease hit close to home. And I'm not talking about the fact that everyone knows Barry loves breasts." Elizabeth paused because the room erupted into laughter. Barry looked at Elizabeth in surprise, not expecting she would make him the butt of a joke. He wrinkled his eyes, put his hand on his heart and mouthed "Ooooh," as though he were wounded, then broke into laughter.

After the audience settled down, Barry spoke. "I lost my wonderful mother to breast cancer, and the world lost a great light. So I said to Elizabeth, 'Let's change the world and give hope to others.'" Barry paused, took a deep breath. "And all of you are making that vision a reality. Because breast cancer research is more than a pursuit of medical advancement; it's a beacon of hope for millions. As you will hear from our keynote speaker, we stand on the cusp of breakthroughs that not only enhance our understanding of this complex disease but also revolutionize the way we diagnose, treat, and, hopefully one day, prevent it altogether."

Elizabeth continued, "Breast cancer still kills over 40,000 American women each year. Many fight the battle against cancer in silence, but tonight, we give the battle a voice. We give it our attention and the funding it critically needs. Our contributions fuel the tireless efforts of scientists and doctors, enabling them to evolve cancer care and treatment."

Barry resumed, "As we continue to support this vital research, we're investing in a future where every diagnosis is met with a viable treatment plan and a cure. Every contribution helps, no matter the size—but hopefully large because you can all afford it," and again the audience laughed for several seconds. Then Barry closed his portion of the speech by being Barry. "Remember, breasts aren't just for ogling, they're for saving!" Once again, the audience laughed.

"There he is, ladies and gentlemen, the Barry Roman you know and love!" Elizabeth exclaimed. Applause filled the room as Barry put his arm around Elizabeth's waist and they bowed to the crowd.

As the attendees applauded, Barry and Elizabeth stepped to center stage directly under the hanging star and posed together for photos, with Barry's hand on Elizabeth's lower back. Their smiles were authentic, and many in the crowd wondered if their divorce was as bitter as they'd heard. All appeared to be cordial, but a silent fury was storming inside Barry's girlfriend. "I don't care if it's to make him look charming, how dare he touch that old hag!" Tiffany thought.

Dr. Sparano then turned his microphone back on and said, "Now I ask you to welcome our keynote speaker, Dr. Sofia Sapientiais from the University of Michigan, who will tell you how her team is using your money to save breasts, and more important, save lives!"

After handing the microphones off backstage, Barry said to Elizabeth: "That was a blast! We still got it."

It was Elizabeth's turn to whisper to Barry. "Let's go tear each other's clothes off like we used to," she said.

"I can't just leave Tiffany here, that would make me a jerk," he whispered back.

Humiliated once again, Elizabeth's jaw tightened as she displayed a large, forced smile while she looked down and her false lashes hid the stinging tears that were suddenly threatening her eyes.

Malosi began to steer her toward the ballroom, but Elizabeth said quietly: "Take me home."

With Steve and Malosi in the front seat, Elizabeth stretched out in the back and practiced deep breathing, slowly regaining her composure as the car wound through I-92 eastbound. Her cell phone rang only once before she answered it and she heard Emily asking, "Where did you go? I thought we were going to show everyone how much fun we're having without Barry?"

"I thought I could do that, but I can't. But you guys have fun, and tell me all about it tomorrow."

"Well, we're here at your table with our studly hubbies, eating this fabulous food and playing hostess in your absence. We're having a great time and I don't plan on leaving until my feet hurt from dancing. I promise we'll tell you all the details after I regain consciousness in the morning," Emily said. Elizabeth heard Phil's robust laughter in the background as she ended the call.

Nearby, Tiffany kept looking toward Elizabeth's table. "Where's that bitch, isn't she going to sit down and stuff her old face with dinner?" she wondered, while turning back toward Barry and smiling. Everyone was laughing at something that Barry said, so Tiffany chuckled too. She worked hard to keep an interested look on her face for 20 minutes, but was relieved when some of the couples excused themselves to enjoy the live band and the dance floor, signaling the end of the forced dinner conversation.

Tiffany turned to see what Elizabeth was up to at her table. Surprised, she saw there was currently only one elderly couple at that table, engrossed in what appeared to be a happy conversation. The woman wore a blue brocade gown and the most stunning sapphire jewelry Tiffany had ever seen. Barry had taken a break from talking, so Tiffany asked him: "Who are they?" nodding sideways toward the silver-haired couple.

Barry turned to see who she was curious about, then furrowed his brow and looked at Tiffany, without a glimmer of warmth. He replied, "Pritti and Bhaskar Khan, VCs and pillars of the Valley. Longtime friends of my family." He stood up and walked over to the Indian couple, who stood and opened their arms and hugged Barry with joy on their faces. Tiffany waited for Barry to beckon her over. She stood beside her chair and watched the conversation intently, but Barry did not seem to remember she was there. Suddenly realizing what Barry meant by "friends of my family" and embarrassed that he didn't intend to introduce her, Tiffany picked up her sparkly purse and walked toward the ladies' room.

The dance floor was full of beautifully clad couples who moved gracefully together. "I should have had dance lessons when I was a girl," Tiffany rued. The chandeliers and brightly lit stars hanging over the dancers radiated off the sequined gowns and gems worn by the women. "All these old, wrinkled rich people, acting like they're happy when their lives are mostly over."

Theresa and Marc were demonstrating how much they loved dancing, while Emily and Phil were more interested in swaying and looking into each other's eyes. Then Emily caught sight of Tiffany watching the dancers. "Theresa, look left," she said.

"That's the face of a very unhappy side piece," Theresa responded.

Instinctively, they both turned to look for Barry, and saw him at Elizabeth's table, talking to Pritti and Bhaskar, all their faces aglow. "They love Elizabeth and wouldn't give Tiffany the time of day," Theresa commented. "No wonder the trash is moping."

"Wish Betsey were here to see that, and how great her party turned out," Emily replied. Turning to their husbands, the ladies motioned toward the bar. "Who wants another drink?" Emily inquired.

As the couples made their way to the bar closest to the dance floor, Marc saw Phil take his cell phone out of his jacket breast pocket. "Check the game score, let's see how much we're up by."

■ ■ ■

At Polestar, eight seats in the boardroom were filled, and on the table in front of each person sat a Crisis Management Plan binder. In addition to the Chief Counsel and Barry's executive assistant were the Chairman, Chief Technology Officer, Chief Financial Officer, Chief Security Officer, Chief Information Officer, and Chief People Officer. No one asked the topic of the meeting. These normally impatient, very opinionated people simply looked at Maria Albright, who had retrieved a basket from the refreshments station in the back of the room, tipped it over to remove the napkin-wrapped silverware, and placed the basket in the middle of the table.

"Please place your phones in this basket," Maria told them. There was moment of silence broken by Swanson. "What the heck, is Edward Snowden here or something?" They looked at each other and one by one put their phones in the basket. After each attendee had complied, she turned to Alisha. "Please put this basket in the cupboard in the next room."

Maria finally dropped the bombshell. "Our CEO is missing. His car and his dead bodyguard were found in a ravine along Woodside Road several hours ago," she announced. Expressions of shock and distress filled the room, one voice layered over another.

"You are here in your capacity as members of our Crisis Management Team," Maria said loudly, over the din. "Remember the millions of dollars we paid McKinsey to develop our Crisis Management Plan, and all the hours of training we had? I cannot tell you how grateful I am that all we have to do now is follow every single step of the plan for Situation Two in the book. There are templates and timelines in each of your sections for you to utilize. As detailed in the plan, Mr. Grisham will serve as our Interim CEO and I will be the spokesperson for all external communications regarding Barry, as well as the point of contact for law enforcement. We'll be using the template in the CMP to draft a press release, which I'll run by the San Mateo County Sheriff. The FBI has been brought in, but I haven't met any of their agents yet. Whoever the Grand Poobah of the investigation is, will review our press release."

Maria said, "Mr. Swanson, please refresh your familiarity with Regulation FD and review the predrafted 8-K form. We'll discuss that more later."

"I want you all to open your binders to page 87. Memorize this section. You are to tell no one, not even your executive assistant or your spouse, that Barry is missing, until we have made our official disclosure. I am dead serious here. Unless you want to do prison time, follow every single word in that section. And don't even think of taking any action with regard to your stock positions, or your family's or friends'. After Barry comes home and all is well, an independent audit will be conducted per the terms of the agreements you signed with Polestar. The audit agency will know every phone call you and your family members made, every banking transaction, every email from all your IP addresses, etc. And the audit agency will turn over any relevant findings to law enforcement."

Maria cast her eyes around the room and seemed to settle on one or two more than the others. She continued, "This is a day we never thought we'd see, and we will remember this for the rest of our lives. I recommend that you all take your binders and work from home—using only the Polestar VPN—until we make our announcements after the market closes today. That's all I have for now. Any questions?"

Every executive in the room started talking at once.

Later, as they all filed out, John Grinder, the Chief Security Officer, turned to a few of the others and asked if anyone would like a coffee before going home. Chief Technology Officer Tina Chang, Chief Information Officer Vijay Mehta, and Chief People Officer Sharon Leone accepted his invitation.

. . .

While the crisis management team was meeting at Polestar headquarters in East Palo Alto, the San Mateo County Sheriff, Carrie Respeto, was meeting in her office with the lead FBI Case Agent, Regina Williams, and the San Mateo Sheriff department's Senior Detective, Lars Jensen.

Sheriff Respeto was a petite Latina in her 50s, and in many ways the most powerful woman in the Bay Area. The gold braid on her uniform jacket appeared oversized on the small sleeves, and the pistol on the right side of her waist looked too big for her hands, but the four gold stars on her collar and epaulets left no doubt that she was leading this meeting.

Lars Jensen, a California-born man of Danish descent, had worked with Sheriff Respeto a few times, and was pleased that she requested his involvement in this case. His eyes, however, were on Regina Williams, who he had met only minutes before. He knew she was assigned to this investigation based on her competence, but at the moment he was fascinated by her beauty. She was African American, late 30s tops, with shoulder-length black hair in natural ringlets, and her skin was flawless.

While Lars was looking at Regina, she was also sizing him up. She thought he might be the whitest White man she had ever seen. The first thing she noticed was his white-blond hair and pale blue eyes. About 6'2" tall, he was muscular but didn't look like he was obsessed with the gym. His crooked nose had obviously been broken more than once, he had a scar on his left cheek, and the wrinkles around his eyes indicated his 50th birthday was a few years past.

"I know you've both read the case file, so let's start with introductions. I assume you know who I am, now I'd like to learn more about you," Sheriff Respeto said. "Agent Williams, you were born in Detroit, went to Michigan State University on a full-ride scholarship, majored in criminal justice, minored in psychology, were Dean's List all four years. Recruited to the FBI straight out of college, have been with the agency 18 years. You're married. No kids. Tell me about your husband."

"Please call me Reggie. My husband Javon is a finish carpenter who's in high demand in the area," she said with pride. "And I eat like a queen, because he's a gourmet cook. It's his hobby."

"What are your hobbies?" the Sheriff inquired.

"Organic gardening. Both vegetables and flowers, especially roses. My husband even cooks with my flowers."

Sheriff Respeto turned to the police detective. "Lars, I've worked with you before but Reggie hasn't. You were born in Sacramento, got your bachelor's in criminal justice from Cal State Sacramento, were not on the Dean's List, but you do speak Danish and English. You started with the state police giving tickets to speeders, and now you're a senior detective. The only time I've ever seen you smile was when you showed me a vintage Mustang you restored. Tell Reggie about your family."

"I'm divorced, have two daughters. Heather is 27; Tracy is 25. Both are married and live in Livermore. No grandkids yet. Restoring Mustangs is my hobby."

"Okay, now we're a happy family," the Sheriff said. "I'm sure you understand this may be the highest-profile case you will ever have. Nobody's going to get a full night's sleep until we find Barry Roman and whoever's responsible for his disappearance. Our agencies will be working together until this is solved. Of course, Reggie, as FBI you rank. But first, let me tell you the agenda for this afternoon. You're expected at Lawson & Williams at 1:00 pm, to interview Elizabeth Roman." She stopped when she saw Lars furrow his brow.

"Rich people justice?" he asked.

In response, Sheriff Respeto said, "I've called a press conference at 3:00 pm, to make a joint announcement with Polestar's Chief Counsel. It's a publicly traded firm so that is well after the stock market closes. Until the news of Barry's disappearance is released through official channels, we can't spark speculation by inviting Elizabeth here."

After seeing Reggie and Lars nod their heads in under-standing, the Sheriff continued. "Back to billionaire Barry's wife. You know about the girlfriend and the divorce? There's no prenuptial, so if Barry's dead, Elizabeth can console herself by counting her money. So yes, we're going to be dealing with rich people justice." Silently, Reggie shook her head.

The Sheriff, all 5'2" of her, stood up behind her desk. "The Governor wants daily updates. I'll call him today. Reggie, you're on the hot seat starting tomorrow. Keep me informed. And be safe out there." The meeting ended.

■　■　■

After breakfast, the Oxford group had proceeded to tour the new St. Pete office—Maya's pet project. Maya had been inspired by the German software vendor, SAP and its NYC Executive Briefing Center, which she had visited a couple of times. The panoramic views of Manhattan from the 52nd floor in the Hudson Yards building were breathtaking. Here, she could only work with views from the 14th floor but the eastern view encompassed the stunning bay, pier, parks, and museums. The city fathers had used the Chicago waterfront as their inspiration.

As the entourage walked in from the Vinoy and saw the view, nearly everyone oohed and aahed. One of them asked the obvious question—"This is our new administrative center?" Tucker had explained Maya's absence, while she was conducting the location search, as a quest for a place to move back-office operations.

"No, it is not," Tucker said. "Welcome to our new Research and Executive Briefing Center." Maya then conducted a tour of the labs and the rest of the office space. Afterward, she presented a few slides on her search process and the location's specs. She ran through some of the 25 evaluation criteria she had used to score four candidates—Fort Myers, Sarasota, St. Petersburg, and Tampa. They included airport access, economics, city walkability, and safety. Patrick noticed several of the invited customer executives were peppering her with questions. "I guess we may soon be getting some new neighbors," he thought.

It was time for another walk—this time to the James Museum. Several people posed in front of the Buffalo Bill statue at the entrance. William Cody, probably the most accomplished cowboy in US history, would be honored with this seat so close to the water, after a lifetime on the plains and mountains.

The time had finally come for Patrick to have his say. He kicked off his session by showing a video of a bearded man hiking in the Utah wilderness with his backpack while recording a podcast. Patrick announced, "Andrew is an analyst like you and me. Not a technology analyst, though once he is finished in the next 15 minutes, you will agree he could easily be one. He is a geopolitical strategist. He presents to much larger crowds than we do. His graphics are way denser than ours. But more about him later.

"Listen to the six areas of innovation he discusses: AI, space mining, personalized medicine, next-gen fuels like hydrogen, crop genomics, and future occupations.

After the video ended, Patrick resumed. "Andrew started his career at an oil company, and moved through various global locations. Then he became a geopolitical analyst for a specialist firm like ours. Now he's a best-selling author and runs a successful practice of his own advising corporations like we do.

"I've bought each of you a copy of his latest book. I want you to think about how his view of global trends will influence your research area. More important, I want you to be ambitious like him. Make your mark in your domain, and then maybe start your own business."

Tucker winced at the last statement but knew if they got to be as good as the bearded man they had just been viewing, they could make him a lot of money in the interim.

"You will have to take risks like Andrew. Believe me, he's constantly pissing off leaders in Russia, China, Iran, and Germany, to name a few. Not with his politics but with his deep analysis of their demographics, military assets, and natural resources. I've met him at a couple of conferences and wondered if he actually works for the CIA.

"We have to similarly tell the world the reality of vendors. We will piss off some of the vendors but they will have to respect our analysis and the fact that we're tough on their peers as well. And if technology buyers listen to us, vendors will follow.

"Andrew's clients pay a lot more for his advice than ours do. When he presents at conferences, he has really colorful slides on population trends, military maneuvers, trade flows, etc. And yet here he is huffing and puffing with his backpack, recording a high-impact podcast on a choppy network on his phone. Gives new meaning to the phrase: 'Focus on substance more than form.'

"You guys are very good analysts. But you are mostly horizontal—you cover back office silos. The next opportunity calls for us to be orthogonal—by which I mean we have to be verticalized, globalized, and rearchitected for a world of applications that will be more analytical than transactional.

"You heard from Tucker and Martha last night about how Gartner and others became dominant forces in our industry, but also how the time is right for a disruptor—and that could be us. Correction—it should be us.

"COVID, the Ukraine war, climate change, and massive digital transformations have made many vertical edge applications viable—telemedicine and personalized medicine in healthcare, EV battery management and billing in utilities, intelligent returns and reverse logistics around eCommerce, direct-to-consumer and related last-mile, small-lot logistics in consumer sectors, CPQ for industrials to handle complex outcome-based pricing which bundles products' spare parts, all kinds of monitoring and maintenance services . . . the list is virtually endless.

"There's also a growing number of application areas aimed at rapidly growing economies around the globe—they must factor in unique business practices, local languages, scripts, currencies, taxes, customs, payroll, and other nuances.

"Beyond these new vertical and geographic applications, we're seeing a new generation of AI and data-enabled applications. The vertical and global data sets of most enterprise vendors are skin deep. Given how expensive GPUs and good AI talent is likely to be for the next few years, enterprises will prioritize unique products and market-insight projects, like drug discovery, mineral insights, product design advantages, trading patterns, etc. Smart customers will protect that data for themselves, train their own large language models, or LLMs, and commercialize that data asset. Vendors will continue to generate proposals, job descriptions, demand forecasts, etc. with their AI—clearly useful stuff, but not deserving significant premium pricing. We need to be associated with the first group of customers, the smart ones."

Finished with his presentation, Patrick looked at two of the customer executives in the audience. One was smiling at him; the other gave him the thumbs-up.

Patrick next invited Henry Novak, the head of Oxford's labs, to show off the AI copilot named Curmudgeon that

Oxford analysts were busy developing. It would access tools like OpenAI and Google Gemini to gather news, reports, and press releases about vendors. It would also tap into Wall Street and other proprietary databases for more vendor analysis. In addition, it would access Oxford's own client query database to see how corporations were using vendor capabilities. Finally, analysts would enter details from vendor briefings, vendor events, their own observations on each vendor, and their competition. The human expertise would validate and enrich the machine learning. The tool would help generate first drafts of Oxford's twice-a-year Golden Circle report for each market category. The analyst group clapped loudly when Henry finished describing the multifunctional tool. Several analysts offered to be guinea pigs for the project.

Next up was Irene Kaplan, an "AR consultant." Raised in the public relations world, she now helped vendors make themselves more coherent to analyst firms like Oxford. She had the audience in titters as she shared anecdotes and "inside baseball" stories of what vendors thought of individual analysts. She highlighted "Bill Lou"—the analyst who spoke with a pronounced Southern drawl like the senator from Louisiana, but with devastating impact. And Megan Lewis—Ms. Multitasker, who was physically at one event while tweeting about another on the other coast. And Jean DePasquale, who asked softball questions but made sure he announced his name and company, so it would become part of the event transcript. And "Vinnie Vertical," who managed to squeeze in a healthcare, banking, or automotive sector question at every event. All super sharp, all quirky.

Talking about quirky, she shared with them that she, too, had built an AI tool, called Gideon—presumably out of respect to the late founder of Gartner—to keep track of analysts with details on their spouses and hobbies, links to their latest research, and more. "It's fascinating how many analysts are good musicians. One of you has amassed a giant collection of mobile devices, covering the last couple of decades. Another has a collection of soda cans from around the world. A couple of your peers have been to over 100 countries. It is amazing how many of you know the byzantine rules of the game of cricket."

Patrick made a note to talk to Irene and compare Gideon, Curmudgeon, and Sherlock, a law enforcement digital agent that Henry's team had developed and which Polestar was now enhancing and commercializing.

Irene then changed tone. "You analysts are under the delusion vendors want your intelligence. They may pretend to, just to stroke your ego. The vast majority of them want you to take their slides and just include them in your research reports. They seem to forget if they can convince you to do that, so can every one of their competitors. Honestly, they should use you more for intelligence. It should bug the heck out of them their customers have 100, 400, or 900 application vendors. Each of them is just a small piece in the customer's jigsaw puzzle."

A vendor executive in the audience raised her hand and said, "Irene, not a question, more of a suggestion: Don't spill our secrets to all these analysts." Everyone laughed.

Patrick chimed in. "Every time I present, I need brain food. I am famished. I hope you are too. We're going to take

61

another walk across the street to the Yacht Club. If you want to skip lunch, please feel free to walk around the museum." Pointing to the roof, he said, "I especially recommend going upstairs to the John Coleman bronze rendition of the three Native American principals at the Battle of Little Bighorn in 1876, better known as Custer's Last Stand. There is Gall with his tomahawk, Sitting Bull with his pipe, and Crazy Horse with his Winchester rifle. The intricate details on each are quite amazing."

■ ■ ■

Meanwhile, at Polestar, John led the way to his office. As he passed his assistant, John told her to take a breakfast break as they were not to be disturbed. His office was large, and had seats for all of his guests.

John liked his cappuccino and had installed a top-of-the-line coffee machine, so the first few moments were spent getting everyone their favorite beverage. Finally he sat, looked around, and asked, "Well, what do you think?" At first, the executives all just looked at each other, each remembering the last time the entire C-suite had spent this much time together. It was a much happier occasion that had happened a month earlier and was held at the Inn at Spanish Bay in Pebble Beach, CA. There, they had hosted an Analyst Day event, prior to the launch of Polestar's cutting-edge GenAI product suite. The theme was "It's Our Time." It had been a small gathering to which 30 analysts, including Patrick, had been invited. Robert Lonigan, CEO of GPUMagic, a Polestar customer and partner, was one of the few outsiders who had joined them. It was a very successful and enjoyable event, bolstered by its location—the stunning resort on the Pacific next to the legendary Pebble Beach golf links.

Vijay broke the silence. "It's just unbelievable! And very worrying to hear that the security guard is dead. It must have been a horrific accident. I hate to think of Barry just lying injured somewhere without help. I always saw Barry as somehow unbreakable. I can still see him at Analyst Day walking on stage led by a robot doing backflips, and another walking menacingly next to him as his bodyguard."

Vijay went quiet but he was relishing the memory of the four drones that were flown into the audience, with two of them dropping music boxes at a couple of tables. When the boxes were opened, they played Lumiere and Friends singing "Be Our Guest" from Disney's *Beauty and the Beast*. One of the drones with sensitive mics amplified the music, and the other with a high-resolution camera projected Barry and the bots on stage onto a large screen.

Sharon finished his thought, saying, "Barry sure knows how to make an entrance, and he's definitely not modest about Polestar's accomplishments. It was impressive the way Barry kicked it off with a slick video that showed Polestar products on shop floors, hospitals, labs, delivery trucks, and warehouses. That was beautifully produced."

Vijay nodded and added, "And I loved how Barry said that he'd be bragging if he claimed to know that GenAI would take off in the last couple of years. He conveyed how we have been architecting our company for this moment. I think he said, 'We have been preparing for it for at least the last eight years when we started investing in vertical automation.'"

Sharon brought them back down to earth. "Guys, Barry is the 'star' at Polestar. We were worried about his absence yesterday. Today, the panic notched up several degrees."

Tina chimed in, "Look, the company is on a solid foundation and the direction has been set. I think we can stop worrying about the stability of the company and perhaps think about the hit our shares will take. I hate to say it, but it won't be pretty."

John laughingly said, "You're fairly new to the company and don't have as much invested in the stock. So you have less to lose. By the way, you were the star of Analyst Day."

Tina actually blushed.

Sharon added, "I loved it when you said we want to make every worker a Luke Skywalker. And perhaps build a Starfighter. My son is a huge fan of *Star Wars*, so I loved the analogy. And my daughter would have loved it when you sang, 'Sally the camel has no humps 'cause Sally is a horse.'"

Tina could distinctly remember her talk.

"Now if AI were a camel," she had said at the time, "it would have at least six humps. You know Gartner has hype cycles for emerging technologies. It shows how different technologies go through expectations of success. If Gartner had a time series going back to the '50s, it would show multiple AI hype cycles.

"How many of you saw *The Imitation Game*? In 1950, Alan Turing defined his famous test to measure a machine's ability to exhibit intelligent behavior equivalent to that of a human. In 1959, we got excited when Allen Newell and his colleagues coded the General Problem Solver. Have you seen *2001: A Space Odyssey*? In 1968, Stanley Kubrick sent our minds into overdrive with HAL, the computer in that movie. We applauded when IBM's Deep Blue supercomputer beat Grandmaster Garry Kasparov at chess in 1997. We were impressed in 2011 when IBM's Watson beat human champions at *Jeopardy*. And in 2016, when Google's AlphaGo showed it had mastered Go, the ancient and incredibly intricate board game. In the last decade, we've experienced Siri and Alexa and our cars 'getting' our voice commands. We've seen vendors like Salesforce with Einstein and SAP with Leonardo—wait, they have Joule now?—bring AI into corporate halls. That was broadly what we now call predictive AI. Better maintenance planning, demand forecasting, etc.

"However, the most exciting recent development is LLMs and GenAI. You guys, of course, keep the scorecard. ChatGPT from OpenAI reached 100 million monthly active users just two months after launch, making it the fastest-growing consumer application in history. I've been exposed to some of the scaling problems they hit scampering to beg, borrow, or steal GPUs. And that of optimizing the KV cache in GPU RAM and moving data at a speed of around 3TB a second.

"Now, even as vendors like Microsoft, Google, Workday and Salesforce are introducing digital agents, many of you analysts are saying it's reaching the top of its hype curve. I get much more sobering feedback from geeks in labs. They talk in terms like 'double descent.' Look it up in the context of machine learning. They say there is so much we don't know about these language models. As one said, 'We are where physics and chemistry were a century ago. Plenty of witches' brews. So many unknown 'unknowns.' AI the camel may just be growing yet another hump. No point telling tech marketing guys and Wall Street to tone down the hype. Or telling the media to not just focus on deep fakes or politicians' fearmongering that all jobs will be lost to AI."

Vijay said, "Your talk was amazing, and I hope you know I'm a huge fan of yours. You learned a lot at Boston Dynamics which uses the tagline of 'Leaps, bounds, and backflips' for its robots. Very impressive to hear how they are improving robot mobility, dexterity, perception, and intelligence. You also mentioned your experience working at Kiva which makes the robots that zip along at the Amazon distribution centers. I have visited one of the centers and see how they bring work to the worker. Which removes miles of walking and carrying huge loads. Quite impressive."

Sharon added, "My job is to focus on employee satisfaction and their productivity, and so it was super exciting to hear about the world of humanoid robots, drones, satellites, machine vision, different kinds of sensors—all turbocharged with AI, which can make all of us super workers in every one of the nearly 900 occupations the Bureau of Labor Statistics tracks."

Tina nodded and said, "Look, that's where we have a long lead, as Barry mentioned in his talk. The coming convergence of Agentic AI and Humanoid Robots positions us very well. We don't want to try to be everything to everyone. But if we can keep adding new professions and automating specific tasks for each, our growth will be endless. Other vendors talk about five or six verticals. Well, to us every one of the occupations we address is a unique vertical. It is amazing to see how far ahead we are in so many areas.

"With my experience at other automation companies, I feel reasonably confident Polestar is on the right trajectory. I don't wish anything to happen to Barry, but the company can glide for a while."

Sharon decided to lighten the mood a bit and recount one of many humorous Barry anecdotes she had heard. "I cautioned Barry not to mimic accents of employees born overseas or tease them about long, hard-to-pronounce names. He recounted to me the scene from *The Godfather* where the Hollywood bigshot Jack Woltz tells the lawyer Tom Hagen: "I don't care how many dago guinea wop greaseball goombahs come out of the woodwork!" and follows up, "my kraut-mick friend." Of course, Barry conveniently neglected to mention that Woltz's attitude resulted in him waking to find his prized horse's severed head.

"Barry would lament that we've become too PC. He'd say, 'When did we forget to celebrate and make fun of our ethnic differences?'

"I had to remind him, 'Barry, this isn't the underworld. Careful with your words.'"

John pointed out that Barry had touched all of them in some way. "For example," he said, "I'll be forever grateful to him for introducing me to Tommy 'Bespoke' Chu. Barry told me that on a trip to Hong Kong in the '90s, he'd gone to Tommy's store in the Kowloon district and ordered three custom-made suits and 10 dress shirts. They were delivered to his hotel two days later. Tommy had done a stint at a Savile Row tailor in London and then went home and built a thriving business. Barry would visit him every few years. One day, Tommy showed up at our headquarters. He told Barry that he'd immigrated to Canada after the British left Hong Kong and recently started a tailoring service in San Diego. Most companies, especially in Silicon Valley, had moved to business casual dress codes, so he'd evolved his business to tailoring nice trousers and blazers. He'd also expanded into ladies' clothing and leather.

"Anyhow, Barry convinced him to open a small store in this building, right next to our corporate gift shop. Our salespeople now can—and do—order tons of suits and dress shirts through him. There's usually a line of people waiting for him to take measurements when he shows up every couple of weeks. I've had to wait in that dreaded line. The rest of the time, having a store here allows customers to pick up their custom-made wear. In fact, our employees are his single biggest source of revenue."

Sharon chimed in, "In my role, I've seen dress code standards get way looser over the last couple of decades. Business casual has morphed into 'anything goes.' Barry has tried really hard to raise the sartorial standards in Silicon Valley. His bulky Rolex is a big contrast to all those Apple watches around. He wears blue wool blazers instead of the windbreaker jackets that show off our corporate logo. And his custom-made Tommy Chu shoes stand out in a world of Nikes, let alone his carefully cuffed trousers in a sea of blue jeans. I know he loves shopping at Hermes when he's in Paris and picks up several of their ties with the distinctive little patterns. I love silk scarves—and he's gifted me with their scarves several times."

A notion occurred to Tina that prompted her to change the subject. "On another note, could you tell me a little about this Patrick guy that Barry seems to really like. He positively beamed during my talk so I can tell he is a big fan of robots. I just met him briefly and I know only that he works at Oxford Research in Cambridge, a technology research and analyst firm. And that he worked for us a few years back. He still seems to be a close friend of Barry's, which seems a little strange."

The others looked at each other for a few seconds, and then John asked, "Okay, who wants to tell the long and involved story of Patrick? The man who many people think is as brilliant as Barry and is 'the one that got away.' I know Barry regrets to this day not keeping him in the company. Any takers?"

After a brief pause, Sharon said, "I'll start. His full name is Patrick Thomas Edward Brennan and he loves to use his full name when signing any documents. He's kind of quirky that way. Both of his parents emigrated from Ireland, and he's very proud of his Irish ancestry. Barry hired him on the spot when they met at a Stanford alumni meeting—must've been love at first sight." Everyone chuckled.

"Patrick was sold on industry verticalization from the start, and Barry immediately put him in charge of the automation group because of that. Basically, Patrick's five years here creatively transformed the company and helped greatly expand our offerings. Patrick helped Barry look at how each occupation could benefit from emerging technologies and how we could develop applications for them. Meanwhile, Barry was brilliant at working with product placement agencies in Hollywood so that a lot of our robots and devices have shown up in movies.

"Patrick traveled to trade shows all over the world and reached out to companies on the cutting edge of automation. He was all about the 'future of work.'

"Everything worked great for five years. At that point, Patrick wanted to move east to be with his aging parents. He asked to move the automation group and Barry said 'No,' flat out. I later heard Barry say he should've allowed Patrick to move the group and also that he should've been way more generous with the equity he offered to him."

Vijay added, "Patrick then got the job at Oxford Research and as an analyst he tracks us, among many others, so the relationship between Barry and Patrick has continued. Thanks to Patrick, Barry has become friendlier with the Oxford CEO, Tucker Newberry. I know that Barry has sometimes complained to Tucker about Patrick's analyses of our company. Yet it doesn't seem to have ruined their relationship. I also know that when Oxford decided to open a Florida office, Patrick asked Barry for advice since Barry grew up in that state. It's obvious to the other analysts how much Barry likes Patrick and so naturally there's some jealousy. You may have noticed some of that at our recent Analyst Day. It's just one of those relationships that is hard to explain and seems to transcend their business association. They're very different, but Barry and Patrick are great friends. Mentor and mentee. Hard to explain, but so it is. So that's Patrick in as few words as possible.

"Oh, and by the way," Vijay continued, "analysts love to snark when midlevel execs kiss ass of their superiors in their presentations. They use the Twitter X tag of #TYFYL—Thank you for your leadership. I hear Patrick gets teased with that slur every time Barry compliments him in public. I thought it was really mean that one of them tweeted photos of Barry and Patrick both wearing Tommy Chu blazers and French-blue button-down shirts with the tag line of TYFYL, suggesting that Patrick wears what Barry does."

Sharon interjected, "Very few people knew the back story behind Patrick's introduction to Tommy. Introducing Patrick at a Polestar event, Barry had teased him for his 'Sears Roebuck polyester' jacket. Apparently, that really stung Patrick, so he ordered some shirts and a jacket from Tommy. Barry then complimented his new wardrobe and said, 'All you need are some Hermes ties and some Tommy custom-made shoes. Your feet will feel buttery soft.' Patrick was not about to spend $250 for a tie when few tech events are that formal anymore. As for the $1,500 Tommy shoes, he thought he could run through several Johnston and Murphy's for the same price."

Vijay said, "All of us should know that when one of the analysts tweets the #TYFYL tag, they're hardly being complimentary. Same when they make fun of the mandatory Safe Harbor Statement that attorneys make us include about future-looking product statements. Especially when a vendor executive actually reads that slide, with its over 200 legal words, rather than just glosses over it."

"Thanks," said Tina, "that is important to know. It explains a lot of what I saw at the Analyst Day event. Well, I guess we just need to wait and pray for Barry's safe return. I'm going to take Maria's advice and work from home."

Just then, Maria popped her head in and asked if John and Sharon could stay.

. . .

Maria waited for Tina and Vijay to leave John's office, and then said, "Guys, the next few days are going to test us all, but especially the two of you. Every one of our employees will be traumatized, and the likely stock drop will make that shock worse.

"Sharon, I'm particularly worried about a few employees who are about to retire and a few with divorce settlements coming up. A 30, 40, or 50 percent stock price drop is going to make them extremely unhappy. Let me know if I can help you, as HR will have to deal with them."

She then turned to John. "Here we've spent the last year convincing employees to come back to the office after working from home during COVID. Our cafeteria and other office perks are very attractive, but we never planned for this kind of buzzkill in the office. Think about if we need to beef up security?"

On his way out, John told his assistant he would work from home, and then drove home. On such a weird day, he had no idea how much work he would actually manage to do. Nothing seemed that important to him until Barry was found. It was consoling to hear that the company was rock solid no matter what happened to Barry. Yes, he believed, the shares would probably take a hit but they would recover. He planned to be at the company long-term so he was not overly concerned.

He grossly underestimated the roller-coaster ride of the PLST stock price over the next few days.

4

You Did What?!

Tuesday pm PST

Reggie and Lars spent several hours reviewing the details of the case, then drove separately to the law office where Elizabeth was to be interrogated.

At 1:00 pm, the west side of the Lawson & Williams building was lit up with amber sun reflecting on its glass exterior. The building appeared to be 90 percent glass, inside and out, with just enough steel and concrete to keep it standing. The exterior reflected clouds, sun, and a mix of deciduous and palm trees, selected to survive California's cycles of drought and low-pressure systems that sometimes create "atmospheric rivers." Inside the building, most of the walls of the law firm's offices and conference rooms were also glass, providing an airy modern aesthetic. The largest glass-walled conference room was the most luxurious, with chrome-framed, well-padded white leather chairs around a glass conference table. When in use, the mirrored credenza was topped with plates of cookies, fresh fruit, and pitchers of iced water. It was hard for opposing counsel to identify a reason to request a room change for depositions, but the architect had designed the room to intimidate. The nameplate on the door said Millennium Room but employees knew it as the Fishbowl.

Elizabeth had attended meetings with her estranged husband in the Fishbowl as part of her divorce proceedings, when her family law attorneys were trying to unnerve Barry. During those meetings, Barry looked uncomfortable while Elizabeth was impeccably dressed with perfectly applied makeup and a cool, unworried demeanor.

But the firm's attorneys knew better than to reserve that room for today's meeting. In a far less glamorous interior conference room, Elizabeth sat on one side of a long wooden table, flanked by the firm's managing partner, Geoffrey Nels, and its famously successful criminal defense attorney, Fred Bibikov. She wore loose blue jeans, a navy University of Michigan football champions sweatshirt, and tennis shoes. Her hair was in a ponytail and the only thing on her face besides a tired expression was moisturizer. Except for the blazing diamond wedding band that she still wore on her left hand, her attorneys hardly recognized her. And today, it was Elizabeth who was the target of the meeting.

Lars and Reggie were seated across from Elizabeth and her lawyers. In a corner of the room sat a young woman, an audiovisual recording technician, who wore headphones and monitored a computer that showed the output of two recording cameras, one pointed at Lars and Reggie and one aimed at Elizabeth, as well as two audio feeds. At the opposite end of the room hung a 75" television where they would presumably watch the Sheriff's press conference.

Elizabeth was keenly aware the detectives were watching her closely. At the moment, she didn't feel much, thanks to the Xanax she had taken earlier to minimize her anxiety. For the past year, she kept a few pills in her purse at all times. After the short break in the questioning, Fred whispered to her: "You ready to resume?" She nodded.

While Fred Bibikov was known to instill dread in prosecutors, and had embarrassed many detectives in court, his voice was warm as he spoke. "Let's continue. We had been discussing security videos. The Romans' security team is in the process of downloading all camera files, interior and exterior, for the estate on Stadler Drive in Woodside, covering the past two weeks. You'll receive them by tomorrow morning."

Fred then placed papers in front of the detectives. "Here's the document we discussed earlier. Stadler Drive, where Mr. Roman has been living for the past nine months, is community property. My client has granted your team access, with certain provisions: The property's security team will be present in every room your team is in. All actions will be filmed by the property's security cameras. And the utmost care will be taken to return every moved item to its original location, and to avoid touching artwork. These restrictions are, of course, in addition to all standard provisions such as preparing an inventory of items retrieved by your team."

"Good on the camera footage," Lars replied, "but your white glove requirement for Mr. Roman's house is going to slow down our investigation."

"There's millions of dollars of art, antiques, family heirlooms, and historical documents in that house. We're making a reasonable request," Fred said.

"What about access to the marital home, where Mrs. Roman lives?" Lars asked. Elizabeth turned to look at Fred, her eyebrows raised almost imperceptibly, but Fred noticed her anxiety.

"As I said before our break, you'll have the past month's exterior camera recordings for Mrs. Roman's residence this afternoon. And my paralegal, Rachael, will get you the detailed invoices from both Mr. Roman's and my client's personal cell phones, which include call logs." Fred's voice had lost its warmth. "Anything else will require a search warrant, and you don't have enough evidence to get one. And your team's presence on the property, where Mrs. Roman lives with her children, will be deemed harassment."

Reggie and Lars looked at each other. Reggie shifted in her chair, crossed her arms in front of her on the table, and leaned slightly toward Elizabeth. "You wouldn't lose half your wealth if Mr. Roman were dead, would you? Now let's go back to the last time you saw Mr. Roman."

"I already answered that," Elizabeth sighed.

"First you said the last time you saw him was Thursday night. Then you said it was Friday morning. Please clarify," Reggie said.

"Thursday night didn't end until about 5:00 am Friday morning." Elizabeth no longer looked tired; she was fully animated.

"Please elaborate."

"Barry came over Thursday to visit the kids, who went to bed by 11:00 pm. Then Barry visited with me." Elizabeth mimicked Reggie, crossing her own arms in front of her and leaning forward toward the detectives. "In my bedroom, naked. And he slept next to me until he got up after 4:30 am on Friday, and left around 5:00 am. Can I make it any clearer to you? Between me and Barry? It's not over. It will never be over."

Reggie laughed and said, "Now you're quoting Mark Dantonio," referencing the rivalry between Elizabeth's university and her own—Michigan State.

"Oh God, you're a Spartan," Elizabeth groaned.

"We've answered your questions," Fred said, and stood up.

Geoffrey Nels also stood, and opened the conference room door for Elizabeth.

As Elizabeth walked toward the door, she looked over at the audiovisual recording technician, who didn't dare raise her eyes or show any expression, but was thinking to herself: *"This just got interesting."*

■ ■ ■

Tiffany was not sleeping well. She had not heard from Barry since Sunday afternoon. Alisha had called her the day before to ask if Barry had spent Sunday night with her, and then . . . silence. His voicemail was full. She called his office this morning and Alisha had told her she didn't get involved in Barry's private business and to please wait for Barry to call her. She took this to mean Barry was at the office and avoiding her calls. The unknown was killing her. Why didn't he call her? Had he gone back to Elizabeth? Was it a new romantic interest?

Then her friend Ashley called. "Did you see the news? There's been an accident and Barry's car has been found in a ravine. He's reported missing and his driver is dead." Tiffany immediately started to cry, and moaned, "Oh my God, I figured that when I never heard from him for the past two nights, that he had gone back to Elizabeth or maybe a new lover. I feel awful, as I was calling him all kinds of names for not letting me know what was happening. Now I just see him lying injured or dead."

Ashley said, "Look, the police are out in full force looking for him so please don't start imagining all kinds of things. Let's wait for him to be found. I'll come over and spend the night with you."

"Thanks so much," Tiffany said, "that would be wonderful as I just feel so alone." They hung up and then she settled down to glean all the information she could from a variety of news networks and websites.

■ ■ ■

At the Polestar office, after the announcement about the accident and Barry being missing, Alisha immediately put in her call to Patrick. She had wanted to call him earlier but couldn't until it was official. Somehow, she had this ridiculous faith in Patrick, like he could do something that the police could not. It was silly, she knew, but he just inspired so much confidence. They had become good friends in the years Patrick had spent at Polestar. The call went into voice mail. She did not leave a message.

. . .

At a few minutes past 6:00 pm EST, Patrick's phone started buzzing with text messages, emails, voice mails, Tweets, LinkedIn messages. He had just sat down with Henry to discuss some lab projects, when Tucker barged in and shouted, "Have you heard about Barry?!" The world knew the news, now that Carrie Respeto's press conference had aired.

"Holy shit!" Patrick yelled. He excused himself and called Alisha. Alisha was sobbing. He felt bad he had ignored her earlier call. He tried to console her, saying, "Alisha, you and I have been preparing for this possibility for nearly the whole decade that we've known him. He will be fine."

He gave Maya the news, and told her he might need a backup for next morning's sessions.

. . .

The Oxford offsite dinner was again at the Vinoy. It was a slightly smaller crowd as the customer guests had left town. And the mood was more subdued as word of Barry had spread.

Patrick kicked it off with an announcement. "Guys, you know I have a long relationship with Barry, so I'm going to skip dinner and make some calls from the room. And Tucker and Martha will take over for my sessions tomorrow."

Then he choked up, but continued, "I wanted to share a tidbit of just how popular Barry is with his staff. His assistant told me 15 members of the company's hiking-and-climbing club with axes, ropes, and walkie-talkies drove to the ravine where his car was found. They were all set to descend into all these thick brushes in the ravine and look for Barry. The cops had cordoned off the area so it wasn't allowed, but I suspect sooner or later that search party will be beating the bushes. And you'll see them from TV helicopters hovering above."

The group again sat at six tables, but some tables were especially popular. Henry's table, for one, was mobbed as people wanted to hear about Curmudgeon. Henry was engaged in a heated conversation with several analysts about when and if the tool would replace their jobs. Henry said, "Not for a long time. It will take away all the tedious stuff you guys do in building your Golden Circles. It actually should make your analysis a lot richer."

At Maya's table, meanwhile, the hot topic was her location search, and the others peppered her with more questions about it. She proudly shared anecdotes from her whirlwind, fortnight-long search up and down the west coast of Florida. A couple of analysts fished around and asked if anyone would be required to relocate from Cambridge. Maya diplomatically responded, "St. Pete is easier to recruit into than Cambridge, so I expect more new analysts to join here."

And at Martha's table, she was hotly railing against an industry behavior she abhorred. "There is a third thing I did not mention in our session yesterday. Something I dislike even more in a vendor—negative selling and competition bashing." The table was agape when she described how she'd often received unmarked envelopes from vendors with dirt on a competitor. "Sometimes they'd arrive at home. One was a thick package, back when the Unabomber was active, and my husband almost called the bomb squad to check it out."

In his corner of the room, Tucker was in fine form, discussing the history of the analyst sector. He reminisced about colorful, high-energy analysts like Howard Anderson who founded Yankee Group in 1970, George Colony who left Yankee and started Forrester Research in 1983, and Gideon Gartner who founded his namesake firm in 1979.

One younger analyst asked whether the AI tool 'Gideon' was named after him. Tucker said wryly, "Yes, presumably Irene named it in his honor. In fact," he joked, "perhaps we should trade names with her—she can have Curmudgeon."

He then went around the table and asked everyone what they thought of the new office. Most of the replies were flattering, though one said he would like to reserve judgment till he walked on a hot and humid July day from the Vinoy to the office. What he did not mention was that he had espied a couple of other Marriott properties much closer to the office, where he planned to stay on future trips.

This quip gave Tucker an opening to show off. "I will gladly sweat a bit. I can fly my plane into the small airport—Albert Whitted—next to the Dali, and walk to the office. Do you know how many world leaders would kill for that kind of convenience?"

Meanwhile, up in their room, Maya had brought Patrick dinner from the buffet downstairs. Patrick was busy entering notes about suspects and motives in the Sherlock tool, and it was busy crawling the web for information about each of them.

He also made a call to Ramon Rodriguez in the FBI Tampa office, who he had worked with on a few cases. They had also broken bread several times. Once they went to the Columbia in Ybor City, which claims to be Florida's oldest restaurant. He asked Ramon to order the food—"This is your cuisine, right?"

Ramon had burst out laughing, then said, "They call themselves the largest Spanish restaurant in the world, to convey the Old World image. You want real Cuban food, come to one of my barbeques. Straight off the bone, roast shoulder of pork with mojo sauce. Or let's go to one of the many neighborhood dives in this town—buffets full of black bean soup, fried plantains, arroz con pollo Cubano. By the way here's a pro tip on Cuban sandwiches: Don't listen to anyone from Miami; Tampa has the best ones. And don't dare screw with the original recipe. Toasted, not limp bread. Cuban, not French or Italian bread. Mustard, yes. No mayo or ketchup. Lettuce, no. Pickles, okay. And you WILL get shot if you put pineapple or cranberry or jalapenos on it."

Having worked with Ramon on UPC and QR code scams, Patrick now listened in awe when Ramon told him of gangs that scoped out neighborhoods with night-vision-equipped drones, selected a car, and then broke into its CAN –Controller Area Network—bus. Then something as simple as a USB cable would allow them to start some of the cars. The modern day crowbar!

Patrick said, "Ramon, this is not about some two-bit criminal. This is about the disappearance of a tech billionaire and the demise of his bodyguard. It may have a national security angle. I'm afraid local cops in California will muck it up. The FBI needs to be involved." Patrick had not watched the replay of the press conference and did not know that this was already the case.

"How are you involved?" Ramon asked.

"I used to work for the missing executive and now I track his company. I know him, his wife, his customers, his competitors—including lots of people who could wish him harm."

"Patrick, I cannot get the FBI involved just because he is a buddy of yours." Neither knew Reggie had already been tapped to lead the investigation.

"Ramon, you told me once I think like a criminal. I plan to sit down tonight and assemble a short list of possible suspects and motives. Call your San Jose office. Ask them to get involved. They won't be surprised. It's huge news in Silicon Valley. Then offer an open line to me."

"Patrick, everything we have done so far has been local and off the record, which has been essential. That's why it's worked so well. You sure about this?"

"Would you rather me dial 1-800-CALL-FBI or go into your Guardian system and type in a bunch of anonymous tips, and watch them get lost among a million others?"

"Okay, let me call my colleagues out west."

Ramon quickly found out that Reggie was leading the case, and he pitched Patrick to her. Reggie responded,

"Ramon, you clearly trust the guy and he sounds very competent, but defense attorneys know how to weaken cases when outsiders help us."

"Reggie, you're thinking ahead to evidence and trials. How about the more immediate search and rescue of this billionaire?"

"As you know," she replied, "we work closely with state and county resources. They should know much more about the missing executive than someone from Florida."

"Normally that would be true," Ramon said. "If this is in fact a kidnapping, well, Patrick used to work for the guy and probably knows most of the suspects. Could he help you from our local office or his home office? Or is that too insecure? He is an hour's drive away but I could see if he could work from here."

"You're way ahead of me. Let me talk to Lars, the local guy on the case. He's a bit old-fashioned and may nix the idea. Then let's set up a video interview with your guy."

As Reggie expected, Lars showed little interest. "Who the hell is Patrick? Can you imagine the field day the defense attorneys would have with Florida Man? Why didn't we invite Governor DeSantis himself to help on this case? You know Sheriff Respeto said Governor Newsom wants to be kept updated on the investigation. There's little those two Governors agree on."

She repeated what Ramon had said: "You're thinking ahead to trials and evidence. How about the more immediate search and rescue of this billionaire? One of your residents, right? Let's do a video interview then you can decide."

Reggie called Ramon back and said, "Okay, can he do a video call with us in a couple of hours?"

"It's late here but he's still working so let me try." Ramon called Patrick and asked if he had access to videoconferencing.

"Yeah, in the office. Give me a couple of hours."

"Perfect."

Patrick took the elevator down at the Vinoy. He saw a few Oxford people around a piano. One of the analysts, John Quinlan, was entertaining them. He waved at them, and then found Henry's table where attendees were finishing dinner.

Patrick said to Henry: "Can one of your guys go ahead and set up the videoconferencing? Tell him I will be there in an hour. Keep this to yourself, but I'm talking to the FBI detectives leading the investigation on Barry."

"How cool is that, man. I'll set it up for you myself."

"You sure you can't ask one of your guys? Keep enjoying your table. It looked pretty animated."

"Yeah, folks excited about AI and Curmudgeon."

Patrick spent a few more minutes at Henry's table, where Jonathan, one of the new analysts, engaged with him. "Henry mentioned that you've studied the history of automation in detail, and believe that humans always overestimate its likely impact on jobs. Is that correct?"

Patrick said, "Yes, I can send you a link to a presentation where I talked about a century of automation—UPC scanners in the grocery sector, ATMs in the banking sector, autonomous cars in the auto sector, and numerous others. In many cases, automation actually increased jobs in the sector. It typically targets individual tasks, not complete jobs. It tends to reduce dull, dirty, and dangerous activities. I expect AI will do similar. You have likely heard the expression—'Those that fail to learn from history are doomed to repeat it.' But try telling that to journalists and politicians who would rather just take advantage of people's fear of automation."

He then walked up to Tucker, who said, "Pull up a chair and answer this table's questions about hurricane risks." Patrick pointed to Maya's table and said, "You folks should be at that table but let me give it a shot. She had a weighted table of evaluation factors as she scored the four towns we looked at. Hurricane risk was 15% of the weight. Fort Myers was scored the lowest on that because it was hit by Hurricane Ian in 2023 using the assumption that lightning does not strike twice. This place, St. Pete, was scored pretty high using another perverse assumption—that it has not seen a direct hit in 90 years, so it's overdue. Yet St. Pete easily beat out the others on other factors. You know, we've done some work with NOAA, and I've visited the National Hurricane Center in Miami. For all the talk of global warming, the average hurricane season over the last few decades has been consistent with the past—an average of 15 named storms, seven hurricanes, and three major hurricanes a year which threaten to make landfall. You should talk to Maya—she has a bunch more fascinating data.

"And of course, we have evacuation guidelines for the office. By the way, you should see how this state starts prepping for a major hurricane as its track firms up. It is quite an impressive exercise. Multiple bulletins from the Guv—I think it is a requirement here that they are bilingual," he joked. "There's a long list: defined evacuation zones and escape routes, major toll roads are declared free, hundreds of utility trucks on standby for fallen lines, and tons of other prep items. They have to factor what we have heard from our neighbors who have lived in Florida forever that each hurricane is different. They can hurt via flooding, strong winds, massive storm surges, waves of tornadoes, all kinds of yard waste missiles and plenty of electrical fires. And at times high tides and the moon's pull join the party and cause even more chaos."

Patrick asked Tucker if he could borrow him for a few minutes, and then told him: "I may need to spend a couple of days with the FBI team on the Barry case. Please work with Martha and handle my sessions tomorrow."

Tucker said, "Wow. Break a leg, young man!"

Patrick then asked Maya if she could take a walk with him. She was finishing at her table, and excused herself by telling the table: "Behave yourself at the bar."

Patrick told them: "Go join Quinlan at the piano."

As they walked to the Oxford office, Patrick told her about the call to Ramon and the resulting chain reaction.

"You did what?!" Maya yelled.

"Barry may not have been too nice to me with equity, and morally we're opposite, but he has been a long-time mentor and friend. It is hugely important to me to contribute in any way I can to help find him."

Maya said, "You know I don't like to watch scary TV or movies. I cringe at physical violence."

"I told Ramon any help I provide will be remote," Patrick told her.

"I know. But I'm so new to this job and the new office. You'll be so distracted and sucked into the case. Sorry, I'm thinking about myself, not your friend."

Patrick hugged her shoulder tightly as they walked past the sprawling banyan trees in North Straub Park and the Bombax on the south lawn of the Museum of Fine Arts. Maya never failed to gush about those giant trees but she was awfully quiet today.

Patrick mimicked her silence but knew she came from far grittier stock. He had heard from his in-laws, Harish and Indra, how their clan had been uprooted overnight when the British divided India in 1947. As Hindus they had ended up as refugees in Bombay, clawed their way out over a couple of decades, then emigrated to the US. Harish had also proudly told him his clan could take credit for stopping Alexander the Great's eastward march across Asia. Maya had joked, "I will believe it when my parents show me their 23andMe lab results with Macedonian or Greek DNA."

∎ ∎ ∎

Patrick did his video call with Reggie and Lars from the St. Pete office, but the connection had dropped a couple of times. He thanked Henry, who had been chatting with Maya.

Reggie called him back on his mobile phone and said, "You come highly recommended by Ramon. We could use someone like you who knows Barry and his well-wishers and not-so-friendly-wishers that well. However, we will need to have you agree to several protocols. Video technology will not work. When can you be here in person?"

Patrick panicked—he had thought he could work with them remotely. Now he would need to really comfort Maya.

Reggie called him again. "There is a nonstop from Tampa to San Francisco in the morning. If you can jump on that, we will work out expense reimbursement later."

"Sure," said Patrick half-heartedly. Ramon called him a couple of minutes later. "I'm booking your flight," he said, "and will pick you up and take you to the airport."

"You sure? Thanks. I'm not home. We're at the Vinoy."

"Ooh, fancy schmancy."

"Can we swing by my house so I can pick up some clean clothes? Actually, pick me up at home. I will take an Uber and get there before you."

After the call with Reggie, Patrick suggested to Maya they take a walk by the James Museum. He told her he needed to fly west the next morning. Maya looked terrified.

They sat on the bench next to Buffalo Bill. Patrick reeled off his bio.

"What a polymath. William Frederick Cody started his career when he was 11. He worked on a wagon train and crossed the Great Plains several times. Then came mining, fur trapping, and Pony Express riding. And he was just getting started. He scouted for the US Army, then hunted buffaloes for meat for railroad workers. Later in life came show business. Probably the most famous cowboy to have ever lived."

Maya was not interested.

"How long will you be gone?" She asked. "Will your team carry guns?" Patrick could see she was already traumatized, and said to himself, *"You're leaving your digital cocoon. Welcome to a hostile, terrifying physical world."*

He hated it when people used the trite quote, "You can check out any time you like, but you can never leave."

Nobody had put a gun to his head—he himself had volunteered to check into Hotel California. Worse, he was dragging Maya into it.

■ ■ ■

Later that evening, Bill Swanson was emotional while talking with his wife, Allison. "I hope Barry's okay. He's been very good to us."

Bill had an amazing collection of French red wine and he had decided to open a bottle of the 2006 Chateau Petrus Pomerol which has been described as "powerful, structured, and masculine." Bill decided he needed to feel powerful and masculine at this moment. He felt somewhat helpless having watched Clive during the Crisis Management meeting and the earnings call. Clive had hardly said anything. Barry was conspicuous by his absence. And he had the foreboding feeling he would be seeing a lot more Clive than Barry.

Unable to think of any better way to demonstrate the sense of his world being turned upside down, Bill had decided the most appropriate course was to drown his sorrows, and to open that bottle, worth thousands, to honor the catastrophic events of the day. He had already checked his BP; it was very high and he had taken an additional tablet. *"Probably not a good idea to mix extra meds with alcohol,"* Bill thought, *"but who cares."*

As Bill and Allison sat enjoying the bottle, they thought of the tens of millions of dollars, their whole retirement, which was at stake. They knew the SEC would be watching closely as Polestar stock fell, which would be normal when a CEO suddenly disappears.

Allison, a former Wall Street banker, managed their finances. She patted his shoulder and reminded him that he was in shock—and bade him not to judge himself. "It's been a traumatic day and you're very worried for Barry and Polestar. That's perfectly normal. Let's pray Barry is found and he's okay."

"You're right," Bill replied, "but I just can't help feeling an era has come to an end. You know Clive hits the ceiling when he sees Barry's expense reports. Often, there are interesting charges from nighttime establishments." They both laughed. Bill had told Allison of the increased tension over these expense reports.

He continued, "Do you remember how the VP of sales once told me he cringed when Barry asked for more direct access to his folks. He thought Barry was just using this as an excuse to meet more ladies. In reality, Barry just likes to hang out with salespeople at group dinners. Now of course, Barry's dinners are legendary, but you know, despite his rudeness, his love of women, and his drinking, there's never ever been a harassment complaint about him from any of our female staff—or male, for that matter.

"You remember that 360-degree review we had, where employees confidentially rated their supervisors and peers? We all knew that Clive really did it to get some confidential feedback on Barry. Clive was worried about Wall Street and wanted to know what he was dealing with. He wanted to know what the staff really thought of Barry, and just because there was not a complaint, it did not mean there were no problems.

"Well, as you know, much of the feedback was fairly vanilla. Clive told me there were many comments calling Barry 'brilliant,' 'inspirational,' 'high-energy,' 'charming,' and so on. But there were also quite a few who called him 'annoying,' 'exhausting,' 'crude,' and 'racist.' Clive discussed the negative feedback with Sharon in HR. Apparently, Barry's views on DEI and his teasing foreigners for their accents were viewed as racist. Sharon had reassured Clive that she'd worked with Barry forever and that while he is all those other adjectives, and more, 'racist' he isn't. Barry has created a very diverse organization, given how many occupations we have solutions for. His view on diversity, which is well known, is skills-based, not related to ethnicity or gender. After all, we have a new Chief Technology Officer named Tina Chang, who is a woman and has a Chinese background. Our CIO, Vijay, is of Indian descent. And John Grinder is mixed race. And many more—we have plenty of diversity.

"It's also true that Barry can be rude and crude with his sales team. He would talk about being poor and then becoming wealthy. Very wealthy. He says he much prefers being wealthy . . . 'every fucking time.'"

Allison agreed. "I've never heard him say anything I would construe as racist but he is often somewhat crude, even in mixed company. I've heard you say frequently, 'It's just Barry being Barry.' If his wife, his high-society friends, and the Board can't get him to shape up, then we just have to accept this is part of who he is. Not his most attractive side."

There was a long pause as Bill considered this complex man. He knew the wine had made him feel rather sentimental and made him forget how often he himself had questioned

Barry's soundness of mind. "Allison, do you remember how I told you about Barry's visit to the GE Global Research Center in Upstate New York and that when he went to lunch, he found himself surrounded by chemical engineers, astrophysicists, and nuclear scientists? This was, of course, back in GE's glory days, and the Center had over 1,500 technologists, many with PhDs covering every STEM (Science, Technology, Engineering, and Math) discipline. Remember how he challenged Patrick and Sharon from HR to build him one of those centers? He told them: 'I want us to be able to boast about Nobel Prize winners on our staff too.' Of course, they had to manage his expectations—GE had 30 to 40 times more revenue than Polestar back then. He wanted Nobel Prize winners on staff! Unbelievable! Barry has always dreamed big. You know I've never worked with anyone sharper than Barry, day or night. He's exhausting to be around."

Bill paused to think for a moment, then continued, "It's hard to believe that a month ago I was hosting a foursome on the golf course with Wall Street analysts at the Analyst Day event. It was such a fun day where I picked up some wicked jokes, and many of them have ended in the Polestar joke network. Boy, I don't feel like telling any jokes at the moment."

Allison looked at her husband. "Bill, I'm not sure the wine is helping. There's nothing you can do at the moment so maybe it's time for bed. I think you should be able to sleep with the wine you drank, so perhaps you don't need to take the sleeping pill."

Bill had drunk most of the bottle while Allison coolly considered how executive stock sales are closely scrutinized to slow down insider trading. Like many other companies,

Polestar took advantage of SEC Rule 10b5-1 to allow its officers to sell a predetermined number of shares at a predetermined time. She knew the next couple of weeks would be intense for her husband, and considered several possible scenarios:

A) Barry does not reappear.
B) Barry is back and survives Clive's inquisition.
C) Barry is back, is fired, and her husband is named CEO, at least for an interim.
D) Barry is back, is fired, and the Chairman becomes CEO.

She thought it was fair to say that, to a varying degree, everybody at the company was traumatized. Some as emotionally upset as her husband, no doubt. Barry was pretty popular. And almost everyone had a decent amount of stock.

Allison was aware of the tension between Clive and Barry. She agreed with her husband—that some people were not meant to be caged. She also had sympathy for Clive, who was just trying to help steer the company through the storm with an unpredictable captain at the helm. She shook her head. *"I'm jumping the gun. Let's see what happens when Barry is back."*

Patrick, like Allison, refused to believe Barry was dead. Neither of them factored a very different scenario—had Barry turned fugitive?

5

Hail Chad Caesar!

Wednesday am EST

At 5:45 am EST, a black sedan with a federal government plate pulled into Patrick and Maya's driveway. Patrick was waiting—after sleeping fitfully at the Vinoy, he'd taken an Uber home to pack a few clean clothes. He quickly exited the house with a laptop bag over his shoulder, pulling his carry-on case behind him. Ramon was in the back seat while a silent FBI driver was at the steering wheel.

"Good morning!" Ramon said. "I wanted to refresh you about protocol on the ride to the airport. It's extremely important not to contaminate the case in any way that could hinder prosecution. You didn't hear this from me, but Lars is likely to be standoffish, because you're a civilian. Also, Reggie is likely to be impatient. We still have no ransom note, if it is a kidnapping. The search parties have not found anything new in the ravine. And we're getting tips of Barry sightings from all over God's good earth."

"Let's hit the drive-through. I really need coffee and I know you love cinnamon buns," Patrick replied.

"Sure. And hey, good news!" Ramon said. "The only seat available this morning was in first class. I hope the rest of your day goes just as well."

Once in his 3rd row aisle seat, Patrick requested a Bloody Mary. *"That should knock me out for a couple of hours,"* he thought. The intensity of the offsite and the light sleep last night justified a siesta. He needed to be ready to pull an all-nighter, if necessary, when he got to the Bay Area. He told the flight attendant to wake him up over Oklahoma and to save him an omelet and an English muffin. He fell asleep even before his plane taxied to runway 1L/19R at TPA.

Right on time and place, Patrick's wake-up call and meal arrived. He munched the food down with some juice, asked for some club soda, pulled out his laptop, and fired up Sherlock. The plane's Wi-Fi appeared unavailable, and this digital tool was not effective offline. Patrick continued entering his list of suspects and motives that he had started the previous evening. He figured he would use his mobile Wi-Fi in the Uber from SFO to have it catch up. He fidgeted with the screen on the seatback—hoping to catch some news about Barry—and was told the entire flight infotainment system was down.

Six hours in the air is a lifetime for an analyst without any connectivity. On his way back from the restroom, he asked the friendly attendant to check with the pilot if he could reboot the system. No luck.

He was reminded of a sign at a restaurant: "No Wi-Fi here. Talk to each other. Pretend it is 1995."

So, he made polite conversation with his neighbor till the gentleman said, "I cannot believe how bad the Bay Area has become. Even a billionaire isn't safe anymore." Patrick did not take the bait but rather went back to his laptop and reviewed some vendor ratings on the Curmudgeon app. Again, it was far less useful without Wi-Fi connectivity.

So he looked over the downloaded personal emails he had received as part of the Oxford joke network. Patrick had inherited a good sense of humor from his mother. It went latent while he was at MIT, but reemerged at Polestar. When the two of them were in Barry's office, there was a continuous stream of giggles and laughs, and afterward Alisha would beg Patrick to share some of the best punch lines. Polestar had a joke network but HR shut it down. It migrated to a mailing list of personal email addresses.

Patrick was pleased to see Oxford had a similar joke network and HR, in a private company, could tolerate it much more than at Polestar. Tucker's guidance was also to keep it to private emails, and to keep the jokes within Oxford. And no making fun of any of Oxford staff. Vendor staff were fair game! And if you don't like the jokes, get off the mailing list. Don't get HR involved.

April 1st was typically a day of total confusion. You could never tell what was real or a joke among the fake resignations and press releases analysts floated.

Tucker also coached the analysts about presentations. Start off with a joke when you present but nothing political, religious, or sexual, he advised. Avoid jokes overseas where English is not their first language.

Patrick admired Tucker's public speaking polish. Tucker invested considerably in staff coaching, presentation aesthetics, Zoom backgrounds, etc. It was a transition for Patrick to present on an uncluttered stage, with no props except clickers, and the images or videos projected on giant screens. At Polestar, the products were the stars—they would always have tables to demo devices and such.

Maya would complain to Patrick that the jokes circulating were mostly juvenile. Patrick would remind her how humor is the best therapy on Wall Street, especially for traders. In a job where you constantly monitor world events—or any event, really, which can move a stock or commodity price—there is no shortage of material to opine on. Supposedly, the only topic off limits for them was plane crashes.

Patrick also told Maya: "The world needs more humor. The darned nighttime comedians have forgotten their job and turned into political commentators."

On this flight, however, he just got quizzical or dirty looks from everyone as he laughed aloud at several of the jokes. Unlike yawning, laughter is not always contagious.

∎ ∎ ∎

Reggie and Lars began Wednesday by interviewing Barry's direct reports, looking for insight into who might want to harm Barry. For the convenience of the company's executives, the meetings took place in the Polestar conference room affectionately known as the Command Center. It was an interior room with walls covered in whiteboards and video monitors. Eight automated video cameras, spaced equidistant, recorded every detail of the meetings held in the room. With microphones at each seat, and bright but surprisingly flattering lighting, there was no doubt every word and expression shared in the Command Center would be captured and archived as Polestar history.

Maria joined Reggie and Lars for the day. She explained the day's agenda and how the cameras and microphones worked, and promised that the FBI could download the recordings of the interviews at the end of the day.

First on the agenda was Jennifer Danielski, Polestar's Chief Marketing Officer. She had been at Polestar for six years, but only five months serving as CMO. Having already attended meetings in the room, she was less intimidated by the Command Center's technology than Reggie and Lars were.

"Before we discuss Mr. Roman's absence, please explain to Mr. Jensen and me how marketing is set up at Polestar. It would really help us know how things work, what the various groups do," Reggie said.

"As CMO," Jenifer started, "I lead all marketing efforts at Polestar. Our C-level execs work together to define our company's mission, values, and strategic objectives. From these, we distill our corporate branding. It is a focus area Barry Roman really enjoys. He views himself as the leader of the corporate branding team, and that includes personally reviewing all advertising and corporate level messaging.

"We continuously perform extensive research to maintain a keen understanding of our market, competitors, and customers. The findings from this research influence our brand strategy, defining who we are, who we serve, and what sets us apart in the marketplace. The Polestar leadership team sets the direction, but it's our marketing team that brings the C-level vision to life.

"Our marketing team is comprised of subteams for handling marketing analytics, product marketing, content marketing, digital marketing, corporate communications, and event marketing. All report directly to me. I'll give you a two-minute overview on each one.

"I'll start with marketing analytics, since their work is used for our corporate branding and everything else we do. Our analysts identify trends, examine customer behavior, and measure the effectiveness of our campaigns. Their data helps us continuously optimize our marketing strategies and execution.

"Next, product marketing is the bridge between our product development teams and the rest of our marketing groups. They're responsible for understanding our products' strengths and weaknesses, identifying key benefits and differentiators, and creating compelling messages that highlight their value to potential users.

"Our content marketing group takes the tools they get from product marketing and the educational materials that come from product development, and they produce our "thought leadership"—everything from in-depth blog posts and white papers to engaging videos and infographics. They help our audiences understand why our solutions are the best in the markets we serve.

"Digital marketing is the group that takes the content from product marketing and content management and leverages the latest digital techniques to ensure that our products not only appear prominently in search results but also engage and convert online visitors into leads. They rely on analytics to refine strategies and maximize ROI. Digital marketing, which includes social media, brings in roughly half the leads that we feed to our sales force.

"Next, we are responsible for corporate communications which includes analyst, media, and investor relations. We work with our product teams and constantly brief analyst firms like Oxford Research and media outlets like ZDNet. We work with our CFO to brief Wall Street analysts at banks like Sheldon Freres and at publications like *Barron's*.

"Those briefings have become extremely complex. About a decade ago, Workday pioneered an Analyst Day where it encouraged analysts to tweet. It was an electric environment as management took loads of questions and analysts live tweeted the exchanges. Soon after this, many vendors adopted the same approach. An Indian vendor, Zoho, had taken it to a new level as they flew selected analysts for a week-long trip to its HQ and to its CEO's farm in South India. It was meant to showcase the firm's culture and how it was a family to its employees and provided for schools, hospitals, and other facilities."

Reggie looked at Lars as if to implore, "Please do not tell her Patrick from Oxford is coming to visit us."

"Last but not least is our event marketing team. They bring our brand to life in the physical and virtual world by organizing and executing everything from webinars and online conferences to international trade shows. We spend a hundred million dollars on events because they bring in a significant percentage of our leads, and Polestar's sales team loves such events the most of anything we produce. The sales guys attend these events with prospects and turn them into customers."

Reggie asked, "Do you have any favorite venues?"

Jennifer replied, "Personally, I would prefer not to fly. We have some great venues for midsized groups in the Bay Area. My absolute favorite is Cavallo Point in Sausalito which blends the history of Fort Baker with stunning views of the Golden Gate Bridge. The Inn at Spanish Bay and the Ritz-Carlton in Half Moon Beach are excellent resorts for hosting. I just love listening to the bagpiper and watching the sunset over the Pacific at the Inn. For larger events we use the San Jose Convention Center or Moscone in San Francisco. But as we all know, our downtowns are not that pleasant or safe anymore and so we've been periodically hosting events in Vegas and Orlando—and in Barcelona for our EU events. I have a couple of team members that are constantly checking out new and interesting venues, their cuisine, ease of access, etc."

Reggie wanted to ask her next about the cuisine, but resisted. She did observe to herself that this lady is passionate about everything she does.

"What about advertising?" Lars asked. "I've heard the first thing that every new CMO does is fire their old advertising agency and get a new one to come up with a whole new ad campaign. I heard the Taco Bell ads with the talking chihuahua disappeared for a long time due to a change in marketing leadership. I loved those ads."

Jennifer laughed and said, "I loved them too. There's a lot of truth to what you're saying. We sell to companies, not to individual consumers, so our ads are not as fun, though enterprise tech marketing is starting to use rock stars and golf players. But we're satisfied with our current ad agency, which collaborated with our C-suite to develop our latest campaign. And we didn't just vote on concepts that the agency presented. Since everyone feels like they influenced the campaign, it would be hard for one person to decide to kill it. Although if Barry decided it was time for a new campaign, I'd have my marketing analytics team run numbers. If the numbers agreed with Barry, the C-suite would start exploring new ideas.

"Let me add another area where Barry adds to our marketing muscle. Polestar has an open line with product placement agencies in Hollywood. Many of Polestar's robots and other devices show up in movies and TV ads. It works both ways, though, because the corporate auditorium shows early-release versions of movies that focus on occupations like linguists, beekeepers, and astronauts. Then the younger staff have spirited conversations about how technology had 'evolved' that profession."

"You seem pretty down-to-earth for a CMO," Reggie said.

Jennifer laughed again. "Don't forget, I've only been in this role for five months. And I started my career in product marketing, where I spent half my time understanding what the markets want, and communicating that to our software engineers. Engineers can quickly detect marketing bullshit and they'll just say that they don't have time to work with an asshole. But if you're ready, I'd like to tell you about a marketing asshole who you might want to check out as a suspect."

"Okay, go for it," Lars said.

Jennifer started, "When I heard you wanted to interview Barry's directs for input on potential suspects, I immediately thought of Chad Rogers."

"Who is he, what was his relationship to Barry, and why do you think Chad might want to harm him?" Lars asked.

"Chad Rogers was my predecessor, the former CMO. Let me tell you about him. He's about 5'9", completely over-groomed with eyebrows plucked more than mine, and a meticulously sculpted beard. He wears heavy hair gel and overpriced contemporary fashion. He cycles through girl-friends so fast that no one on his team ever asked if he had a nice weekend with Sherry, in case he'd already moved on to a Tracy or a Michelle."

"And?" Reggie prodded.

"Five months ago, Barry fired Chad for misuse of com-pany resources and it didn't take long for most of Silicon Valley to hear about it. Chad was literally a laughingstock, and a vain guy like him has to be filled with rage," Jennifer responded.

"Okay, go on."

She continued, "This was three months before the launch of Polestar's biggest AI product. Chad scheduled a full-day meeting of the entire marketing department, ostensibly to finalize plans for the product launch. All the North American marketing employees attended in person, and the overseas team members attended virtually.

"So, everyone's in the auditorium, well-caffeinated, waiting for the meeting to begin. Then we hear trumpets and here comes Chad, dressed as "Chad Caesar," on a chariot wagon pulled by six hired actors dressed in togas. Suddenly, the volume in the auditorium went way up.

"Most of the audience was laughing, and saying things like, 'Holy fuck, I don't believe this.' As Chad was brought onto the stage, out come about a dozen female actresses, dressed in low-cut mini togas, holding large fans made of white feathers, and they started fanning him. Chad was stretched out on that wagon, face plastered with a shit-eating grin. Then he stood up and gestured to the slide on the 40-foot screen behind him. The crowd quieted down to hear what he had to say. But instead of getting to the agenda, those toga babes chanted 'Chad Caesar, fearless leader,' and everyone lost it again.

"Eventually people shut up and the meeting got started. All morning, before each presenter walked through their product launch plan, the AV team lit up the screen with short videos showing scenes of actors playing Julius Caesar in various victories, with Chad's face edited over the faces of Jeremy Sisto, Rex Harrison, and Laurence Olivier. I sat there thinking, *'Now I know why I'm still waiting for my beta customer testimonials from our video team. What a self-aggrandizing asshole!'*"

"Still sounds like gossip," Reggie said.

"All right, I just wanted you to understand the whole situation. During the lunch break, I got a call from Barry's executive assistant, asking me to come to Barry's office.

When I got there, it was a very short meeting. Barry told me he had just fired Chad Rogers and that he wanted me to take over as CMO. He said he'd been watching my work as VP of marketing for AI products and felt I was a good fit. Of course, I said yes. Then Barry said he'd make the announcement himself in about an hour and I should not tell anyone before he did. So, I went back to the auditorium and waited."

"And why do you think Chad is a suspect?" Lars prodded this time.

"So, after lunch, Barry made a surprise appearance on stage, and the place went silent. Barry praised the hard work of the marketing team and talked about how the new AI product was revolutionary and how glad he was to have a world-class marketing team to launch it. Then he announced me as the new Chief Marketing Officer. So then everyone realized this meant that Chad had been fired, and you should have heard the noise in the auditorium! Everyone was talking about how Barry might as well have fired Chad in front of all of us. Some people started chanting 'Chad Caesar, fearless leader,' and howling with laughter! And Barry started laughing too." Jennifer was laughing loudly, herself.

"Later, I went back to my office, which was next to Chad's. A security guard was standing outside Chad's office and Chad was in there, literally throwing things in boxes, and swearing up a storm. And I heard him say, 'I'm going to kill that fucking asshole,' and other threats. I remember the security guard used his radio and suddenly there was a second guard in the hallway. You should ask them about it.

"Chad was beyond humiliated, and I'm sure he still is. I'm serious. The story of 'Chad Caesar, fearless leader' was all over the Bay Area. I went to a party a week later, with non-Polestar folks who were telling the Chad Caesar story, and a couple of women were laughing so hard, their mascara was all over their faces."

A flicker of a smirk crossed Maria's face for a millisecond.

"Thank you, Jennifer. We'll call you to follow up with more questions," Reggie said.

After the door closed behind Jennifer, Reggie and Lars burst into laughter.

"Oh yeah, we have to check Chad out," Lars said, nodding emphatically.

Jennifer failed to share another detail. Barry had not abruptly decided to fire Chad. He had been impressed by Jennifer in a meeting where she said "MQLs bring curiosity, SQLs bring cash."

"Is that SQL as in Structured Query Language?" he'd asked her.

"No, SQL as in Sales Qualified Leads. Very different from MQLs—Marketing Qualified Leads," she replied. "In our digital world, we get plenty of curious visitors. We may count them as leads, but they are not ready for our highly paid sales teams to spend time on. We have to watch for signals from our website, social media, and phone calls that they are ready to become SQLs."

Soon after, Barry had asked Jennifer to review Chad's processes and budgets and give him a candid summary. Her results: "We are spending too many marketing dollars and deriving vanity metrics. We're investing in some channels which get us plenty of eyeballs but very few enterprise class prospects. In some, we're getting lots of web bots with not a cent to their name. Our marketing is not verticalized enough, given our product portfolio. No wonder our sales teams complain they aren't getting decent leads so they are out prospecting on their own. I feel really bad for our sales teams outside North America. We are not doing them many favors."

Chad was an old-school marketer—big on flash and vanity. Barry had blamed himself for that—*"I encouraged Chad to be brash. But not to piss away dollars. And sure as hell not to spend money glorifying himself."*

. . .

Patrick established access to the mobile network as his plane landed at SFO. He found a surprisingly light load of messages. Tucker, Martha, Henry, and Maya had kept the Oxford team busy with the breakouts today. Most of the offsite event attendees must be getting ready to fly out.

He saw a text from Reggie. "Lars and I are at Polestar HQ this morning. Check into your hotel and we will call you when we are ready to leave. We will meet at my Campbell, CA, office."

Before the pandemic, Patrick would have headed to the rental car center. While travel in general had deteriorated, he found renting cars had become miserable. It used to take minutes to rent one, and a few minutes to check one back in with an associate and their mobile device. Not anymore. That sector needed to rethink automation and employee productivity. He took an Uber to the Marriott near the San Jose Convention Center. He had stayed there for an event a few years earlier and the Concierge Lounge had been especially nice to him. He also remembered they had given him high-intensity glow sticks, as they were expecting power outages. He marveled at the useless trivia jammed in that brain of his.

He asked the hotel receptionist if there was anything touristy that he could squeeze in for a couple of hours. She rattled off a list of places including the Municipal Rose Garden and the Guadalupe River Trail. She then said, "How about something really unique?" Patrick raised his eyebrows.

"The Winchester Mystery House." Patrick immediately said "Yes!" He thought it would have some of the history of rifles and the FBI. She arranged for a ticket for a mansion tour.

■ ■ ■

Smiling, Maria said, "We need coffee refills. What would you like for this round?"

"I want to try a mocha with foam," Reggie replied.

"This time," Lars blurted, "I want a regular black drip coffee. No *Americano* crap. Real Americans drink regular drip coffee."

Maria made a call and 10 minutes later three large coffees were delivered to the door in Polestar mugs, followed soon after by the president of Polestar's venture capital division, who carried his own coffee mug and a manila folder.

"May I introduce Fabrice Legrand, president of our VC division," Maria said. "Fabrice, this is Regina Williams of the FBI and Lars Jensen, representing the Sheriff's department." Fabrice nodded to the investigators and pulled business cards out of the inside breast pocket of an impeccably cut, double-breasted suit jacket and handed them to Lars and Reggie.

Looking at the card in his hand, Lars said, "Fabrice means 'the craftsman' and obviously Legrand means 'the large.' So I'll remember you as the large craftsman."

Reggie rolled her eyes at Lars, then handed her own card to Fabrice. "Nice to meet you, Fabrice."

"It is my pleasure to meet you, Regina and Lars. I would prefer the circumstances were different," he said with a French accent. Both Reggie and Lars looked surprised.

His man-purse had given Reggie a clue, but she politely asked, "You're French, or French-Canadian?"

"Regina, I spent my first 30 years in France, mostly in Paris. My entire career has been in technology, some of it with the advanced research branch of the Ministry of the Armed Forces. A joint project with your DARPA led me to Lawrence Livermore National Labs. I then discovered the joys of venture capitalism on Sand Hill Road, and I have been in my present position at Polestar for five years."

"It's going to be very pleasant listening to this man talk," Reggie thought.

"She is a brown goddess," Fabrice thought, smiling.

"Fucking frog in a fancy suit," thought Lars, scowling.

"Let's get started," said Maria. "Our VC team evaluated some AI software from a startup firm called Nested Models, owned primarily by Amin Mehdi, about two years ago. At first their product looked promising, but we decided not to invest. That ended very badly."

"Yes," Fabrice agreed. "The details of the software product that we reviewed are not especially important for me to tell you. It is the outcome that you should know."

Reggie asked, "Give us some background here—what's the process when someone comes to you for VC funding?"

"To start with," Fabrice said, "I run Polestar Ventures, which is largely funded by Polestar. The Roman family has its own fund, a separate legal entity. They tend to make smaller, early round investments. In VC vernacular, that is called 'seed money.' We invest in later stages where startups are more mature—they have a growing number of customers and revenues, far beyond being just an idea. There is a very disciplined hierarchy of investments in the VC community. Startups get ever larger rounds of funding before they finally go public or get acquired. This way, entrepreneurs have to go through several gates and milestones before they qualify for the next check. Another aspect of the VC community is that we're always part of a consortium to diversify our risks. We either lead a consortium of investors or we're invited to join one. And at every stage, each of us does our own due diligence to decide if we want to make the additional investment.

"When we got to the due diligence stage for Amin's software, all the references came back positive. Tina Chang, who heads our R&D, was intrigued by its architecture. I am not a technologist but she explained to me that they were using large language models for some of the processing, then branching out to small language models and to what they called narrow models for others. They said it would minimize utilization of expensive graphical processing units, or GPUs, and their energy demands. Also smaller models tend to be easier to reuse across many functions.

"As you may know, Nvidia is going gangbusters with its premium-priced GPUs. Let me give you a quick tutorial on the massive computing power it takes to process the prompts millions are posing to ChatGPT, Claude, and other large language models. The text that we humans input is translated into tokens. A token is a couple of Unicode characters. Unicode is a standard with a mission to allow everyone around the world to use their own language on phones and computers. It supports 150,000 characters across languages and scripts—right to left, top to bottom, and every variation in between. Also, nearly 4,000 emojis, which as you know have become a universal language of sorts.

"The tokens are then converted into vectors. Vectors are multiplied by billions of weights. And there is plenty more before ChatGPT responds to a prompt. That's because we are not limited in what we can ask it. Its model has to be extremely large. In turn, large models require GPUs with large amounts of memory to hold the model, its parameters, and the data being processed.

"Sorry for that detour—Tina can spend hours on what I described in a couple of minutes.

"So we began a deep investigation into the software. It performed some valuable functions that we wanted to add to our AI solutions. We thought about acquiring this small software company, to save us time, rather than to develop this functionality ourselves."

"So the startup firm wanted you to invest in their company and you wanted to buy and take over the entire company?" Lars asked.

"Yes. That is very common, and not what caused the problem," Fabrice said. "The issues arose when we tested the software on our large test database. It required us to parse the data into smaller chunks to feed their models and it still caused performance issues. So we examined the software code and found that it was poorly written. It could never scale. Meaning, it could never process the large data volumes needed to make it valuable. We also got concerned about the data fragmentation. Customers increasingly want detailed audit trails on how AI generates results. You may have heard about machines 'hallucinating'—when misleading results can be caused by insufficient training data, incorrect assumptions made by the model, or biases used in the training data.

"They did not really have a software product; they had an idea. We already had the same idea, but we were trying to buy software that took the idea to a completed and patentable product. So we terminated our evaluation and rejected the funding request."

"Is this an unusual situation? How might this be relevant to our search for Barry Roman," Reggie asked, more politely than she had questioned the CMO earlier.

Maria interjected, "We decline most funding requests. In fact, most never get this far into due diligence."

Fabrice continued, explaining, "At first, there was no worry on our part. Our AI design team simply returned to designing our own solution for the same functionality. We feared it would take several years before we completed our own product. But we hired additional engineers from MIT, and they had new ideas. They looked at our designs and improved them, and we started coding within three months. We finished coding the new product last month. And then Barry started receiving death threats."

"Now you're talking," Lars said.

Fabrice nodded. "Phone calls came to Barry's direct line, accusing him of stealing the design for our new product, and saying that he would be killed. But we couldn't trace the calls, and the voice was identical to Barack Obama's. Of course, the calls were created using an AI speech generator."

"East Palo Alto Police and San Mateo County Sheriff personnel can tell you about their investigation," Maria said. "Of course, we suspected Nested Models immediately. Theirs was the only AI solution we evaluated that had functionality similar to the product we'd just launched. The threats stopped once the Sheriff brought the entire team in for questioning. And we sent Amin and other founders of Nested Models a letter detailing how our technology and functionality is vastly different from theirs."

Lars piped up, "So you saw their prototype, stole their idea, and that gave you a head start on your own product. You already found out what wasn't going to work by looking at Nested Models' code. They did the hard work, and you used them to school your designers."

"That's naive," Maria replied. "You can't patent an idea; you can only patent a solution."

"We did only what every VC firm does," Fabrice said. "We looked to invest in the software to complete our product functionality. Their software did not work when we tested it. So we made our own."

"And what's the status of Nested Models now?" Reggie asked.

"They're shutting down. The website is still up but the office is up for lease and their sign was removed," Maria said.

"Our team will investigate. Thank you for the information," Reggie said.

"He's charming but he's a snake," she thought as Fabrice exited the room.

6

Are We Here for a Software Demo?

∿➤

Wednesday pm PST

T he clock on the wall showed nearly 1:00 pm. Reggie asked Maria, "Can we get an In-N-Out Burger delivery? Will security have a problem with that?"

"Alisha already scheduled you for lunch and a tour with Alex, one of our Customer Visit Center administrators. We thought you should see the full campus, as it might offer you some insights into life at Polestar," she replied.

"What time?" Reggie asked, while thinking, *"I'd rather have an Animal Style cheeseburger and fries."*

"No more than five minutes. He's on standby."

"That'll work," Reggie nodded, as Maria left the room and closed the door.

Lars had a scowl on his face. "What the hell? We're not here to be convinced to buy software or Polestar stock."

"I'd rather eat In-N-Out and keep working," Reggie said.

"Who would name their company In-N-Out—you know what I mean?" Lars said.

Reggie smiled and said, "When I first moved to California, I blushed the first time someone asked me if I wanted to 'grab an In-N-Out for lunch.' It didn't help that it was a male colleague, in the first few days we'd worked together. He saw my reaction and burst out laughing and said 'Let me explain!'"

Lars opened the door when Alex knocked. "Hi, I'm Alex Brocato and I'm delighted to take you to lunch and show you around Polestar HQ," said a tall, sandy-haired young man dressed in crisp khaki slacks and a polo shirt with a Polestar logo. "Shall we start with lunch or the tour first?"

"Lunch!" replied Reggie and Lars in unison.

■ ■ ■

At the Winchester House, Patrick's tour concerned itself with a lot of rifles but in a way he found profoundly spooky. Sarah Winchester, heiress of the gun-making business fortune, was advised by a medium to move West in the 1880s upon the untimely deaths of her husband and child. She was told to build a house and continue adding to it, to atone for the many deaths the rifle had caused. The Winchester Model 1873 rifle and the Colt .45 were called "the guns that won the West."

She started with an eight-room farmhouse, and kept building nonstop for 38 years with a team of 13 carpenters. The house ended up with 10,000 windows, 47 fireplaces and plenty of other eye-popping details in a sprawl of 160 acres, costing her a total of $5 million (nearly $75 million in today's dollars). It would be a significant overstatement to say she had a master plan—there are doors that open into walls of brick, doors that open to the air outside, staircases that go nowhere, and so on. She spent $1,500 on a Tiffany window glass designed to act as a prism and cast a rainbow of colors in the room. But she had it installed on the north side of the house which the sunlight does not touch. The San Francisco area earthquake of 1906 leveled some of the house, leading to other construction changes and costs. Not surprisingly, the construction came to a halt when she died.

Patrick thought he had seen a sign for a "Café 13" at the mansion, but found out it was only open on weekends, so he made do with slim pickings—a bag of chips and a candy bar he bought in the gift shop. He wished he had arranged to meet Reggie and Lars at the Polestar Café but that would have led to all kinds of rumors.

Patrick walked around the gardens at the house. Sarah Winchester had also managed several botanical beauties like a Saucer Magnolia tree, a few Spartan Juniper trees, and some Creeper Trumpet vines. Equally as interesting, he saw a hedge in the shape of number 13—which must have been Sarah's favorite number, Patrick imagined.

As he walked around the grounds, Patrick chuckled at how little he had learned during that tour about the history of the FBI. He had picked up much more from any conversation he'd had with Ramon. At one of their lunches, Patrick had asked Ramon: "Is it true what the media says about the politicization of the FBI?"

Ramon responded, "Nothing new, and true of most federal agencies—the FAA, IRS, and so on. The field staff are very driven, loyal citizens." (And, as he often thought but did not say, understaffed and underpaid.) "The regional offices are bureaucracies," Ramon said. "The headquarters in Washington, DC, are the political hives. I can tell you most of my fellow agents are incredibly proud of the FBI's history. And most of us are regularly embarrassed by what goes on in DC."

■ ■ ■

Patrick had read in one of the leaflets that Sarah was also a keeper of exotic birds. He wondered what descendants now occupied the aviary.

He was thinking, *"Now that was interesting—not something you see every day and in every city."* That was an understatement. It has been called the most haunted house in the US.

■ ■ ■

Reggie and Lars took the elevator to the first floor and Alex led them to the Polestar Café, which bore no resemblance to any company cafeteria either detective had ever seen. While the Café's layout was like a food court, that's where any similarity ended. The walls were covered in what looked like silk wallpaper and the tables and chairs were blond wood.

There was no plastic laminate in sight. Alex gave them a quick tour of the food stations.

The wood-fired pizza kiosk was extremely popular. Large margarita, pepperoni, and grilled vegetable pizzas were sold by the slice, while 12" individual pizzas were made to order. Two toque-blanche-topped chefs were tossing pizza dough to the rapt attention of employees waiting in line.

The vegan station appeared to be the favorite of many of Polestar's Indian employees, and the meals on display were a colorful assortment of food art. A 20-foot-long salad bar had lettuce, spinach, kale, arugula, and what seemed to be every type of greenery and legume one could desire on a salad. Reggie saw a bowl of Black Seeded Simpson lettuce and took a photo of the sign to later show to her husband. Next was the delicatessen food station, replete with New York City décor, but the staff smiled while asking, "What can I make you for lunch today?" instead of yelling "What'll you have?"

The food station that caught Lars' attention was "The Grille," where steaks, chicken, and sausages were sizzling over flames. "This look okay to you?" Lars asked Reggie.

"Damn good, especially the chicken," she replied.

After the investigators had placed their orders, Alex asked them to sit at one of the tables in the open center of the Café.

"My husband would love this place. He'd probably eat a different dish each day and then try to replicate them at home," said Reggie.

Lars agreed, "It smells absolutely fabulous in here. Lunch has to be the highlight of each workday."

Alex came to the table accompanied by a white-aproned man pushing a cart with their meals. Employees at surrounding tables looked to see who was receiving the special delivery service not normally afforded to Café patrons.

Taking a seat, Alex gave a small wave to onlookers. "Oh, it's that guy from the CVC, with customers," an employee commented to colleagues at his table.

Lars cut into his perfectly cooked steak. "If I worked here, I'd definitely gain weight—if I could afford it." Since Alex had made clear they were his guests for lunch, Lars hadn't noticed the food prices.

"Actually, take a peek at the pricing boards on our way out," Alex said. "All the meals are subsidized by Polestar. We encourage employees to take a break and get good nutrition to fuel their day. Having so many excellent food choices right on campus makes life easy for our team."

After finishing their meals, Alex escorted the detectives through the far side of the Café where they passed the omelet and Mexican food stations. At the exit, a sign reminded employees that "grab and heat" dinners were available from 5:00 pm to 7:00 pm each evening.

They then proceeded down a hall into another wing of Polestar's central campus building. They passed the frosted glass doors of Alejandro's hair salon. Alex opened the door to show the salon with eight chairs, where mostly male clientele were getting haircuts. Next, they peeked into the Relaxation Center, a suite with low lighting and lavender-scented air where employees were receiving chair massages to relax their shoulders, necks, arms, and hands—the standard areas of pain for keyboard-bound employees. Next door was the gift store with all kinds of swag with Polestar logos—coffee cups, polos, jackets, etc. He pointed to a corner with a "Tommy Chu's" sign hanging and where Savile Row bespoke quality suits, dress shirts, shoes, and other clothing items were hanging or wrapped and waiting to be picked up.

"Tommy comes here every few weeks and takes measurements," Alex said. "The rest of the time, this is the delivery location."

"Are these services subsidized?" Reggie asked.

"They're at the lower end of market prices," Alex replied. "Food is essential. The rest of the on-site services are primarily a convenience for our employees." He added, "Tommy Chu is premium-priced. I can't afford him, but our salespeople swear by his custom-made suits and shoes."

The three passed the dry-cleaning center, where employees were dropping off nylon drawstring bags or picking up plastic-covered clothes on hangers. Exiting the main building, they walked on a brick-paved walkway to the employee fitness center, a three-story building with large windows where fit-looking employees were exercising. Surprisingly, the fitness center didn't smell like sweat. The ultraviolet light air cleaning system circulated a faint lemon verbena scent, energizing the athletes.

Next, Alex showed Lars and Reggie the company's childcare center. "We provide top-notch care and education for children eight weeks to five years old." A large playground featured tiny equipment for toddlers and standard play equipment for older children. "The hours are 6:00 am to 7:00 pm, and the food options are diverse enough to accommodate all the religious preferences of our multinational employee families. On Saturday, our hairstylist, Alejandro, opens up the salon to parents with young boys. You should see how proud they look when they leave."

Next on the campus tour was Polestar's conference center, the site of the "Chad Caesar, Fearless Leader" incident. The 4,000-seat main auditorium was empty, but the two wings of standard meeting rooms were fully occupied.

Alex completed the tour by walking his guests back to the Command Center conference room. "So, what do you think of our campus?" he asked.

"This is amazing," Reggie said. "Except for sleeping, you could practically live here!"

"That's the idea," Alex said. "We want to make life as easy as possible for our employees."

"So they can work 60 hours or more each week," Lars said.

"That's one way to look at it," Alex replied. "It's been a pleasure. Thank you for letting me show you around." He smiled as he left.

■ ■ ■

Maria returned to the Command Center with some file folders and a full mug of black coffee. "There are two more situations that could be relevant to your investigation. The first one dates back four years, when East Palo Alto approved our request to rezone the residential neighborhood, which is now our headquarters campus."

Lars and Regina nodded.

"Barry had wanted to expand our HQ, so for many years our real estate division had been buying properties for a new campus. So, in each of these potential office locations, we bought every property that came on the market, under the names of multiple trusts and entities. In response, prices edged up and property owners became more interested in selling. We let the properties out under short-term leases.

"Our current location was always Barry's favorite of the potential targets. He wanted to be able to say that we have a campus right across I-84 from Meta. He liked the idea of having an unobstructed view of the bay, and the location was an easy exit off 101. Four years ago, when we had acquired more than half of the neighborhood under dozens of different names, we requested rezoning from East Palo Alto."

"And that would be when this situation erupted?" Lars said.

"Yes. The remaining homeowners didn't join in the protest; it was the renters who were upset. As is standard for any big development, our real estate division made generous offers to the remaining homeowners, which were contingent on all of them agreeing to sell and vacate by a specific date. It was the offer of a lifetime for people who owned those homes, and we closed the sales quickly. It was the renters who got a nonprofit to plead their case with the planning board and the city council. They bought billboard ads and staged protests, which were covered by the local newspapers and television stations."

"I assume you expected that reaction? Just because this is a common story across the country doesn't mean it's fair to force out lower-income families," Reggie said.

"There were three residents who joined together to incite others," Maria said. "Their common denominator was that each had been a long-term renter and had extended family packed into their houses. They'd lived in those houses for over 20 years, since the days when East Palo Alto was considered dangerous and undesirable. Way before the Four Seasons went in on the west side of the city and woke up developers to the potential." Maria paused to sip her coffee.

"Sounds pretty typical," Lars said. "This kind of push-back happens everywhere."

"Well, these protesters knew they couldn't harm Polestar by boycotting their software—that's one of the beautiful aspects of selling enterprise software where deals start at a million dollars. So, anonymous threats were made on Barry's life. All the details are in this folder," Maria said, gliding the folder across the table to the detectives. "We sweetened the deal with moving expenses and rental deposits for long-term, multigenerational renters. But the threats kept coming in."

"Net it out for us. What did East Palo Alto police do?" Regina asked.

"They traced the threats to the three ringleaders and arrested them. All three of them had priors and were held without bail. The fire went out of the protests when the prosecutors charged the three men who made the death threats. Within three months of closing the sales on the houses, they were vacated and the residents were relocated. We razed the buildings immediately to avoid a squatter situation. We've been in our new HQ for a year now, and it really helps us with recruitment and retention."

"So why is this something we should investigate now?" Regina asked.

"All three of those guys have completed their sentences and are out. With Barry missing, you might want to find out where they are and what they're up to."

"Got it. What's next on your list?"

Maria shifted in her seat and decided she needed another coffee. She walked over to the beverage station in the back corner of the room, lifted a thermal carafe, and took her time pouring the steaming liquid into her mug. Reggie and Lars both recognized that she was suddenly uncomfortable.

"I didn't hear the announcement that this is break time. But if you insist . . . ," Reggie said, and pulled a canned, flavored sparkling water from the ice bucket on the beverage station. *It was so difficult to get a plain old Diet Coke anymore,* she sighed.

They both returned to the conference table. "You asked me to tell you of anyone who might want to harm Barry," Maria said. "This involves a situation that we settled out of court. The police were never involved. It's a sad story."

"Sounds interesting," Lars said.

Maria began, "Two years ago, before the Roosevelt Club ceased operations, Barry and Scott Bates, the CEO of Pumpkin Technologies, were on a panel for an event discussing AI. I don't know if you already know, but Barry and Scott were close friends since the early days of Polestar, and Scott had been a big investor. So they shared a limo to the event, had a couple of drinks in the car, and arrived just in time to take the stage. Scott led the discussion, and Barry and others shared their thoughts, normal panel stuff. Then this other panelist, a guy named Greg Carson, highjacks the discussion, says

Barry and Scott are way behind the times in their thinking, and he goes off on some rant. If you've heard anything about Scott you know he's not afraid to tell someone they're an idiot, but that night he just kept saying, 'Really, tell us more.' The guy thinks Scott is really impressed and reaches out across Barry to hand his card to Scott, and the *Jupiter News* included a photo of that faux pas in the next day's paper.

"So, after the event, Barry and Scott drank several shots in the limo on the way home, since traffic was so slow. Then Scott calls Greg and says he and Barry were impressed by his brilliance and that they want to meet with him to discuss a role at the new joint venture the two firms are launching. The guy's so excited he can't wait, wants to talk to them immediately. So, they end up picking up Greg and driving around in the limo, pouring Greg drinks and talking about this nonexistent joint venture and a nonexistent Chief Scientist role. Then they drop Greg off at his house. Turns out the guy is an alcoholic who'd been sober for many years, but ended up taking a fifth of Chivas Regal as he left the limo, and drank it at home." Maria paused to sip some more coffee.

Regina and Lars had been silent until now. "Please continue," Lars said.

"Greg drinks more of the booze and is so excited he decides to call the reporter from the *Jupiter News*. He tells the reporter that he's in discussions with Scott and Barry for the Chief Scientist position at the as-yet-unnamed new joint venture between Polestar and Pumpkin. He tells the reporter what his plans would be for the new firm, tries to convince the reporter he's a genius. The *Jupiter News* tried to confirm with our PR department, and Pumpkin's too, but no one knew what he was talking about, so they decided they needed to do some research—and neither company called the reporter back. Based on the Roosevelt Club event, the reporter thought that Greg might be credible. So, the *Jupiter News* ran two stories. One was straight-up about the panel discussion. The other story was labeled as 'valley gossip' and they quoted Greg talking about what his vision was for the rumored joint-venture firm.

"Being publicly traded, both Pumpkin Technologies and Polestar had to issue press releases saying that no joint venture was in consideration between the firms, that no Chief Scientist positions were open at either firm, and no interviews had been conducted with Greg. That poor guy was so embarrassed, he went on a bender and ended up in the hospital with alcohol poisoning."

"I'm not hearing how this guy could be our suspect," Reggie said.

"I'm not proud to say that the incident really ruined the guy's life. Once he recovered, he sued us and Pumpkin Technologies, and Scott and Barry personally. Scott played hardball, but Barry felt horrible and personally paid for medical costs and rehab, and cofunded our settlement with Greg. The guy got enough millions to start his own firm, if he wanted to. But still, Greg swore that someday he would get even with Barry and Scott."

"Wow, from your story I guess CEO stands for Chief Asshole?" Lars suggested.

"The two men are no longer close, if that provides any consolation," Maria said.

"We'll check Greg out. Have anything else for us today?" Reggie asked.

"That's all we've got for now. I'll leave you to read the files, but I've cleared my day of meetings to help answer any questions you might have. So, never hesitate to call me on my mobile, anytime. And I mean that." Maria closed the door as she left.

■ ■ ■

Reggie looked at Lars and asked, "Are all CEOs such jackasses, or is it just in this industry, or just in Silicon Valley?"

"The valley is notorious for jackasses, assholes, ego-maniacs, and sociopaths who believe in success at any cost," Lars said.

After the two had reviewed the files' contents for an hour, Lars stood up and stretched. "You have any questions for Maria, or shall we move on?"

"Let's move on," Reggie said. "I'm going to initiate checks on all these folks when I get back to the office." She put the files in her briefcase, and they walked to the elevator.

As Reggie drove south on 101 toward San Jose, Lars silently read though his phone messages. When Reggie exited at the Lawrence Expressway, Lars asked, "I thought we were going back to your office."

"We are, but first we're going to In-N-Out Burger."

"If you're as tenacious with investigations as you are about hamburgers, we'll find this billionaire by tomorrow night. What's the fascination with In-N-Out?" Lars asked.

"You know how I said my husband is a gourmet cook? The downside is he hates fast food. I tell him In-N-Out is gourmet fast food, but he won't listen."

Reggie turned right on Bridgewood Way and took another immediate right. A homeless camp had been set up under the trees separating the Lawrence Expressway from Wildwood Avenue. "Did you know that half of all homeless people in the United States live in California?" Lars asked. "And at least 40,000 of them are here in the Bay Area. That's up around 35 percent in the past five years."

"You memorized these statistics?" Reggie asked.

"I volunteer at various shelters," Lars said. "I just read a new report on the topic. The problem just keeps getting worse, even though the state increased funding from less than a billion dollars to almost five billion a year. The report said we have created a 'Homeless Industrial Complex.' Over the last five years, the state has supposedly spent $20 billion which it cannot explain, and the homeless numbers have gone up! So many hoteliers and businesses thrive on those big dollars. And our state's welfare generosity is a magnet for homeless from other states. When you call yourself a 'sanctuary city,' you're setting up large billboards attracting runaway teenagers and dropouts from society."

"Detroit had unhoused people," Reggie said, "but when I moved here, I was shocked to see how much more prevalent homelessness is. I wonder if it's the great Bay Area weather . . . because no one will freeze to death living outdoors?"

"When I first started volunteering," Lars replied, "I had preconceived notions that it was mostly substance abusers and the mentally disabled who were homeless. Now I know the issue is way more complicated than that. I can hook your gourmet cook husband up with a shelter in your area, if he'd consider making basic food for grateful people."

"I'll talk to him. He really might want to do that!" Reggie said as she pulled her car into the In-N-Out parking lot. "Now I'm feeling guilty for this feast I'm about to eat. But I can't solve a case on an empty stomach."

They walked into the restaurant, and Reggie placed her order. "What the hell is Animal Style?" Lars asked. The college student working behind the counter sighed, which Reggie noticed.

"We don't have time for that. Do you like pickles?" she asked him.

"No."

"Then just order a Double Double with fries and a drink."

When their order number was called, Lars carried over their tray. "Quick, I have to salt the fries while they're still vulnerable!" Reggie said.

"What the hell is a vulnerable fry?"

"The salt will only stick to the fries when they're really hot and moist from the oil," she answered, reaching over to salt Lars' fries too.

"You obviously learned that from your gourmet husband. Wait, I don't like too much salt."

"Try them," Reggie ordered.

His eyes opened wide. "Damn, these really aren't fast food fries! They're amazing."

"Told you," she said. "Now taste your burger. You'll be hooked too."

They ate silently while checking their phones for status updates. For security, Lars waited until the walk back to the car to tell Reggie: "The security cameras didn't catch anything helpful at Barry's home. He and his bodyguard were laughing as they exited the property. Probably the last laugh the guard ever had."

Reggie said, "Patrick Brennan should have arrived to my office by now. Let's go meet this know-it-all and see if he's going to add as much value as we've been told."

■ ■ ■

In his mind, Patrick thanked Sarah for the tour of the bizarre estate she called Llanda Villa, and prepared to make the trek to Campbell to meet with Reggie and Lars.

In the Uber, Patrick caught up with Maya, who sounded satisfied with how the offsite had gone. She added, "It's so lonely without you. I just realized how little either of us has traveled in the last few weeks. I suspect we will have to get used to more people visiting us in St. Pete."

Patrick talked about the mystery house and Maya observed, "Patrick, that must be some kind of a touristy record for you. Dali, James, and now Sarah's house all in a week!" Patrick wasn't flattered. He thought to himself *"Instead, I should have gone into the ravine and looked for Barry"*

■ ■ ■

At Reggie's office in Campbell, Patrick, Reggie, and Lars walked into the meeting room holding hot beverages in paper

132

cups. "You missed out on our meetings at Polestar, Patrick," Reggie said, trying to get the analyst to relax so he'd open up a bit. "We were offered any kind of coffee we wanted. First, I had a cappuccino, and then I had a caffe mocha with a heart in the cream. Probably a thousand calories in those drinks. Now we just have drip coffee, but hey, at least we have real half-and-half, none of that powdered stuff."

Lars was reading something on his phone. Patrick asked Lars, "What did you drink?"

Lars looked up. "What? Oh, I asked for black coffee. I was given an Americano—diluted Espresso. I was like 'What the hell is this, it's terrible.' So, after that I made sure I got plain black drip coffee, like this," he said, raising his paper cup.

Patrick reached into his bag and said, "I usually just ask for a cup of very hot water and some half-and-half." He pulled out a Ziploc filled with Starbucks Via sachets and opened one. "Portable and only 70 cents a serving. It's micro granules of Columbian Arabica beans which dissolve very easily. I try to have only one cup a day." His coffee choice helped Reggie build a mental profile of the man. *"He is likely a bean counter in more ways than one."*

They sat at the laminate-topped, metal-legged, rectangular table in the room.

Reggie set the stage. "Patrick, let's start with some of your background."

But Patrick started with a tutorial: He described what a technology analyst does, the current excitement with the Magnificent Seven, the new AI boom, the difference between Wall Street buy side and sell side analysts, the changing role of industry analysts, and the new generation of bloggers.

He then described his long relationship with Barry—his time at Polestar, his coverage of Polestar with Oxford, and his social interactions with Barry and Elizabeth. "When I heard the news about Barry's disappearance, my mind went into overdrive and a list of suspects and motives just wrote itself," he concluded.

He explained to them how he populated a tool called Sherlock that he had previously used with Ramon. Polestar was developing the AI tool further and he would be using it to present on the big screen, when it was his turn.

Reggie interrupted, "Save that for the morning. For now, I'd like your input on some of the suspects on Lars' and my list."

Patrick was pleased to hear that. "I believe Barry is still alive and we should all be hustling." He was going to propose an all-nighter but he needed to hear what progress the law had already made.

Reggie started with the obvious. "We don't have a ransom demand yet, so we need to consider if Barry himself orchestrated this and has absconded."

Patrick explained that analysts did a lot of scenario planning when they look at new technology markets. "We assign probabilities to scenarios that add up to 100."

Reggie said, "I guess we do something similar. So in this case, I would assign 60 percent to the scenario that Barry has skipped the country, 20 percent that he has been kidnapped, and 20 percent that he is still stumbling around in the brush or murdered in the ravine."

Patrick raised his eyebrows, then said, "Mine would be the exact opposite." He did not say it aloud but one of the enhancements planned for Sherlock was to factor probabilities from sites like Polymarket which allow users to speculate on outcomes in political, sports, and other events using crypto currency.

Reggie said, "If there was a ransom demand, my kidnapping probability would be much higher. Patrick, I'm sure you know the tech sector has plenty of criminals and fugitives?"

Patrick said, "You thinking of the tech executive who met the same fate in a jell cell as Jeffrey Epstein?"

Reggie said, "Let's not jump to conclusions. Look up the FBI's most wanted fugitives list, which is on our website, and see how many are wanted for cybercrime."

Lars added, "And Homeland Security has FASR—the Fugitives and Absconders Search Report—which is used to screen immigrant applicants. The tech sector has a lot of immigrants and it's certainly not lily-white. Barry could easily be in Belize or China. We can't rule that out."

Patrick replied, "Barry was unpredictable, no question. But Polestar was his baby. He was always full of positive energy, exhaustingly so. I can't see him running away."

Lars looked unimpressed. "We hear a lot about ethics in AI. Is there a possibility that Barry suddenly caught religion? Could Barry's disappearance be a calculated move to expose vulnerabilities in the very systems Polestar has created, forcing a reckoning with AI's societal impact?"

Patrick paused and looked at Lars to see if that was a serious question then said: "I am a technology analyst, not a philosopher, but like you say ethical AI is a hot topic. Many people are behaving like ethics only applies to AI. Every new technology brings out new ethical issues for society. As far back as the 1940s, Isaac Asimov, the science-fiction writer, developed an ethical framework for robots. These days, as we evolve autonomous driving, the auto industry is being forced to answer the question—if an accident is unavoidable, should the vehicle protect the driver or a baby in a stroller on the sidewalk?'

"When I was part of Polestar's executive team, our philosophy was that society broadly has to play Socrates, and our politicians then enact laws to embody that guidance. Individual companies can only go so far when it comes to defining ethical boundaries. You also have to realize that the ethical AI conversation is being stoked by academics and activists and they often talk in the abstract. You have to look at ethics as they apply to specific scenarios. We adopted a best practice from the healthcare world. Many hospitals can quickly convene a committee of nurses, local priests and rabbis, lawyers and healthcare ethicists. Such a committee is available to doctors or to family members of a patient for guidance on thorny issues from genetic testing to euthanasia. Our Chief Counsel, Maria, was responsible for convening our ethics committee, if and when needed.

I have been gone from Polestar so not sure if that protocol has changed, but I doubt it. You are suggesting a scenario where Barry had a sudden, dramatic change of heart on AI-related ethics, and then lost his moral compass and went to the other extreme and killed his bodyguard along with his escape? I would call that highly improbable."

Reggie changed course and asked, "Was Barry under any unusual pressure?"

"You know how hot the AI sector is," Patrick said. "That race is huge pressure all by itself. He has a new boss—actually a Chairman who is supposed to mentor him. Here's a man who does not like to be caged. Finally, he is going through a fairly bitter divorce with his wife. Pressure enough? However, everything I know about Barry tells me he chooses fight over flight. So, my absconding probability is still the mirror opposite of yours, Reggie.

"By the way, concerning your third scenario—is there any update on the search in the ravine? I heard a hiking group at Polestar drove to the ravine yesterday, all ready to tear the place apart, and were turned back by the police cordon."

"You've been flying, so probably did not watch the many news helicopters hovering over the ravine," Reggie responded. "There is a massive manhunt going on—I would say as many dogs, two-way radios, and axes are involved in the search as humans. Since you are convinced it's most likely a kidnapping, let's see if you and Sherlock can help in identifying suspects we don't know much about. Let's first share what we do know."

Lars looked at Patrick and said, "You appear to have known him far longer than most of the folks we met at Polestar. So perhaps you can help fill in the blanks. Was Barry involved with any drug dealers?"

Patrick appeared offended. "Barry's vices are alcohol, cigars, and ladies. I've never seen him indulge in any drugs, not even weed. Having said that, I know Barry by day, extremely well. But he needs only four hours of sleep. I don't really know the nocturnal Barry."

"How about Elizabeth? My team finished reviewing the exterior security camera files for Elizabeth Roman's home," Lars said. "They confirm the timing of Barry's visit last Thursday into Friday. What she said checked out. There was a passionate, groping kiss outside the side door, and she was only wearing a thin, short robe. Bet that was interesting."

"Great!" Patrick said. "So is Elizabeth cleared as a suspect now?"

"No way," Reggie replied.

"Why not?" Patrick asked.

"The cameras confirm only what she told us," Reggie replied. "They don't prove she didn't orchestrate his disappearance. We never thought she hit him upside the head and dumped his body off Pillar Point Harbor. We have a lot more investigating to do before we can clear her."

"Do you have unlimited resources, or will that take resources away from finding Barry alive?" Patrick asked. "Because I think time is a-wasting."

"We're running all kinds of inquiries on several people," Lars started to explain.

Normally, Reggie would not have interrupted, but her childhood growing up buying the cast-off clothes from the Saint Clair Shores Salvation Army, just north of Grosse Pointe Shores, had just bubbled up in her memory.

"Listen, I know all about people like Elizabeth Roman. She lived a pampered life in Grosse Pointe Shores before she married Barry. I lived in Detroit, about 20 minutes from her parents' lakefront mansion. I know those people. Every time you'd hear about a missing wife or a dead husband, the culprit was the spouse. The Grosse Pointe police would always suspect some gangbanger from Detroit—but nope, it was the spouse. Usually not the spouse themselves, of course. They paid someone to do the dirty work. And that could be what we have here too."

"Listen, I know Elizabeth," Patrick said. "She's not responsible. Go find the real bad guys."

"Let me tell you about Grosse Pointers. You drive through the east part of Detroit down Jefferson Avenue, through some of the most run down parts of the city. Good luck finding a cop when you need one. Then you drive across Alter Road into the village of Grosse Pointe Park and all of a sudden, the road turns into a landscaped boulevard, with a cop on either side of it. You go three miles over the speed limit and if you're Black or in an old car, their cops pull you over. 'You're not like us, you're trouble,' they think. There's so much money in the Pointes you'd think it was a great hunting ground for burglary or robbery. But everywhere you look, there's a cop. And some of the neighborhoods supplement the real cops with private security firms.

"But what happens when one of *their* kids breaks the law? Nothing. Their cops and security details look the other way if the perp is a privileged White boy from the Pointes. Some guy from Detroit? He's cuffed, jailed, and charged within a few hours."

"What does that have to do with this investigation?" Patrick asked.

"They're not regular people. They think they're special, above the rules, above anyone who's not like them. If your outfit costs at least $2,000 and your watch or diamond ring cost at least $50,000, then you obviously come from a 'good family' and so *of course* you're not guilty of a crime. And if somehow, someone made an error and they think you're guilty, well there's always a liquid $100,000 in the bank for a defense attorney who understands they need to clear up that misunderstanding right away. 'You just go work on your tennis serve while everything gets straightened out.' Grosse Pointe kids grow up with no consequences, and that creates monsters."

Patrick had no idea how to respond. Lars nodded and said, "I hear you. Rich people justice is like that everywhere."

"It's not just about the justice system," Reggie said. "Let me explain. When I was a Girl Scout in Detroit, our white troop leader sometimes shopped at the Kroger grocery store on Mack Avenue in Grosse Pointe Woods. She knew the troops who sold cookies there were always sold out by 2:00 pm. So, she loaded up her SUV with cookie boxes and we girls manned a table just like other troops had done. But we hardly sold anything. All those Grosse Pointe shoppers pretended they didn't see us. Or they said they were on diets. They acted like we didn't even exist. We were cute, smiling, 11-year-old girls but our skin and hair made our cookies invisible."

"I'm sorry that happened to you, but I'm not sure it's relevant here," Patrick said.

"It is," Reggie replied. "People like Elizabeth grow up to have cold hearts. And every time a husband or wife goes missing, it's their spouse who set it up. Barry probably humiliated Elizabeth one too many times. She was brought up to ignore a certain amount of adultery, so long as no one found out. But he crossed that line and now he's missing. So we're not clearing her yet. Our only challenge in this case is that

140

we can't just go out with sonar and find Barry's body in Lake Saint Clair where the Grosse Pointers sail their ocean-going yachts. So, it's more of a challenge here."

"This is ridiculous, and you're wasting time!" Patrick insisted.

Lars looked directly into Patrick's eyes. "I can't show you Elizabeth's FBI profile, but let's just say you got a sneak peek from Reggie. Moving on."

Reggie smoothly segued into the next suspect on the list, seemingly unruffled by her walk down childhood memory lane. "Everything we've found on the girlfriend, Tiffany, says she's not our perp," Reggie said. "The security cameras on the condo that Barry was letting her live in, and the location tracking on the car he leased for her, and locations of the cell phone Barry was paying for, show where she's been for the past 90 days. The team has tracked her phone calls and interviewed people she talked to. There's nothing. Tiffany's luxury lifestyle ends if Barry can't keep writing checks, and she's already freaked out that she might have to get a job."

■ ■ ■

A knock on the door of the conference room brought Reggie to her feet. "Dinner is served," said the department admin, handing Reggie a brown paper bag. The three of them took exactly 18 minutes for a break, and then got back to work. During the break, they encouraged Patrick to make small talk.

He mentioned he had been to the mystery house. Neither of them had. He asked if the Guadalupe River Trail was also a tourist trap. He wanted to go jogging there. Reggie said, "I've heard it is more of a tent city these days."

He shared that Maya and he mostly lived on salads, turkey, and tofu. When they did eat Indian, he liked the grilled kind, no curries. Very little alcohol.

"My drug of choice," he said, as Lars leaned forward, "is sleep. Seven hours ideally, but six at minimum."

Lars asked him about sports. Patrick was tall and lean.

"Lots of jogging, especially with Maya in the morning and after dinner. Occasional golf and pickup games on the court. Some softball, some flag football. I'm blessed with good Irish genes, but have little time for recreation, especially with my frequent travel. Or at least that's my excuse, and I'm sticking to it."

Lars couldn't resist saying, "I thought the Florida heat and humidity would be your excuse?"

Patrick was starting to get impatient, and Reggie sensed it. "Patrick, we have to explore every option. You've probably heard of the murder in San Francisco of Adam Roy, the tech entrepreneur. I can only share what has been reported in the media but originally the perp was supposedly someone homeless. The toxicology report showed a cocktail of drugs in Adam's body. The suspect arrested is a tech businessman who Adam appeared to know. So many twists and turns."

Reggie continued, "The tech rich are very different from those who come from generational wealth. Many in California can trace their wealth back to the mining riches from the 1800s. The wealth these days can be accumulated very quickly, and the temptations today are far more lethal than those faced by previous generations. In your role, you see the wealth creation from technology. We see the many negative effects of people splurging on that wealth."

Patrick had heard about Adam Roy during a previous visit to San Francisco. He had also heard, during that dinner, about the spectrum of chemical substances available if you had lots of money in today's Silicon Valley. Much stronger cannabis than their "flower children" parents had popularized. Cocaine to boost energy levels—the purer the better, ideally straight from the labs, with no middleman or dealer cutting, diluting, or contaminating it. MDMA to heighten your senses. Ketamine as an antidepressant. Adderall to sharpen focus. Xanax to treat anxiety and panic disorders. Deadly Fentanyl if you weren't careful.

Then there were all kinds of startups focused on plant-based foods, alternative diets, anti-aging concoctions. Patrick was reminded of what a local had told him that chemical dependence in today's Silicon Valley was very different from that in *The Valley of the Dolls*, which Jacqueline Susann wrote in the '60s.

Moving the meeting along, Lars said, "We hear Barry was a lady's man. Did he have any more mistresses?"

Patrick appeared even more offended by this question, but responded, "That is, of course, the mythology around Barry. He bragged a lot more than he did in reality. I don't know of anyone other than Tiffany, and frankly don't know her very well."

Half in jest, Patrick followed up, "I mentioned I don't know nocturnal Barry. But Tiffany may be able to fill in the blanks about that. Barry is definitely a Man in Full."

Reggie nervously laughed.

Lars, unamused, said, "If I were to guess, I'd say your loyalty is to Elizabeth?"

"I wouldn't say that. I spent most of my time with Barry and am still loyal to him. I find Elizabeth a very warm person, a caring mother, and I consider her a friend. I like them both equally."

Sensing the tension, Reggie said, "Patrick, you've had a long day. Go grab a few hours of shuteye. Can we start at 7:00 am?"

Patrick pointed to his roller bag. "I came ready to pull an all-nighter. My friend and mentor, Barry, is alive and needs rescuing."

Reggie said, "Lars and I have teams working all night tracing every lead."

"Cover your notes, gentlemen," segued Reggie as she opened both the vertical and the horizontal blinds covering the window of the conference room in two layers. "There's nothing on the white board so I wanted to get some of the dipping sun in here, but look at that sky. You'd think it's a hazy kind of cloud but that's smoke."

Lars stood up and moved to the window. "Man, this was just a little fire in a park in Uvas Canyon a couple of days ago. Amazing how fast it spread." He looked at the weather app on his phone, and it showed an Air Quality Index of 121. "AQI says our air is unhealthy for sensitive groups."

"It better be below 110 in Fremont," Reggie said, "because I'm already overdue on weeding my garden. Organic gardens can quickly get overrun with weeds if you don't keep up with them."

Patrick said, "I apologize. You do have to take a 360-degree view. I only want to see Barry safe. Let me walk you through a couple of my suspects this evening so you guys can start to roll them over. By the way, my body is on east coast time, so we can start as early as you want."

"Okay, don't put your phone on silent in the hotel. We'll call you if we need you earlier."

Patrick asked to present from Sherlock on the big screen. Each suspect had their mug shot, brief bio, and a rating that Sherlock's algorithms calculated..

He started with "All Hail, Chad Caesar." Lars had noticed Patrick had taken plenty of notes on each suspect Reggie and he had presented. He asked Patrick about the tool he was using. Clearly, he had been distracted when Patrick earlier introduced Sherlock. Patrick described the tool again and how Henry's team had developed the core features of the digital tool while working with Ramon and that Polestar had licensed and was enhancing for commercial release. Several law enforcement agencies were trying it on pilot projects.

Lars raised his eyebrows and said, "We can't stop you from putting your notes in there, but please don't add any details of the suspects we have independently identified. We may run into all kinds of data privacy violations."

Reggie glared at Lars as if to say "Let the man talk. We are not AI novices in the FBI. This is cutting edge stuff and we know how to balance AI with human intelligence."

"Okay," Patrick said, frowning, "but some of the ones you have talked about like Chad were already on my list. Okay if I present my profiles on them?"

Lars replied, "Glad you're starting with Chad. We heard about him at Polestar. Let's hear your point of view."

"Oh man, that guy's going down in history and not in a good way," Patrick said.

"What can you tell us about Chad, and why would you consider him a suspect?" Reggie asked.

"He's an egomaniac. Absolutely loves to be on stage. Should have been in Hollywood, really. He puts on a persona when he clips on a microphone. He doesn't just walk the stage when he gives a presentation. I've actually seen him practice his blocking like he's Hamlet or something. Oh, and let's not forget the obsession he has with his image. And I'm talking about physical appearance plus reputation."

"So, what's his reputation now?" she asked.

Patrick laughed. "He's famous! For being so humiliated! I don't know if he'll ever get another job in the industry. Maybe he can move to Small Town, USA, and work at a Fortune 500 company in some midlevel position. Pride goeth before a fall."

"Would Chad want to see Barry dead?" Reggie asked.

Patrick stopped laughing. "Yes. He really would. And I think he'd be happy to do the job himself."

"Anything else we should know about him?"

"I don't know much else, but I would consider him a very serious suspect."

"What do you know about Greg Carson?" Lars inquired.

"The guy who got drunk and told the *Jupiter News* that he was going to be Chief Technology Officer for some joint venture between Pumpkin and Polestar?"

"We heard it was Chief Scientist," Lars commented.

"I never met him, but here's what Sherlock has on him. The rumor mill in the Valley states he was on the autism spectrum and clumsily leaked to a *Jupiter News* reporter that he was going to join some AI joint venture between Polestar and Pumpkin Technologies. But then Scott Bates and Barry pulled the plug on the whole venture. I heard there was a lawsuit."

"Where's Greg now? Is there any more gossip about him?" Reggie asked.

"I have no idea. I assume he got a big settlement and left the valley to do something else in AI. Wouldn't surprise me if he was working at Los Alamos National Labs now."

"On some Top Secret project?" Lars asked.

Patrick scoffed, "Seriously, you don't think Top Secret is really the government's highest level of security, do you? Top Secret clearance will just get you inside the lobby of one of the buildings."

"What's higher than Top Secret?"

Patrick pulled up the profile for Robert Lonigan. "I don't know for sure, but you can ask this guy Bob that question. He'd know. He's well connected in intelligence circles. And one of Sherlock's prime suspects. I last met with Bob at the Analyst Day." Patrick explained the concept of the event and how it had evolved over time.

Lars said, "Yeah, we met the Polestar CMO yesterday. The events sound like boondoggles for analysts at fancy resorts in exotic places."

Patrick said, "Some of them can be. But most are full of slides, one-on-ones, person-to-person conversations in a world with too much Zoom." He turned his laptop around and showed off his tweets, transcripts, blogs, LinkedIn posts, and Instagram galleries from that event.

He paused and said, "Well, that day I'd seen Bob fuming at something Barry said and I decided to follow up with him. Bob just creeps me out. I can't quite explain it. I know California is a 'two-party consent' state but I decided to make a recording in case it was useful and delete it if there was nothing to report. I uploaded the conversation to the cloud so let's have a listen. I consider him one of the main suspects in the disappearance of Barry."

The sound was a bit on the low side so they had to listen in carefully.

"You got a minute, Bob?"

"Sure. For you, Patrick, anytime."

"Always stroking analyst egos, eh? Let's go somewhere quiet. Let's walk to the Spanish Bay Club."

"Barry always took care of you. Don't they charge $100 for a martini?" There was the sound of laughter.

"Do we have an NDA with Oxford?"

"You know analyst firms don't sign NDAs. We have so many sources of information, we find NDAs tie our hands when vendors brag to everyone else about stuff that we were already aware of."

"Bet you have not heard about what I think you plan to ask me about," Bob said.

"Bob, let's keep lawyers out. Do you trust me?" Patrick asked him.

"I don't trust how close you are to Barry."

"Nothing you tell me will get back to Polestar."

They heard Patrick praise the view. "The sunset from here is spectacular—the ocean just goes on and on. And between the bagpiper who parades here every evening and the seaside chill, it makes you feel like you're in Scotland. This is the payback Californians get for the taxes and other burdens they carry. The weather and gorgeous landscapes are two of the only things I miss about living in California. Would you like a drink?"

"Vodka tonic please. Barry can afford it."

"Speaking of the devil, I saw you shake your head when he was presenting this morning—a couple of times."

"Patrick, you know many of Polestar's industry offerings—hell, you launched several of them. You know that banking and financial services broadly are very different from retail or manufacturing. I like Polestar's approach of making individual workers much more productive with automation, but in banking there is much more of a focus on automating entire processes, not just individual workers. Surely, you've heard of straight-through processing? They prefer not to have any human fingerprints across processes and make it more like machine-to-machine communication. That's a reason Polestar partners with us—we understand banking, insurance, and other financial institution processes. End to end."

"Bob, here's what I don't get. Polestar does not have many financial industry customers. Where is Barry getting his banking data to feed his AI? He has access to tons of processing power. I understand you're a customer for his GPU as-a-service offering. But AI also needs tons of data and domain expertise. Are you his source?"

"Patrick, did you know I was in the Service? Spent a fair amount of time in the Middle East. I used to hear the expression often, 'Who put OUR oil under THEIR sand?' Sounded funny most of the time. Idle talk, but sometimes it sounded ominously hostile. We are going through something similar in the technology world: 'Who put OUR data in THEIR data centers?' There is zero respect for customer data. There's a land grab happening. Sure you have heard *The New York Times* sued OpenAI and Microsoft for the unlicensed use of Times articles to train GPT large language models."

"What does that have to do with Barry's presentation that morning?"

"As part of our partnership with Polestar, we use one of their data centers as well as their GPU as-a-service offering. Some of our banking customers' data resides there. We have reason to believe that there's been a breach. We thought it was a Chinese gang, and asked Polestar to investigate. But after Barry announced he has banking intelligence, I'm afraid the real thief may be him. He may be dipping into the cookie jar to feed his language models and train his AI algorithms with live data from my customers and other banks. They entrusted that data to my company, and I am afraid Barry has broken that trust."

"Wow . . . You sure?" Patrick asked.

"I'm 95 percent certain, but not sure where the Chinese hackers fit in. However, I'm caught between a rock and a hard place. Barry is my partner. Tony Batista at Sheldon Freres and others are my customers. Who do I inform first?"

"That's a tough one. Barry had always believed in the expression 'Keep your friends close, and your enemies closer.'

We all wish he wouldn't hug us so tight. Bob, I'd start with your attorneys and your Board. We need to get back . . . let's go to the presentation room separately. Don't want to raise Barry's suspicion. I'll stop in my room, and tell them I had to do a Zoom call. Thanks for sharing this, Bob. I promise this stuff will not get back to Barry. No NDA necessary."

Patrick ended the playback. "I wanted to talk with Bob later and when I asked around, I was told he had left in a cloud of smoke."

Reggie and Lars looked at him quizzically.

Patrick said, "According to witnesses, Bob shot out of the parking lot, and had to brake very hard to avoid hitting an Amazon van. There were squealing brakes, the smell of burning rubber, and visible smoke. Then he also hit a stone curb on the passenger side and just kept going.

"What can I tell you? Bob is a drinker, has a bit of a temper, and he can be abrasive and impatient. However, when he's in the mood, he can be the life and soul of a party. He's an incredible storyteller and has an endless store of jokes."

Lars commented, "Let me make sure I understood— when he was talking about 'Who put OUR data in THEIR data centers'—he meant Barry was reaching into his banking customers' cookie jar?"

Patrick nodded yes.

Lars said, "Well, Bob certainly seemed to be angry in this talk with you and he definitely had a drink or two."

"It's such a shame," Patrick replied. "If I had met Bob that afternoon, I would have told him to go ask for a private one-on-one with Barry and double check. I didn't get the chance. I called him afterward and he never called back.

"My last suspect tonight is extremely speculative. That's Tony Batista at Sheldon Freres, that Bob mentioned who is also a Polestar customer. There's a lot of money in technology, and I've seen knockdown, drag-out fights during contract negotiations. It's well known that Barry and Tony love to one-up each other.

"I talk to the sell side analysts at Sheldon and they tell me how tough Tony makes their jobs. He is always comparing margins in technology to that of street drugs. And here they are, yelling at technology CEOs for better margins, year on year."

Lars said, "Sounds like a stretch. Corporate negotiations rarely turn physical."

"Tony's annual bonus is tied to how much he can squeeze vendor margins. Like I said, I may be speculating, but I wouldn't want that Sicilian to make me an offer I couldn't refuse."

Lars reacted, "You've been watching too many *Soprano* episodes and *Godfather* replays. Your mob allusion is trite, even insulting. The Mafia, as it's been known, has been gradually neutered since the RICO Act became the Fed's weapon in the '70s. They're still into white collar crime, but physical, violent stuff they're outsourcing to the Latino gangs."

As Patrick wrapped up, Reggie told him: "Call an Uber. We don't want you socializing with San Jose's homeless late in the day." Patrick realized it was already 11:00 pm by his body time.

After he left, Reggie told Lars, "Boy, we have the polar opposite of Barry here."

"Really? I'd hold my judgment till tomorrow, but if I were to put a bet tonight, I'd say Patrick and Elizabeth are a tag team and probably know exactly where Barry is right now. In fact, I can guarantee that Elizabeth Roman and Patrick Brennan are not profiled as suspects in his Sherlock tool."

"Oh Lars, your Florida bias just came rushing out," said Reggie.

Lars replied, "Yeah, like your Michigan Wolverine bias?"

They both shared a much-needed laugh, a respite from the pressure cooker they worked in.

■ ■ ■

In his hotel room, Patrick paced as he caught up with Maya again. She had slept for several hours so was coherent for at least a few minutes. The roast beef sandwich Reggie served was starting to cause heartburn, and Patrick needed the pacing to help his digestion. He would also keep his Fitbit happy with those steps. It preferred outdoors steps in fresh air but would have to live with this air-conditioned version this evening. He hoped he could go jogging on the Guadalupe trail in the morning.

Then the roast beef led to a dream—or was it a nightmare? He actually spent the whole night out with 'nocturnal Barry.' There were titty bars, drug dealers, half-finished bottles of alcohol, way too many cigars, and bizarrely a number of stops in the haunted Winchester house.

Reggie woke him from that reverie. "Come as early as you can. Lars' team has collected some dashcam video from the edge of the ravine which could be interesting."

Patrick knew he desperately needed a shower to get rid of the cigar smoke. Wait, was that a dream or not? It had to be a dream. He usually needed seven hours of sleep. No way could he have pulled an all-nighter with Barry.

Somebody wise had once counseled him: "You can get into all kinds of trouble if you have money. You can get into even more trouble, if in addition, you have too much time on your hands." As Patrick pondered that, said to himself quietly: "*Oh Barry, who needs just four hours of sleep a night, what kind of trouble have you been getting yourself into with your billions?*"

7

Welcome to High-Tech California

~~→

Thursday am PST

Lars told Reggie and Patrick what the local cops and troopers had gleaned from knocking on doors in the neighborhood near the ravine. Most of the occupants wanted to know if the TV helicopters would be gone soon.

"Unfortunately, the houses are set pretty far back in the hills," Lars said, "but we did get follow-up calls from several residents to confirm none of their security cameras captured anything of interest.

"However, we have had some amazing luck. A teenager has only just come forward, who captured, in his front cam, Barry's car slipping and sliding and the car behind him with masked tags speeding away. This car-cam fellow—sorry

Patrick, for privacy reasons I can only call him John Doe in your presence—stopped at the edge of the ravine to look for the car. He'd been drinking and didn't want to get into trouble with the police, so he drove off. When he got home he thought of calling the police, but fell fast asleep. The next morning, he convinced himself the car would have been found by now or that the driver had made his way up to the road, so he did nothing.

"Anyway, he's 17, goes to school, has a part-time job and a girlfriend, so not much time to watch the news. At some point, he noticed the presence of helicopters and eventually listened to the news. Then he realized that the car he saw go into the ravine must be related to Barry Roman's disappearance. Still scared, he told his mother. She made the call. Frankly, I don't think he's the smartest kid, but we got lucky. If it weren't for the mom, he probably would have been too scared to call us.

"He told the cops when they arrived that he had footage on his SD cards from his 360-degree cam setup. Welcome to high-tech California! He also thought the four night-vision cams in his car were illegal, which added to his reluctance to contact the police. They're not, in fact, illegal. Teenagers!

"When the cops reviewed the footage, they noticed in the rear cam, a few minutes later, that another person had stopped and used their drone to look in the ravine. More high-tech California. That car left shortly thereafter. It was a beat-up blue Kia. Reported stolen. In high-tech California, surprised he did not pull up in a driverless Waymo."

Patrick perked up. "A drone? Can I see the video?"

"Why?" snapped Lars.

Patrick looked at Reggie and said, "Your colleague in Tampa—Ramon—talked about high-tech petty crime and how many auto thefts now involve drones to identify potential marks. Could it be that Barry and his bodyguard were targeted by one of these gangs? It may be far-fetched, but could we have Ramon look at the footage and see if he has any ideas?"

He looked at Lars and said, "I realize John Doe is a private citizen and you want to protect their privacy. I don't need to see the video or know his or her identity."

Reggie sent a link of the video to Ramon, with a note: "Patrick sends his regards. Take a look, especially at the last portion where the guy launches a drone into the ravine, then call me. Thanks."

Ramon called shortly after, and asked, "Are you near Patrick? Can you put me on speakerphone?"

Ramon sounded excited. "Patrick, how are you, man? You know who the drone jockey looks like? It's our boy, Paulie!"

Patrick looked confused. "Paulie?"

"Remember the work you did with us on UPC and QR code tampering. Paulie was the local Tampa gang ringleader for some of that retail fraud and has since graduated to night vision drones for car thefts."

Patrick looked up Paulie in his Sherlock AI tool. There was not much there. He had helped the investigation in background.

"Is he a solo player or is he part of organized crime?"

"Let me check," Ramon said. "I'm pretty sure he's connected to a low-level mobster called Jimmy, who I think we have under surveillance."

Ramon called back shortly. "We have metadata on a call we believe came from Paulie to Jimmy, shortly after the time stamp on the video." Patrick wondered whether the FBI had used a StingRay device, which he had seen demoed at a talk on mobile phone surveillance tech.

"Even more interesting," Ramon said, "right afterward Jimmy called a NYC 212 number. It appears to be an executive called Tony at a New York bank."

"Tony? Tony Batista? I was talking to Reggie and Lars about him last night!"

Lars looked at Reggie and said, "What are the chances?"

Reggie interjected, "Okay, let's get all the information we can on this Paulie guy and start a nationwide search for him, and this car."

Patrick's heart sank. Is the Mob involved in this? There had been no ransom demands. He felt so out of his depth. But he stayed quiet.

Ramon seemed to hear him. "The Italian Mafia in Tampa is long past its prime. We're mostly focused on Latino gangs now. So, I'm not sure what Paulie is doing and why he's so far from home."

Lars confirmed that in California, too, law enforcement's focus was almost exclusively on Latino gangs: Mexican cartels, MS-13 from Central America, and the Venezuelan Tren de Aragua. One more ruthless than the other.

Lars added, "In the rear-cam footage, we noticed another person around the car. This guy's whole face is tattooed, which is a telltale sign of the MS-13 gang."

Patrick's heart fluttered. He had heard the MS-13 was a vicious LA gang with Central American roots. Their main motto was *"mata, viola, controla"*—"kill, rape, control." They may have expanded north to the Bay Area to traffic fentanyl and other deadly drugs, especially to the many homeless in San Francisco.

"Holy Mother of God, what have you got yourself involved in, Barry?" Patrick muttered to himself.

He then told the others: "Guys—I feel so helpless. I know nothing about the Mafia—Italian or Latin. I have a feeling you people would be better off without me in the room. Can I be excused? I'm headed back to my hotel room. Call me if I can help on any digital matters."

Reggie said, "Before you leave, we'd like some of your input on a couple of things we heard at Polestar HQ."

Reggie asked about Nested Models, and Patrick pointed out that Fabrice's unit was technically independent of Polestar and had little involvement with the company. Patrick also noted that he got only secondhand input from Barry.

"But it appears cruel how Polestar benefited while Nested Models crashed and burned," Reggie said.

Patrick looked up Amin in his Sherlock tool. He was born in Louisiana, and he was of Persian descent. But the tool did not have much data about the Polestar investment. In a delayed response to Reggie's point, he spoke up, "Well, it is capitalist Darwinism. Survival of the fittest and the luckiest. Overall, I think the system works. Look at how many immigrant founders have been funded. Look how many immigrants have become CEOs of large tech companies. If the system were rigged, you'd see only second-generation, White sons of tech founders continue to get most of the VC money and top executive jobs."

Reggie then asked about the East Palo Alto rezoning and death threats.

Patrick said, "It was handled by the real estate group and I just heard secondhand from Barry. Living now in Florida, I've had a chance to talk to some folks about how Walt Disney very quietly, back in the '60s, acquired thousands of acres in Florida for what has become Disney World. It's a fascinating story, including a former CIA official and how they kept such a large purchase under wraps so pricing would not spiral. The big difference is they were buying swampland, whereas East Palo Alto was already developed."

Lars interjected, "I bet it's a fascinating story, but it still sounds like more rich people justice."

Patrick did not take the bait, and Reggie gave him an out. "I want you to ponder something in your hotel room. Bob was 'numero uno' suspect on your list yesterday. Has Tony replaced him now? Pose Sherlock that question in your hotel room please."

"I will. My immediate answer is the plot just thickened. Tony is Barry's customer and Bob is Barry's partner.

"But first I have to isolate and delete from Sherlock data about some of the suspects. Remember Lars' comment about privacy?" which caused Reggie to glare at Lars.

8

The Fox in the Henhouse?

Thursday pm PST

Reggie noticed Patrick's face had turned ghostly white as he packed up. She didn't know that he was concerned about possible physical violence. Patrick knew Maya would be very worried as soon as she heard anything that suggested the Mob. After all, she had never wanted him to get involved.

Lars deduced something else. He told Reggie afterward: "I know Patrick has a very high IQ, and appears to know a lot about technology. But I get the heebie-jeebies when I'm around him. Remember when Ramon introduced him to us, he said 'Patrick thinks like a criminal'?

"He knows so much about the victim, his wife, and each of the suspects with his little AI tool. And here he is embedded in the investigation. Reggie, my Spidey-sense tells me we may have let the fox in the henhouse."

Reggie replied, "Tonight is date night. I usually leave early since my husband cooks something special and wonderful. I'll be back online after dinner. Let me ponder what you just said. I'll see you here tomorrow morning."

Lars did not have any reason to leave the office. "I'm expecting the results of the financial investigation on Elizabeth Roman to come in any minute," he said. "That's the last piece we need to evaluate her. I'm going to stick around and wrap that up.

"And Reggie, something wild to consider," he said, holding up a business card. "During the Polestar tour I picked up a card for Tommy 'Bespoke' Chu. Guess where his main office is? San Diego. Could he have hidden Barry in one of his garment trucks, slipped him across the border, and then used his Chinese contacts to move him across the world?"

Reggie rolled her eyes. She thought "*With all our digital fingerprints—mobile calls, toll charges, credit card and ATM transactions, security camera recordings, tips about sightings—people assume fugitives are easy to nail. The reality is there is too much digital data to mine—the proverbial finding the needle in the haystack.*" She told Lars, "I was looking forward to a gourmet meal. Between doubts about Patrick and Tommy, you're already giving me heartburn."

■ ■ ■

That evening at dinner, Reggie told her husband, Javon, about her case in general terms, and she mentioned that an "industry analyst" was assisting them and knew most of the suspects. Her husband's interest was piqued by that highly unusual aspect. With Lars also so suspicious of Patrick, Reggie decided to send an internal request for a more detailed security briefing on him. While most people likely associate the FBI with investigating violent crimes, they stay busy with plenty of white-collar crimes—money laundering, securities fraud, IP theft, real estate fraud, etc. And they are constantly running background checks for gun owners and applicants for naturalization. The bureau even operates the NICS, the National Instant Criminal Background Check System.

She got an answer pretty quick. "Looks pretty clean. You may want to check with the Customs and Border Patrol. Appears to do a lot of international travel."

She knew that checking with Customs would take a while and probably yield little in results. Instead, she called people she knew in security at United and at Delta Airlines. To each of them she said, "I need a quick look at your Frequent Flyer database. Please don't make me get a subpoena. I just want to find out where one of your regular fliers leaves or enters the country."

She got a call back from her United contact pretty quick. "He flew quite a bit with us internationally five to six years ago. Mostly from LAX and SFO to Asia Pac. Not as much recently." That made sense, as those were Patrick's Polestar years in the Bay Area.

Her Delta contact called a little later and said, "Lots of domestic travel on us in recent years through ATL. No international travel." That also made sense, since he was now based in Tampa.

But no international travel did not jibe with what her colleague had mentioned. Was he flying on private planes?

She also sent Maria a text: "We heard about the tailor, Tommy Chu, during our tour of your campus. Can you find out when he last met Barry?"

She heard back, "I can check with his assistant, Alisha."

· · ·

Back at the hotel, Patrick finally connected via phone with Charles Morgan, the financial analyst at the NYC bank, Sheldon Freres.

Patrick started, "Sorry man, been on the road."

Charles chuckled, "I know the drill. But holy fuck— Grisham has gone from chairman to acting CEO since the earnings call. The stock's nosedived. What are you hearing about Barry?"

Patrick told him: "Not much more than you have, sorry to say. How's our friend Tony? I invited him to be part of our offsite on Monday but he declined."

Charles exclaimed, "Please don't give him more of an audience! The guy is a piece of work. Makes my job freaking difficult because he's always publicly saying software margins are too high—and here we are, asking software CEOs to deliver more every year."

"Is he a bully inside Sheldon?"

"Well, he's on the cost and efficiency side of the bank. We're the revenue side. Procurement folks become assholes to everyone, particularly during recessions."

"Is he a tough Sicilian?" Patrick kiddingly asked.

"You mean like Luca Brasi?"

They laughed and signed off.

He reflected on Reggie's question. Bob was still his top suspect. Lars was right—it's trite to think of the Cosa Nostra, the "classic" Sicilian Mafia, as still being as powerful as Hollywood portrays it. Tony was just a tough negotiator.

"Wait, you know nothing about Jimmy. And you don't know much about the China breach," Patrick thought. He was tempted to call Tina at Polestar but didn't know her that well.

So many "known unknowns" and who knows how many "unknown unknowns." And the more time that passed, the less confident he felt that his analytical mind could solve this Rubik's Cube.

Just then, Reggie called.

"Let's begin early tomorrow. Breakfast at 7:30 am to start with?"

Though he agreed to this, Patrick sounded even more distant than he did that afternoon.

"Everything okay?" Reggie asked.

"Oh, just issues in my day job."

That was an understatement. He was having a terrible day. Room service delivered a greasy burger and cheap wine. He had called Maya, who said things in St. Petersburg were not going well. Somebody at Oxford in Cambridge had spread a rumor that every analyst who refused to relocate to Florida would be fired. She wept as she told him that she'd heard they had a nickname for her in Cambridge: "Mallory Knox," the ruthless character from the movie *Natural Born Killers*. "I am not even a blond. That would make you Mickey, and you rescued me from an abusive family."

Patrick felt sick. Analysts could be mean but Maya could also be overreacting. There was plenty of jealousy in Cambridge about her rapid rise, from an intern to Chief of Staff of the CEO, and now opening the spanking new show-piece in Florida.

"Maya, come and spend the weekend with me. Catch a flight tomorrow and we'll go grab a couple of nice dinners here. Best Chinese food in the nation."

"Seriously? But you're on call with the FBI, 24/7," she pointed out.

"Not 24/7. Guess where I am now? In my hotel with a crappy room service meal. I don't want it to repeat the next few nights. Book your flight and send me your details."

He next called his CEO boss. "Tucker, the relocation gossip mill has already started in Cambridge. You might've stirred the pot, but people are blaming Maya and she's not taking it well. I plan to ask Henry to hold down the fort in St. Pete next week while Maya flies out here for a couple of days."

Tucker said, "Patrick, have I ever told you how much I love your late evening calls? Nothing but good cheer. You analysts are always a pain in the ass, but I'll calm things down in Cambridge."

Patrick next called Henry, the manager of the labs team in St. Pete. "Sorry to burden you, but I need you to play office manager next week. Maya and I had planned to take the week off, which I had to put on hold. But I've asked her to join me for the weekend and I may have her stay a few days more.

"So, please—take the whole office out for a happy hour. Go to lunch with a different group each day. Get some catered food another day. Take a few folks to a Rays game. Mix it up."

Henry said, "I was hoping you were going to invite me to be a fly on the wall and hear about all the cool surveillance gear the Feds have. But I'll settle for taking credit being the reason Patrick finally felt comfortable taking a whole week off. Seriously buddy, try and chill for a while. And when you're back here, I hope you're allowed to geek out on details about their gear."

• • •

He should have gone to bed. Instead, Patrick made the mistake of googling "MS-13 tattoos," and the faces he saw spooked him. He remembered a conversation with a lady who used to moderate video content on the web. She ended up with PTSD from a couple of years of watching gang rapes and killings. As she'd said, "The dark web is so full of dark alleys. Danger everywhere." In his nightmare, Patrick had similar PTSD and had wept to Maya, saying, *"Sorry baby—I should never have agreed to work on this case. Why am I allowing so much evil to seep into our lives?"*

He was torn. He desperately wanted to help find Barry. But he was committed to his soulmate above all. They had walked the seven circles around the holy fire in the Hindu wedding ceremony in India. They were equal partners for life. And she needed him. But while he put on a brave face, he needed her even more. He was so comfortable in the technology world. But this was a world of savages. And it was not on the virtual dark web. It was in the real-life dark alleys of urban America. So near to us.

167

He trembled as he thought about the MS-13 motto, *"mata, viola, controla."*

Section B
The Search

9

More Mafia?

Friday am PST

At 5:20 am, Patrick was woken by his cell phone ringing. He was alarmed to see that it was Maya. She was hysterical. "Somebody just called in a Don Corleone accent and hissed, 'Tell your hotshot detective husband he's way out of his league. We'll make both of you offers you can't refuse,' then they hung up!"

He asked Maya for more details about the phone call. "What did the caller ID show?"

"Potential spam."

"My guess is it was just an asshole analyst from Cambridge rattling your cage. But we're not taking any chances. The sooner you catch your flight out here, the better.

I'll meet you at the airport. I know there's a nonstop that leaves around two your time. Please get packed."

"This whole situation is bullshit, Patrick. You're an analyst, not a detective. You're putting our lives at risk!"

"Look," he said. "Let me book that flight and send you details. I'll call Elizabeth shortly to tell her what's going on. I'd really like for you to stay with her in her fortified palace, since I'm doing all this to help her husband." Maya agreed, and Patrick booked her a main cabin seat on a nonstop.

Patrick felt like he needed a workout to clear his mind. How about a jog along the Guadalupe River? He took a cab and the driver warned him: "Be careful out here."

He had not expected to encounter so many unhoused people. He knew homelessness was a complex problem, yet he felt so frustrated by people who, as he saw it, had given up. He did not understand the homeless psyche. He was all about making humans superproductive with automation. *"Why won't these folks give me a shot to make their lives meaningful? Just give me a chance!"*

Still, he was glad he had put small notes in his shorts, while he left his wallet in the hotel room. He mostly gave out singles. But next to a sleeping man was a dog curled up beside him, and he left two fives.

He thought about the walking tour of St. Pete that Maya and he had taken when they first moved to town. The guide was a historian and talked about how the town went through booms and busts every few decades. *"Could that be the face of our vibrant town in a few decades? I hope not."* He had definite views on how town elders should not abdicate their duties in managing the look and feel of their communities.

. . .

Back in the hotel, in a subdued mood, Patrick showered, dressed, picked up breakfast to go from the lounge while thinking about Maya and his nightmare the night before.

He trembled again as he thought about "*mata, viola, controla.*" Kill, rape, control.

"*Snap out of it, guy!*" he advised himself. Time to call Reggie.

Patrick told her about the call Maya received, and Maya's imminent flight to the West Coast. Reggie immediately reached out to Ramon in the Tampa FBI office to tell him about the new threat made to Maya and Patrick and asked him to arrange an escort for Maya to the airport.

Patrick next took an Uber from the hotel to Campbell.

In the car, Patrick called Elizabeth. He told Elizabeth the quick summary of the threatening call Maya received. He asked if Maya could spend a few days with Elizabeth, who immediately said, "That would brighten our household. It's been so tense with all the additional security here. We could catch up on our time in India—that was so much fun. Can you email me her flight details? Let me get my assistant to upgrade Maya and then I'll call her."

Elizabeth suddenly realized she owed Patrick an apology. She took a deep breath, then said, "You know what, Patrick? I was so wrapped up in myself, but I should have thought of this when you first told me you were coming out to help the FBI. Why don't you check out of the hotel and come stay at my place with Maya? God knows we have plenty of room!"

Elizabeth next called Maya. "Maya, I'm really looking forward to having you stay with me. My assistant just sent you the upgraded itinerary on the nonstop flight that'll bring you to SFO, and our security firm will send a car to pick you up. An armed guard will be waiting for you as you deplane your flight, right at the gate. Don't let all the security freak you out. And be sure to pack a bikini because we need to drink lemon drop martinis poolside!"

"Thank you so much, Elizabeth. Patrick told me he may have a surprise hotel for me, but this is way cooler."

"No worries—I should have thought of all that several days ago. Now, on another topic, I was thinking we could lighten the mood a bit. Can you bring along your wedding albums so we could reminisce about our wonderful time in India?"

"I'll see what I can gather up," Maya said. She was flattered but thought Elizabeth was just being kind. Besides, it would be awkward to ferry the "family crown jewels" into that tense, Ground Zero setting. And she didn't really have time to look for them, then unpack and repack her suitcase to fit everything. An unmarked car pulled up, and one of two bulky guards knocked and said, "Fifteen minutes, ma'am." The two guards stood outside.

One of her neighbors called and asked if everything was okay. Fortunately, Maya's sense of humor kicked in: "Yeah, it's the new Uber armored service that they're piloting. We got a free coupon. Actually, I'm going to the West Coast—Patrick is stuck there and asked me to join him. Please keep an eye on our place, okay? Thanks very much!"

The ride to TPA was quick, and airport security appeared to have taken the day off. She said to herself: *"This must be a premium version of the TSA PreCheck and Clear that I signed up for."*

Just as Maya was ready to board, she got a call from Elizabeth, which she let go to voicemail as she stood in line with other first-class passengers. Once she was seated, she played the voicemail.

Elizabeth's friendly voice said, "I'm inviting two girl-friends to visit with us over the next few days. They're looking forward to your color commentary on all the wedding ceremonies. As you can imagine, when Barry and I got back from your wedding, I tried but did a poor job explaining Hindu concepts and Indian cuisine to them. Also, one of them is helping her company evaluate relocation options away from California. She was wondering if you could walk her through your Florida search project. Thanks, and cannot wait to see you."

She noticed some whispering upfront before takeoff. That was explained by the fact that the purser checked on her every 10 minutes on the flight. They kept tempting her with Mimosas and French Rosé. And there was the white linen lunch—no plastic cutlery in sight. Nice rich coffee—one of the best cups she had ever tasted at 30,000 feet. She said to herself: *"I am still mad at Patrick, but not if he can arrange this experience on every flight."*

Maya was also pleased to see the "Wi-Fi on board" sign. She ran Speedtest on her laptop. The upload speed was miserable but the downloads were at an acceptable 20 megabits a second. She could retrieve a few files from folders on Google Drive and update them on the flight. Maya had created a presentation on the wedding ceremonies for a neighborhood event, and had embedded numerous photos and a few videos. She also gathered the slide deck she had presented to Tucker and Patrick comparing the Florida locations she had evaluated. Finally, she retrieved the presentation she had done at the offsite a few days ago about the office location evaluation. *"I love this laptop; thank heavens I back it up every night,"* she thought.

Patrick had told Maya about Barry's stunning home theater. That would work well, she thought, if Elizabeth's friends really were as interested in the presentations as Elizabeth claimed. But Maya's prime reason for the visit was to be with Patrick. She wondered if he had been getting enough sleep.

■ ■ ■

Reggie was inquisitive at the breakfast meeting. "I had a nightmare about flying last night. I'm a really nervous flier. Patrick, can you sleep on flights?"

Patrick certainly did not want to share with Reggie his own nightmare the previous night about the MS-13 tattoos and his resultant PTSD. Reggie's question made him think of Maya on the flight enroute to him; he was concerned about her well-being, but he would rather talk about airlines than MS-13.

"I love the flat-bed seats on international flights," Patrick said. "I am out like a light as soon as we level off and I can push those buttons to extend the seat."

Reggie kept the topic alive. "They must hide those planes from me. Every time I fly United or Delta, I'm squished in the middle seat."

"Actually, I avoid US carriers when I fly overseas."

"Seriously, you forego the frequent flyer miles?" Reggie asked.

"Some of the international carriers are just so much better," Patrick replied. "Newer planes, far better food, attentive service. Nothing can match flying on the top deck of the Emirates A380. They once let me play bartender at the back of that plane. There was a TV showing a live soccer match. It was the most crowded sports bar you've ever been to. Wish I could've collected some tips!

"Another time, I got upgraded to first on Singapore Airlines to Indonesia. My profile shows a preference for seafood and I'm usually lucky to get a couple of shrimps. It was three flights each way, and each leg had seafood from Norway, Alaska, Japan, and elsewhere around the world. Blew me away.

"But it's not always smart to fly foreign carriers," he continued. "When I was a new employee at Polestar, I was not entitled to fly in business class. Had a trip to Tokyo and told the travel agent to book me on China Southern as their business fare was lower than United's economy fare. When I got back, John Grinder, the Polestar security officer took away my phone and laptop and completely sanitized them. He told me: 'Next time you need to go into China, take a burner phone or else I'll shred your phone when you return and then personally fire you.'"

Reggie said, "Wow . . . well, I learned something new today. Still glad I don't fly too much, especially on a government economy fare. Also, Patrick, does Sherlock know anything about Tommy Chu?"

Patrick replied, "My tailor? The guy's an absolute work-aholic. Is he one of your suspects?"

Reggie turned coy. "No, we happened to see his little store during our tour at Polestar. Just wondering if you knew anything about him. Speaking of Polestar, back to work."

Reggie had heard enough from Patrick. He was flying non-US airlines on international trips. Nothing illegal about that and no wonder Delta and United did not know about his travel details.

While Patrick excused himself to join an Oxford conference call, Reggie told Lars: "About the issues with Patrick you mentioned last night—I sympathize with your concern, I really do. I told you I would think on it. I did a lot more than that in the last 12 hours. If it's the Mafia, Patrick can't help us much on that front—and wouldn't even want to. As a civilian, violent crime has already got him spooked. We'll just have him on standby going forward."

Lars started to protest against even that degree of involvement from Patrick, but Reggie cut him off. "You and I would still be on square one if it weren't for him and Polestar's guidance. One of your state's major employers-slash-taxpayer is missing. That should be our major focus. And by the way, I have asked Maria at Polestar to see if we can find out when Barry last met with that tailor. Seems like a real long shot, but given all the loonies reporting Barry sightings from Tijuana to Timbuktu, why not rule out another possibility?"

Patrick joined them after his quick check-in with Oxford and started sipping coffee with Lars and Reggie. Patrick told Lars about Maya receiving a threatening phone call. Reggie said, "Our Tampa office has provided security for Maya, and they're at your house right now, Patrick. They'll escort her to the gate for her flight."

"Thank you," Patrick replied. "The flight should arrive at SFO around 6:00 tonight, and we'll both be staying at Elizabeth Roman's home for the next few days."

Lars had been listening with an expressionless face until this point. He blurted, "Well, it's a good thing we cleared Elizabeth as a suspect last night, then!"

Reggie elaborated. "Elizabeth has no financial incentive to kill Barry. Turns out that she and her parents own more of Polestar than Barry does. Elizabeth's parents put up most of the money that funded Polestar when it was a startup. And Barry had been back in her bed right before he went missing. For the moment, we are ruling out any crime of passion in spite of their nasty divorce. Those two are screwed up, but killing him doesn't provide her any benefit."

Patrick could not resist. "I told you she was innocent! Actually, Sherlock did."

"Yes, it kills me to say this, but he was right."

Patrick laughed. "Best thing I've heard all week!"

. . .

From her home office in Atherton, Elizabeth initiated a FaceTime to Theresa and Emily. "Hey girls, I'm hoping you can pack an overnight bag and come over tomorrow for lunch and drinks, and swimming and drinks, and videos and drinks!"

"Is that a prescription from your doctor, because it sounds like good medicine for what's ailing you right now," Emily replied.

"A seriously good idea," Theresa agreed.

"You remember I told you that Patrick Brennan has been helping the FBI with the investigation? Well, for security reasons I've asked him and his wife Maya to stay with me for a while."

"Smart," Emily said.

"I know you two haven't seen Maya in a few years, but I've talked about her enough that you must feel you know her. I've asked her to bring some videos and photos from their wedding in India that Barry and I attended. All that pomp and pageantry I tried to tell you about is best seen on film."

"True. Remember I had asked you to get Maya to share her info about opening an office in Florida, because my CEO is sick of California taxes? Is it okay if I ask her about that?" Theresa inquired.

"Yes, I did remember and I asked her to bring whatever she can share on the relocation process."

"Okay, what time tomorrow, and which rooms are we staying in?" Emily asked.

"How about 1:00 pm? And do you want to share the pool house?"

"My favorite!" Emily said, though in the back of her mind she went *"wonder if it will look suspicious that we are celebrating while Barry is still missing?"*

She wasn't far wrong.

10

Gaming Laptops—Not Just for Games

~~→

Friday pm PST

The Uvas Canyon wildfire continued to blaze, sending plumes of dark, gray-brown smoke thousands of feet into the troposphere. The area's prevailing winds were offshore, moving in a northwest-to-southeast direction, while the Santa Clara Valley funneled the smoke northward toward the San Francisco Bay.

The heavily forested mountains that nestled the campground where the fire originated included many species of trees and shrubbery. The fir and pine trees were especially flammable, generating more smoke than other trees in the forest, but all vegetation inside the fire zone was on fire.

The mountainous forest was sparsely populated, but Cal Fire had issued mandatory evacuations for everyone west of the Chesbro Reservoir and north of Hazel Dell Road. Roads within that boundary were closed to all traffic, to facilitate air tanker drops of red-dyed ammonium phosphate fire retardant outside the fire perimeter, to help contain the fire. The planes would continue their flights until Cal Fire could confirm a solid, continuous perimeter of red encircling the fire. Once the planes had completed their work, ground crews would move in to clear a firebreak outside the red boundary. Meanwhile the ammonium phosphate would kill all aquatic life in the area's creeks and ponds.

Pacific Gas and Electric had executed Public Safety Power Shutoffs in the evacuation zone, and were proactively monitoring the situation to determine when and where further PSPS were needed.

Those living or working within 10 miles of the evacuation zone reported a sudden and substantial increase in wildlife sightings. Smaller animals like foxes, woodchucks, and opossums, and herds of deer were met with fascination, and many people put out water to help them. The sightings of coyotes, mountain lions, bobcats, and the occasional black bear, however, incited fear and kept many people, with their pets, inside their homes. Birds had flown tens of miles away from the smoke. Residents from the community of Coyote south to the village of San Martin, who remained in their homes despite sore throats, burning eyes, coughing, and congestion due to unhealthy air, saw a furious orange western sky and heard an eerie absence of birdsong.

．．．

Patrick checked out of his hotel and took an Uber to Atherton while Maya was in the air. Arriving at Elizabeth's home, he was shocked to see how much additional security was in place. *"Boy, they have turned this beauty into a fortress,"* he thought. The armed security guard gave the Uber driver the third degree and wouldn't let the car inside the gate. Patrick pulled his suitcase and laptop bag up the long driveway to the house.

At the door, Elizabeth hugged him tightly. "It will be so nice to have you and Maya here! We'll be joined by Theresa and Emily, for quality girl time. The last few days have been such an emotional roller coaster."

A thought flashed through Patrick's mind. *"It will be hugely awkward if Elizabeth and her friends continually unload on Barry."*

He got an out with Elizabeth's next statement. "I know you have to work while you're here. Why don't you use Barry's office?"

"That would be great!"

Elizabeth led Patrick down a hallway with a barrel ceiling and into a very masculine wood paneled room with a window that overlooked a garden with a variety of flowers in bloom. "Is this a copy of the Resolute desk?" he asked.

"It is!" Elizabeth said. "I got that for him as a surprise and he absolutely loved it. He liked to joke that the world's most important leaders sit at a Resolute desk. This one is not actually carved out of the oak timbers from the HMS Resolute, though."

Patrick was about to set his laptop bag on Barry's desk, but noticed a laptop was already there. "Is this your laptop?"

"No, it's the gaming laptop Barry brings to play with the kids. He usually connects it to the home theater. He left it here last week."

"Have the cops checked this out?" Patrick asked.

"No. I never even thought about that. I think it's just a gaming laptop. But maybe you can run some checks on it, see if there's anything more to it?"

"How much time do I have, before I need to leave to go pick up Maya?"

Elizabeth looked confused. "One of the security guards is tracking her flight and will go with our driver to pick her up. They'll probably leave in an hour."

"I'd like to go with them. Can I take this with me to start running some tests on the drive?"

"You'd better turn it on to see if it is password protected first. I'd hate to see you take it and not be able to do anything with it."

Patrick turned on the gaming laptop. There were two user IDs on the computer. The one named Games didn't require a password. The one named Barry did.

"I'll look in our 1Password account and see if I find anything useful. Barry was always diligent about changing passwords on Polestar computers but pretty lazy about passwords on our personal devices. Let's hope he didn't get his own 1Password account after he moved out."

Patrick interrupted her. "You sure he doesn't use NordPass or Cloudflare? "

"Never heard of either," Elizabeth said, shrugging her shoulders. She logged into the password manager from her phone. Then she read off a password to Patrick that he typed in. It worked. "Thank God for Barry's laziness!" she said.

A security guard that Patrick had never seen before knocked on the open door of Barry's office. "I'll be leaving in a few, to go pick up your friend Maya," he said to Elizabeth.

"Maya's my wife, and I'd like to go with you," Patrick said. He slid Barry's laptop into the sleek cordovan leather laptop bag, which had been underneath it on the desk. "Can I use your internet access in the car?"

"Sorry, you can't use the car's mobile hotspot. That would be a breach of our security protocols. We need to have unfettered access to the bandwidth in an emergency," the guard replied. His boss, Terry, had convened a memorial for Phillippe and gently reminded everyone of a core truth. "We are in both the security and hospitality business. We have to be pleasant to our guests, but never forget our Job #1 is to protect them."

"No worries, I have a Nighthawk hotspot device so I'll use that. Besides, there are tests I can run even without the internet."

"I'll be meeting your wife at the gate. You'll have to wait in the terminal."

"I'm okay waiting for her in baggage claim," Patrick said.

As soon as he sat in the back seat of the black car, Patrick got to work on the laptop. When they reached the airport, the driver dropped Patrick and the guard off and went to park. Patrick found a seat in baggage claim and returned to examining the laptop. He quickly became immersed in the project.

"Patrick!" Maya called out to him as she and the guard approached. Patrick stood and embraced his wife as if they had not seen each other in a year. He asked her to carry the laptop while he lugged her rollaway.

"New one?" asked Maya.

"No, but a gold-plated one. Hold on real, real tight."

On the drive to Elizabeth's, the guard noted the two of them slept in each other's arms most of the way.

He said to himself, wincing about his dead colleague, "We are worth every dime Polestar pays us to protect their executives. Especially since some of us literally give our lives for them." His company had a long history of security and detective services. He had no idea that Patrick was a digital sleuth his firm would have loved to recruit.

As Patrick and Maya dozed in the back seat, the driver and guard noticed the hazy sunset. *"Glad that fire's all the way down by Morgan Hill,"* the driver thought.

11

Is He Even Alive?

Saturday am PST

As the sun rose over the Bay Area, Patrick was wrapped in a white terrycloth bathrobe and sitting at Barry's desk, perusing the gaming laptop. Maya, in a matching white bathrobe and slippers, entered the room carrying two coffee mugs, and handed one to Patrick. "Anyone else up yet?" he asked.

"Only the security guards so far," she replied as she sat down in a comfortable leather arm chair across from the desk. "I slept like a dead person last night. How about you?"

"Are you kidding? Curled up with my Miss Maya? Best sleep possible."

"I could tell by your face when I walked in that you're deep in analysis mode. Found anything interesting?"

"Well, I see that there is some kind of program on this computer that is a tremendous data hog. I've just started looking into it. Of course, I won't quit until I've analyzed everything on here. What's your agenda for the day?"

"I'd love to try out Elizabeth's kitchen, maybe make breakfast for everyone. Emily and Theresa are supposed to be here at 1:00 pm, and we're going to just hang out, maybe swim, or stream a movie. I don't know the specifics, just going with the flow. And if the girls really do want to see our wedding videos or talk about office relocations, I have presentations on my laptop ready to go."

Both of them sipped their coffee quietly, Patrick's eyes on the screen of Barry's gaming laptop and Maya lost in thought, until they heard scuffling footsteps approaching. Elizabeth wore a fluffy turquoise robe and matching fuzzy slippers. Her hair was messy and she was not wearing makeup so the dark circles under her bloodshot eyes were obvious. Neither Patrick nor Maya had ever seen her in such a natural, vulnerable state. "Good morning; how'd you sleep?" Elizabeth asked.

"Great!" Patrick said, and Maya nodded in agreement. "How about you?"

"To be honest, I don't think I've slept more than four hours any night this week. And I just looked out the window and saw that the wildfire smoke has gotten worse. You know Barry has asthma, right?" Elizabeth asked.

"No," Patrick replied. "Seriously, I've always thought he was bulletproof."

Elizabeth turned to look out the office door and down the hallway, then spoke, almost in a whisper. "I don't know where he is, but I hope he's away from the smoke, because if he's not, it could kill him. Have you found anything yet, Patrick?"

"I just found a data hog of a program, and I will definitely tell you when I figure out what it is, whether it's helpful or not. I promise," Patrick assured her.

Maya was surprised. Until now, she had thought Elizabeth was handling Barry's disappearance well. She was so upbeat yesterday and had acted like she was throwing an informal weekend party with overnight guests. When Maya and Patrick returned from the airport the night before, a pot of pasta sauce was simmering on the stove, waiting for them, and Elizabeth was putting away a large grocery delivery, talking about the meal options for the next few days. Now Maya realized that Elizabeth was trying to act "normal" for her children's benefit. *"I should be ashamed of myself,"* Maya thought. *"I felt like she owed us for everything Patrick has been doing to help the father of her children. She looks like hell because she's going through hell."*

"Do you and your children like crepes?" Maya asked Elizabeth.

"Yes!" A smile suddenly lit up Elizabeth's face. "Do you know how to make them? I have a crepe pan but have never successfully made any that anyone would want to eat."

"Absolutely! Let's go take inventory and see what kind of fillings I can make. I'll get those done and then I can make everyone the crepe of their choice," Maya said. The ladies left Patrick to his work.

． ． ．

Across town, the mood was much more somber. Neither Lars nor Reggie were pleased to be in a drab office on a Saturday morning. No meaningful breaks yet in the case. No news on Paulie and his tattooed companion. No ransom demands. No communication from Barry. Lots of Barry sightings—even one from Tranquility Base. Some smart-ass thought he would lighten the mood by invoking NASA's lunar landing in 1969.

Was Barry even still alive?

Reggie called Patrick, asking him if he had any new ideas or information. He told her he would call if he came up with anything. Reggie told him that she was going home to spend the rest of the day with her husband and his gourmet cooking, but to feel free to call her.

At home, she told her husband she was disappointed in how little Lars had brought to the investigation. The FBI prides itself for collaborating with counties and cities around the country. "I have worked with much sharper local detectives," Reggie said.

■ ■ ■

Cal Fire estimated that the Uvas Canyon fire was only 35 percent contained. Forward progress had been stopped on the eastern perimeter but the smoke continued to increase as an estimated 2,000 acres were actively burning. Billowing black smoke at the surface of the mountainous terrain moved skyward and became brown, then orange, then tan. Brave fire fighters had arrived from Oregon and Washington to supplement exhausted Cal Fire crews. The US Army had water tanker trucks located on several roads surrounding the perimeter, manned by unnaturally calm personnel who had seen much worse than this fire and were used to breathing through military gas masks.

Air quality had deteriorated quickly in the Morgan Hill area over the past day. An average AQI of 240 led most inhabitants in the "very unhealthy" purple part of the air quality map to vacate their premises. Gang members wearing $40 respirator masks from Lowe's were quietly breaking and entering to hunt for valuables in empty homes. Law enforcement personnel were working overtime to deter criminals, and everyone remaining in the smoke-filled towns was in a foul mood.

12

An Omen of Good Luck?

Saturday pm PST

A few minutes after 1:00 pm, Emily drove her 2002 convertible, in classic Thunderbird blue, which perfectly matched Zeta Tau Alpha turquoise, up to the eight-foot-tall gate at Elizabeth's house, near the end of Ridge View Drive in Atherton. After she answered the armed guard's series of questions to his satisfaction, Emily parked in the small "family only" parking lot, rather than the oval driveway at the front of the house, which was only used for parties or special guests like former Gov. Arnold Schwarzenegger.

A few minutes later the guard repeated the admittance process with Theresa. She parked next to Emily's car and entered the house through the back foyer and keeping room, to the pale yellow kitchen with its cathedral ceiling and skylights. The kitchen and adjoining keeping room, together, were larger than the typical starter home in the Bay Area. Elizabeth was finishing luncheon preparations and looked up to greet Theresa. "Maya, this is my friend Theresa. She went to college with Emily and me, and we three were roommates in the Zeta house." Elizabeth waved her hand toward a tray holding champagne flutes, a glass pitcher of mimosas, and a bottle of French champagne.

Theresa was obviously very comfortable in Elizabeth's home and gave Maya a welcoming smile and said, "Good to see you, Maya. I remember you from the harvest party here the year before last," and she poured herself a mimosa. "Gotta start off with some vitamin C."

Maya somewhat nervously returned the smile and said, "Yes, great to see you again," although she had met so many people at that autumn-themed party that she did not remember Theresa. Luckily, she had remembered Emily from that same event, and had avoided an awkward moment when Emily arrived earlier.

The four women lavished praise on each other's outfits and looks, as per "girl's weekend" protocol, and then it was time for a light meal. Elizabeth had set up a salad bar on the 20-foot island and now placed an overflowing platter of blackened chicken slices at the end of the line. She couldn't remember whether Maya was vegetarian and was too embarrassed to ask, so she purposely hadn't assembled all the salads in advance.

After serving themselves, the ladies entered the casual family dining nook, which faced south and overlooked the

193

patio, pool, and gazebo. The almost two-acre property backed up to acres of protected land surrounding the Bear Gulch Reservoir. All of the grass on the hill leading to the reservoir was brittle and tan, but the hundreds of trees on the reservoir acreage remained green. The trees had adapted to the cyclical weather of the area, and the deep roots that nourished the trees during drought also held the trees firmly into the ground during atmospheric rivers, when mudslides stripped other land bare.

The ladies made polite, positive conversation while eating their salads. Emily was the first to allow any clouds into the conversation when she said, "I brought my bathing suit but it's really hazy outside."

Elizabeth made clear that she wanted to maintain an upbeat mood by responding cheerfully, "We can just ignore the smoky sky. I turned on the pool heater yesterday and the concrete heating this morning. Whatever heat the sun doesn't provide, PG&E will." Elizabeth heard motion in the kitchen. "Let me see if my kids and Patrick, and the security team, have everything they need for lunch. I know I have plenty of staff but it keeps me busy to look after all of you."

Now was the part of the female ritual where each woman praised Elizabeth's hospitality and expressed their concern about what she was going through. As the newcomer, Maya went last. "It's so nice of her to invite Patrick and me, and to put this little party together. Especially with all the stress she's under."

"Having guests and entertaining us is good for her," Emily said. "It distracts her from the agony of not knowing what happened to Barry. And it also helps convince her kids that the situation isn't as bad as it really is. If mom's entertaining, life must be almost normal, right?"

"So you're doing her a favor by being here," Theresa said to Maya.

When she returned, Elizabeth said, "Let's have some lemon-drop martinis! And do we want to swim first or watch Maya and Patrick's wedding videos first?"

Jennifer entered the room and asked, "Can I see the video too?"

"Of course!"

Emily chimed in, "Yes, please!"

"I'll make you lemonade," her mother said, and went into the kitchen.

Immediately after the five ladies opened the French door to the patio, the housekeeper pushed a cart into the breakfast room to clear the dishes. Fifty-year-old Lucia had been a usually silent member of the household for over 15 years. She had undergone a thorough background check and was under a strict nondisclosure agreement, but she earned over $150,000 a year, and felt she was adequately compensated for her discretion.

After Elizabeth made the lemon beverages, the ladies moved into the dove gray home theater. As a movie and music buff, Barry had spared little expense on the audiovisual technology—so there was an 8k resolution screen with Dolby Atmos® and Dolby Vision® built in. The speakers and subwoofers had shrunk in size over time, but they could still produce thunderous sounds. With the smart home technology, there were voice commands for controlling everything including lighting and temperature. Elizabeth had designed the home theater space to contrast with the rest of the house, which had a French chateau vibe. The room had a sleek Art Deco feel with a minimalist décor—no wires in sight anywhere, neutral colors, recessed lights hidden by molding, gray silk curtains with blackout liners. But Barry had won out on fitting in a sleek bar area. Elizabeth placed the pitchers of lemon drinks on the bar top, and showed her guests a hidden refrigerator filled with many other cold drinks.

There was chatter while the women tried to figure out how to connect Maya's laptop to the wall-size monitor, as they couldn't see any connection components. Julian heard the voices and looked into the room. "What's up?" he asked.

"I want to show a presentation and some videos that are on my MacBook, but I'm not sure how to connect," Maya answered.

"I'll do it," he said, and looked at the connection ports on Maya's computer. In less than two minutes the women cheered as the presentation appeared on the wall in front of them, and the ladies sat down in the gray leather recliners with built-in drink holders, while Julian strode away to his drums. Jennifer stayed with the ladies.

"I'm glad Patrick is not here—he was embarrassed by how many times we got married and the number of wedding planners we had involved. He would have been happy to call it done after the ceremony at Civic Hall in downtown San Francisco."

Maya started off with photos of her in a stunning white dress and Patrick in a tuxedo. Patrick had insisted on the Beaux-Arts style structure which blends French, Roman, and Greek design. Maya wasn't as excited—it was an administrative office with city residents lined up for all kinds of paperwork. "He's such a patriot that the rotunda with medallions which honor liberty, equality, strength, and learning was a neat setting for him."

"Next, we had a rehearsal Indian wedding at McAuley Estate Vineyards in the East Bay." Photos showed her in a stunning red-and-gold silk sari and Patrick in a striking blue sherwani and beige salwar trousers.

Maya played a video which included several of the Hindu ceremonies. "They are called by different names around India but roughly follow the same format. *Kanyadan* is the Sanskrit term for when my dad joined my hand with Patrick's, to convey that he was entrusting me to Patrick's care. He united us by wrapping a white cloth around our right hands. The priest then poured holy water which flowed from my parent's hands into Patrick's.

"Here in a ceremony called *Saptapadi*, we are doing seven circles around the fire. In the first four, Patrick led me. In the other three I led him. It's meant to show we can each lead in life. And each circle has specific vows for us chanted by the priest."

Maya showed another set of photos. "This is called *Aashirwad,* or a shower of blessings. The priest is chanting mantras from the ancient holy books, the Vedas. We sought his blessings and, in turn, he showered us with rice and petals of flowers."

Then there were photos of the buffet, of endless tandoori dishes, curries, naan, and other breads. And photos and videos of nonstop dancing. She turned on a video so they could hear the intertwining sounds of Bollywood and western wedding music. There was a pause when a photo of Barry and Elizabeth popped up.

"Damn, you two looked gorgeous!" Emily said. Elizabeth just nodded as she looked at Jennifer to see her reactions. She did not appear upset by the photo of her mother and missing father cuddled up together.

"Now let's move to India. Several guests took advantage of the long trip to add a few days before or after our ceremonies in Bombay, now called Mumbai. Here is a montage our guests shared with us—Elizabeth went to the Taj Mahal in Agra, some European friends went to Varanasi and Haridwar, the holiest Hindu cities on the Ganges River, some went to tea plantations in Kerala in South India. Some of Patrick's tech bros went to Bangalore—the outsourcing capital of the world.

"We had a temple wedding, and then a reception on the lawns of Brabourne Stadium, which used to be a world-class cricket venue. India is absolutely cricket crazy. Don't ask me to describe the game. I went to a game in India and embarrassed myself by asking baseball questions.

"The *Mehendi* ceremony took place a couple of days before the wedding. This is when the bride gets orange henna dye patterns on her hands up to her forearms, and her feet up to her ankles. Female guests, especially young ones, line up to get painted." Maya displayed a photo of Elizabeth showing off her hands.

Elizabeth chimed in, "I was too chicken to have them paint my feet too."

"How long do the dye stains last?

"A couple of weeks."

"Is the dye toxic?"

"In the US, the FDA only allows it as a hair dye but I haven't heard of them arresting Indian ladies on their wedding day," Maya replied.

"Is it unique to India?"

"Not at all. It is said to go back to Egyptian royalty and then spread throughout the Middle East.

"Here is the *Baraat*: Patrick arrived on a horse—because we could not find an elephant in Mumbai—serenaded by a marching band. He was a good sport and even got down and danced in the crowds. A White man doing that in the streets of India is capable of stopping traffic!

"Don't worry, there is no quiz at the end. Even I need a refresher to all the Hindu Gods every time I return to India."

Next, Maya showed the *Sindoor Daan*—where the bright red, actually vermilion, powder is applied to the parting on the bride's hair. "Many Indian women apply that every morning—it is a marker of marital status for a lady. If you stop applying it, people can associate it with widowhood."

Elizabeth then shared some of her thoughts. She turned to the others and said, "The videos give you an idea of the sights and sounds of the wedding. But nothing can replicate the jet lag, the humidity, the smells of India. Or the different taste of food there—so much more intense.

"Now, who wants tandoori chicken for dinner tonight? And rogan josh, and biryani! It won't be nearly as good as what we ate in India, but I think I can get one of the security guards to go pick it up for all of us. I doubt they will let DoorDash in."

The group consensus was that Indian food was perfect for dinner. Then Theresa opened the black-out curtains and sunlight dazzled everyone's eyes. "Pool time!" she said.

"We've barely touched this pitcher of lemon drops, ladies!" Emily said. "I'm taking it out to the pool. Put on your bikinis and meet me out there."

"I'll talk to the guards about picking up dinner in a few hours," Elizabeth said cheerfully. But her primary reason for wanting to speak to the guards was to ask if there was any news about Barry. One of the guards agreed to go pick up Indian food for everyone, but there was no new information about Barry.

Elizabeth had taken Xanax occasionally during times of stress and anxiety for several years. When she learned Barry was missing, her doctor increased her dosage, but as each day passed, she grew more anxious. *"I don't know how much longer I can do this stiff upper lip thing for the kids' sake,"* she admitted to herself. She wasn't due for another pill yet but took one anyway, and then changed into her swimsuit and joined her girlfriends outside. Seeing that her children had decided to join the women and were already in the pool, she said, "I'll race you! I bet I can do two laps in the time it takes you pumpkins to do one." Emily interceded, knowing the combo of martinis and Xanax would not necessarily go too well with a strenuous race in the water, and said, "Elizabeth, can I borrow you?" and took her inside the main house. The lab, Max was happy to take her place with the kids.

Soon the breeze turned cool and the children went into the main house, while the women went into the pool house. Elizabeth took one of the martini glasses from behind the small but elegant white marble bar and poured from the martini pitcher, filling her glass to the rim. She emptied the glass in three minutes. "I love Meyer lemons," she said, then went into one of the guest bedrooms to shower. Ten minutes later she emerged wearing one of the many white terry bathrobes that were in the closets of every guest room in the house. She walked to the bar again and poured the last few drops into her glass. Elizabeth's guests could easily see she was intoxicated.

"You know, Barry and I had those lemon trees planted eight years ago. It was his idea. A few months before then was the first time he cheated on me, that I knew of anyway, and I was deeply depressed. He'd apologized, and promised he'd never cheat again. He said I'd see that our love would grow back and bloom like the lemon trees, and whenever life got sour, we would make lemonade or a lemon meringue pie and remind ourselves we were in this life together."

"I remember that," Emily said.

"Me too," said Theresa.

Maya just listened.

"I told Barry his cheating made me feel ugly and unwanted. And no matter how many times he told me I was beautiful I just couldn't believe him. We'd go to events together and then I'd see photos afterward, and think, 'Wow that photographer is good, because I look okay in that picture,' but every time I looked in a mirror, I saw an ugly woman."

"And you kept asking us what kind of plastic surgery you should get. I am so grateful that Barry told you not to have any work done," Theresa reminded her.

"I should have hated Barry but at that time I hated myself. I thought I was ugly and fat and boring and many days I wanted to die. I couldn't kill myself because of what that would do to the kids. But I wanted to be dead. It took me two years to get my confidence back."

"Thank God for Dr. Jorne. She was wonderful," Emily said.

"Then when Barry cheated again four years ago, Dr. Jorne quickly helped me see that the problem was not with me, it was inside him. Thankfully that was just a short fling. But then he started up with that god-awful Tiffany. All the rage came back and I told him he had killed my love. And he said nothing. Nothing! Then as soon as our new place was ready, he told me he was moving into it alone, and he went public with that whore."

All four women had tears in their eyes.

"So why do I care that he's gone and no one knows where he is? If he's dead then I don't have to be humiliated anymore. I should feel relieved. But I just want him to come home."

Someone knocked on the pool house door. Maya was grateful for the interruption and even happier when she saw Patrick. "Wow, Elizabeth, you open up this charming mini palace for your gal pals and give me the closet?" Everyone laughed, knowing that Patrick was working in Barry's stately office. "Dinner has arrived. May I borrow Miss Maya?"

"You two go ahead, and tell everyone to get started on dinner. We'll be there in a few," Emily said.

After Patrick and Maya left, Elizabeth said, "I can't eat dinner in nothing but a bathrobe, and I don't feel like getting dressed and doing my makeup again."

"I'll go in and ask Lucia to help me fix up three plates and I can use her cart to bring them out here," Theresa volunteered.

"Great idea!" Elizabeth said, and popped the cork of another bottle of French champagne. She was busy getting three champagne flutes out of a cupboard and didn't hear Theresa whisper to Emily: "You stay here." Emily nodded.

Emily stuck her head out the door and called to Theresa: "Put lots of food on those plates, or we're going to get drunk off our asses!"

"That's the plan," Theresa replied. Emily wasn't sure if she meant there would be plenty of food, or Theresa was planning to get drunk.

"Whatever, either works for me," she thought, and went back inside the pool house.

■ ■ ■

After a leisurely and casual buffet of high-quality Indian food, Patrick told Maya: "It's so nice to have you here. Would you mind if I keep working on Barry's laptop? I may have found something but I'm not sure yet. I'll come interrupt you if I need another set of eyes."

"No, of course I don't mind. Helping is why we're here." Maya gave him a tight hug and warm kiss, then went out into the darkening night.

The open land around the reservoir absorbed the sound of I-280 beyond it. She imagined how many stars might be visible if the wildfire haze was not obstructing them. As she approached the pool house, she heard someone sobbing. From a distance, Maya looked through the window to the living room of the small but beautiful house. All three of the women had tears on their faces, but it was Elizabeth who was wailing.

"Bhagwan tumhare saath ho"—Maya whispered—the rough Hindi equivalent of "May God be with you" she had learned from her mother. Then she turned around and walked back to Barry's office. Patrick was surprised to see her. "To what do I owe this pleasure?" he asked.

"The three of them are messy drunk and crying. I don't want to intrude. I would only be in the way."

"Okay, my love. You can help me look over some of the data." Patrick closed the door. Then he said, "Unfortunately, I think it's encrypted, and I don't have the cipher key."

Maya asked him to display the data and she examined it for several minutes. Then her eyes opened wide and she gasped. "It may not be encrypted—look at this data field which repeats every 20 or so characters. It is likely the date field. Create a comma separated values file and sort the file by date. Then you can see if there are common patterns across the rest of each string."

"You're brilliant, as usual!"

"What I am is exhausted. Sorry, Patrick, it's been a long couple of days and I'm still on eastern time. Wake me up, though, if you need me to look at anything else."

"Yeah, sorry, Miss Maya, go crash. I love you."

The couple embraced and lingered inside their hug. "I'm so proud of you, Patrick, for using your knowledge and talent to try to save someone's life. I'm not as optimistic as you, and I think Elizabeth is facing the harsh reality tonight too. But God bless you, keep trying."

Maya walked slowly through the house, noticing how quiet it was now. Lights in most rooms had been turned off. She didn't hear any voices, only the footsteps of a security guard. "Where is everyone?" she asked the uniformed woman.

"The kids have gone to bed and the ladies are still in the pool house. You off to bed too?"

"Yes, my body still thinks it's eastern time. Goodnight."

As she used the restroom, she realized she was in a state-of-the-art "smart" home, and it had more than the fancy theater. The toilet had LED lighting, heated seats, auto-flushing, and even music—features all triggered by handy voice commands. Patrick had told her they were commonplace in Japanese residences and even on their airplanes.

While she showered, she suddenly felt optimistic. *"Barry surrounds himself with so much technology and shows off robotic bodyguards on stage. I would bet he has AirTags somewhere on his body so he can be tracked."*

As Maya slipped between the linen sheets on the most comfortable mattress she'd ever experienced, she prayed once more for Barry and his family. She had been too tired to download an app which would have allowed her to adjust the firmness of the mattress, try the zero gravity setting, turn on the lights under the bed, turn on the foot warmers, and plenty more. She quickly fell into a dreamless sleep.

■ ■ ■

Meanwhile, Patrick had created a CSV file—but he knew he needed coffee before he could study it. Entering the kitchen, he saw a different female security guard, and introduced himself. "I'm Imani Jackson, on the night shift," she replied. "We changed guards at 11:00 pm."

"I'm going to make coffee. Would you like some?"

"Sure—can you make a big pot? Right now, I need to join my colleague outside because we think there's a mountain lion on the prowl. We need to get Mrs. Roman back into the main house."

"I've never seen a mountain lion in the wild," Patrick said. "I'd love to see it!"

"You can watch from the dining room, which has the best view. If the lion is on the property, when I turn on all the exterior lights, you'll see it run. Right now, my colleague is in the pool house. This wildlife show starts in about two minutes, so take your position."

Patrick walked quickly but quietly to the dining room, which was dark. The immense chandelier hanging from its vaulted ceiling showed no fire in its crystals, but Patrick recalled how spectacular it was the last time he attended a party there. The long oval table was ringed with 20 chairs, with more chairs along one wall, ready to accommodate a festive banquet. But tonight, the room was silent, without the laughter and happy chatter Patrick heard on previous occasions.

As he approached the windows overlooking the back-yard, Patrick was startled when all the exterior lights illuminated simultaneously, and he caught sight of a mountain lion standing ankle deep on the steps descending into the pool. In a fraction of a second the lion was off, running toward the reservoir, its legs fully extended front and back, then drawn together, moving as fast as a car. A minute later, when the lion could no longer be seen, the lights were extinguished and Patrick's eyes began to readjust to the dark.

Back in the kitchen, Patrick poured himself a cup of coffee and looked in one of the two refrigerators for milk. Even better, he found a pint of cream. Imani and Elizabeth entered through the glass French door. "That coffee smells wonderful," the guard said.

"None for me," Elizabeth said. "There's nothing like watching a mountain lion cross your path to get the adrenaline flowing! Sobered me right up."

"In many cultures, the mountain lion is seen as a guardian spirit animal," Imani said. "It's a symbol of courage, power, and strength. It is very good luck to see one."

"From a distance," Elizabeth added, making everyone laugh.

A moment later, Maya entered the kitchen, wrapped in her white bathrobe, hair tousled. "My sleeping beauty!" Patrick said, delighted to see her.

"I heard lots of excitement," Maya explained. Imani told her about the mountain lion, and Patrick described the beautiful way it ran. "Wow! That's not something people see every day," Maya said as she smiled, suddenly reenergized.

"Are you refreshed enough to work with me for a while?" Patrick asked his wife.

"I'm off to bed," Elizabeth said. "Goodnight."

13

The Fudge Factor

Sunday am PST

Holding mugs of coffee, Patrick and Maya returned to Barry's office. "I ran the CSV. You're just in time to help me analyze it."

Maya sat at Barry's Resolute desk, admired its carvings, then leaned in toward the monitor. She studied the screen for a few minutes. "The first field is the date as you structured it, second the time stamp, the next few could be GPS coordinates in degrees, minutes, and seconds!" she said delightedly. "Not sure what the rest of the string is about. If I'm right, Barry is limping around somewhere—see how the GPS coordinates change ever so slightly every few minutes? But oh, dear God, if this is correct, he was alive as of yesterday and moving about! Do you have more recent data?"

Patrick said, "You may be right about the GPS coordinates. But it appears to arrive at random intervals. Almost as if whoever is transmitting is moving in and out of network coverage.

"I should contact Reggie and see if the FBI can look at the data."

An hour later, Reggie called back excitedly. "If those are the GPS coordinates, he is not very far from us."

"Actually," Patrick said, "we may be speculating from a CSV file I created from the raw data. Can one of your code breakers look at it and see if they find similar patterns?"

Reggie said, "Patrick, I think I should also send an agent to the last GPS coordinates you have. If the location looks plausible, I'll then send a SWAT team."

Patrick said, "Probably a good idea if, indeed, that is the location data. We don't know what is transmitting it, how often, or what else is in the data string."

Reggie told Patrick: "Stay on standby—let me see if I can have one of my analysts look at it, and the two of you can validate that it's the location data."

Maya went back to bed and Patrick went into the kitchen and made himself a small plate of leftover food. "*I need some fuel to keep me awake the rest of the night,*" he said to himself.

But Patrick was asleep, head on his arms at Barry's desk, when Reggie woke him at 6:00 am. "Good news," she said. "Our analyst thinks the data is not encrypted, and your mapping to specific data fields looks plausible. Bad news—I sent a vehicle to scope out the location for the last coordinates you sent and it's a pond."

Patrick, now more awake, muttered, "Oh shit. They found him dead?"

"No bodies. The coordinates are off."

Patrick thought for a while, and then nearly yelled. "You know, in my vehicles I store a wrong address for the Home button on the navigation system. I remember telling Barry this and him saying that was clever. So, if the car is stolen, they will be trying the garage door opener for somebody else's house and hopefully give up. If, indeed, this is Barry, I wonder if he has added an error in the data it transmits. It may add three or four, or deduct one or two degrees from the actual GPS coordinates.

"Each latitude degree difference would cause a roughly seventy-mile distortion on earth. Longitude error would vary by how close you are to either pole. In California, a longitude degree difference would throw us off roughly fifty miles. We need to talk to Elizabeth—she may know if Barry has an AirTag or some other chip which transmits location data."

Reggie said, "Patrick, wait for Lars and me. We're in charge here, as you know."

"Of course, hurry over."

■ ■ ■

Patrick went back to their bedroom to take a shower. Even though he'd slept only about three hours, he was wide awake and very hopeful.

After a quick shower, Patrick told Imani, who was still on duty: "The FBI special agent in charge is on her way over to look at some information that I found on Barry's laptop. Could you please wake Elizabeth and ask her to grant them access?"

"Oh, that sounds very promising!" Imani said. "Absolutely—I'll go wake her now!"

Imani knocked on the door to Elizabeth's bedroom suite. It was a very tired and disheveled version of Elizabeth who opened the door and asked, "What's going on?" When Imani explained the situation, Elizabeth said, "Fabulous news! Please have them use the media room, and ask Patrick to connect Barry's laptop to the wall monitor. I'm going to shower. I'll be out in 15 minutes."

After she showered, Elizabeth made coffee for all, and called the others to convene in the kitchen for sustenance— coffee and pastries. Witnessing Elizabeth's graciousness, Reggie thought, *Who is this woman, and where did that Grosse Pointe bitch go?*

They regathered in the media room where Patrick summarized his findings, and Reggie explained that the last GPS location turned out to be a pond. "Oh God, you found Barry in a pond?" Elizabeth exclaimed, shock on her face.

"No, no! That's not what I meant," Reggie assured her. The realization hit her: *She still cares about her husband.*

Patrick explained, "I found a GPS tracking program on Barry's laptop. Regina's team went to check the most recent coordinates and it was a shallow pond on a farm, too shallow to hide any bodies. So, we think there's something off on the coordinates. We need you to help us figure out what's going on."

Lars asked Elizabeth what Barry carried on a regular basis which could potentially hide a transmitter. "An AirTag, maybe?"

Elizabeth thought quietly for some moments then said, "The only thing I can think of are his cell phones and his clunky Rolex President watch. He never goes anywhere without it. If someone asks to look at it, he always points out that it has a bark finish. And they usually retort that it's the thickest, bulkiest gold watch they've ever seen."

Reggie asked her: "Do you have any documentation for the watch?"

Elizabeth excused herself, then came back 15 minutes later. "No printed manuals, but I found this receipt from a store which services our watches and jewelry." The receipt for $7,500 only said NAV in the service description.

Lars said, "NAV could stand for navigation. It could be a custom, tiny GPS coordinate transmitter they fitted into the watch."

Elizabeth pointed out some scribbling in Barry's handwriting. It said +1 and -1. Above that was written +2 and -1, but a line had been drawn through those numbers. "I have no idea what that means," she said.

Patrick immediately pulled up the software code, while everyone else in the room watched the lines of code scroll by on the wall monitor. After what seemed like a long time, Patrick yelled, "Barry, you rascal!"

All three faces hopefully turned to Patrick. "Barry added a branch in the code that adds 1 to the longitude degrees and deducts 1 from the latitude degrees from the raw data transmitted."

Reggie said, "Okay, that accounts for the +1 and -1 that Barry scribbled on the receipt. But I'm puzzled. Why would Barry add a transmitter to his watch?"

"Maybe simply to track the watch if it was lost or stolen."

"And why would he distort the location coordinates to throw someone off by 50 to 100 miles?"

"Maybe because he did not want his Chairman or his wife to hack into his laptop and see exactly where he was all the time?" Patrick offered.

"I believe that!" Elizabeth agreed.

"And what about +2 and -1 that Barry had scratched out on the receipt?" Lars asked.

"Perhaps, like his passwords, he changed the distortion factor in the code every so often and noted it on the receipt?" Patrick grinned. "Barry, you sly one."

"Thank God he was as lazy about changing those numbers as he is about his personal passwords, or that receipt wouldn't help us," Elizabeth said.

Reggie was already adjusting the coordinates from the ones Patrick had given her. Then she immediately called the agent who had found the pond and asked him to do a drive-by around the revised coordinates, and to use a drone to get close to any buildings in the area.

"While we wait, let me make us breakfast. And please, if my children come in and ask any questions, let me answer them," Elizabeth said.

"I'm going to wake Maya and tell her the news," Patrick said. He and Elizabeth left the room.

Lars pulled the door shut and asked Reggie: "Doesn't it strike you as odd that Patrick conveniently seems to have all the answers?"

Reggie quietly lost her temper, her words brandished like sharpened swords. "You worried about evidence contamination? You're still suspicious about someone who has been invaluable to us? And how did your guys miss seizing the laptop or finding out from Elizabeth about the Rolex? A very important man is still missing. Shouldn't we all focus on finding where he is and rescuing him?"

Lars' face turned bright red, but he said nothing.

Two hours later, after everyone on the Roman property had feasted on the breakfast Elizabeth cooked, Reggie received texts with drone photos of a nondescript warehouse-type building. She waved to Lars, Elizabeth, and Patrick, and they returned to the media room. She held out her phone to show the image of the building. "I'm going to send in the SWAT team. I have a good feeling Barry is in that structure."

Reggie made two phone calls, then moved close and took Elizabeth's right hand in between both of her own. "We've got our best people out there. I will personally call you when we know anything. Thank you for your hospitality this morning. Now Lars and I have to leave to meet up with the SWAT team."

"Thank you for everything," Elizabeth replied, with a hopeful look on her face.

"We'd have gotten to this point earlier if you had let us have that laptop when you gave us the security camera footage," Reggie said.

Elizabeth's face turned solemn. "Sorry. It was just a gaming laptop he used with the kids. I didn't even remember it until Friday evening, when I asked Patrick to check it out."

"Well, we're here now," Reggie said, suddenly feeling a little bad for adding to Elizabeth's emotional load. "And I don't really know if our guys could have figured it out as fast as Patrick did."

14

Well, Hello There, K2

Sunday pm PST

An hour later, Reggie and Lars, wearing armored vests and helmets, arrived at GPS coordinates 37°01'05.5"N 121°30'29.9"W in Gilroy. A single-lane dirt road led to the parking lot of a white cement building clad in peeling paint. The building sat alone in the middle of a corn field. The next closest building, a quarter mile away, was a small store selling fertilizer and farm implements.

With pistols drawn and respirator masks on, the detectives walked the perimeter of the building and saw no signs that it was occupied, but they were unaware that a silent alarm had been triggered the minute Reggie and Lars' cars pulled up.

A few minutes later, a caravan of armored SWAT vehicles pulled up and surrounded the building, mowing down corn stalks. The SWAT team leader saw the detectives calmly approaching, emerged from an armored truck to confer with Reggie, and then gave the order for the team to deploy.

The SWAT team first ran a wall-climbing bot packed with heat, vibration, and sound sensors. As it crawled the outside of the building, it transmitted exception data which was painted on a 3D model of the building on the team's computer. The thick walls made the job difficult but the sensitive sensors managed to capture a location where it appeared to hear someone's frequent hacking. It also picked up vibrations of a water pipe—presumably the same person cleaning up after a coughing fit.

While two armored personnel cut through the heavy steel front door of the building, 20 additional SWAT team members attired in full armored gear and gas masks held automatic rifles at the ready. After cutting through a couple of additional interior doors, the SWAT team next sent in a bomb-sniffing bot which sent back its readings along with camera images to the controller device.

The SWAT team leader told his team "Not sure what he's saying, but looks like our guy. Go get him."

Barry had seen the bot approaching the cell he was locked in. He recognized it as one that Polestar had helped assemble for customers and shuffled excitedly in its direction. "Well, Hello there, K2. How are you, my old friend?" The robot development project had been a difficult one, and its code name within Polestar, K2, was a reference to the second highest mountain peak in the world.

Barry's excitement about K2 soon turned to terror. He saw several officers clad in attire he had only seen in movies, and thought his life was about to end. He fell to his knees and folded his hands pleading for mercy mumbling, "Please, no, no . . . "

But then one of the armored men lifted his mask and asked, "Mr. Roman, are you alright?" Barry let out the breath he had been holding. Then he burst into tears of relief, sobbing through raspy coughs.

Reggie pushed through the officers inside the building and was elated when she saw Barry. After minimal questioning, she helped Barry walk outside to the life support vehicle. Once an IV and oxygen tanks were started and Barry's vitals were checked, the medical vehicle was escorted to a Kaiser facility in San Jose.

Reggie pulled her cell phone from her pocket and placed a call. Elizabeth answered on the second ring. "Barry is alive and in damn good shape considering what he's been through."

Reggie had to hold the phone away from her ear as Elizabeth screamed her thanks, over and over, to Reggie.

"He's on his way to the San Jose Medical Center. You can go see him in about three hours, but perhaps longer. Wait for us to tell you when you can come. Let the doctors check him over first. I have some things to take care of, but I'll make sure you're an approved visitor."

Reggie walked over to the SWAT team leader, and confirmed his team was ready for their second location, which had been relayed when Reggie made her earlier call from Elizabeth's house.

"It's a nondescript stucco house in an average neighborhood in South San Jose," Reggie told him. "Local police are on standby. I'll call them and let them know we're on our way. Based on the location tracking system, someone wearing Barry's watch was at this address every morning and evening, and I hope they're home now."

When the team arrived at the house, a Spanish-speaking crew had just finished cleaning the house after the Airbnb tenants left. The cleaners did not know who had been staying in the house, nor when they left. The only information they could provide was the phone number for their supervisor at the cleaning company contracted by Airbnb.

Members of the SWAT team took photos of each cleaner, their cleaning company identification cards and driver's licenses, their work van, and its license plate. Then the cleaning team members were loaded into one of the SWAT vehicles and taken to the FBI office for questioning. A tow truck was called to impound the truck, then the SWAT team, Reggie, and Lars departed.

The cleaners' van was stolen before the tow truck arrived. It was never recovered.

■ ■ ■

Barry had gone through the ER, where he was given a nebulizer treatment. He had an IV running in his left arm and a nasal cannula delivering oxygen. He also had been given a whole-body MRI to double check there were no undiagnosed injuries. Barry let them know he was told he had a concussion following the accident, and they told him that his brain looked normal. His bruises were fading, but he still had some back pain. They gave him a mild analgesic and after looking him over, called him "incredibly lucky." The doctor told him: "Not many men walk away from a car accident where you fall 50 feet down a ravine, and not break something."

He was in a clinically clean hospital room with semi-closed blinds filtering the light, and felt very comfortable as he lay in bed. It felt luxurious in comparison to the plastic pad he had been sleeping on for days. He was astonished to hear it was Sunday, exactly a week since he had been kidnapped. The doctors also felt he was lucky that the asthma attack triggered by the smoke was not worse, but also thought it helped that he had been symptom free for several years. His throat still felt somewhat raw.

Barry was happy he didn't need to go to the ICU. When he was a child, he had a few serious asthma attacks which required trips to the hospital. He had once ended up in the ICU, which had been very scary. As he got older, his attacks got rarer. He had worried when they got Max that he might be allergic to the Labrador's hair. That turned out to be a false alarm, and he got to enjoy playing with Max along with the kids.

He remembered his doctor telling him that asthma is a lifelong disease that can go into remission over time, but it doesn't mean you outgrow it. He did carry an inhaler but couldn't remember the last time he had to use it. Obviously, the smoke acted as a trigger and all those asthma symptoms came back. When he was in the cell and the inhaler became less effective due to the increased smoke, all his childhood memories came galloping back. He remembered the fear, anxiety, tightness in his chest, difficulty breathing, and shortness of breath. He practiced mindfulness breathing to help calm his mind and reduce his anxiety. This had helped to a point, until he was sure he was being left to die. Then his cough got worse, for what was the point in managing your breathing if you were waiting for someone to kill you? When the rescuers had come through the door and he was convinced they had come to kill him, he remembered he almost fainted. He was embarrassed to remember how he cried with relief.

Everyone in the hospital knew who Barry was and that he had been missing for days. They also knew he had just been found, but no other information was shared. Barry was pleased that one of his personal bodyguards was on the other side of the curtain, which was partially drawn around the bed, and that police were stationed outside the door. He had never been more grateful for strong, watchful guards. He now realized that he had not once fully appreciated their role in his life. He promised not to give Clive a hard time in the future when he advised him to take care and increased his protection.

■ ■ ■

Reggie and Lars then joined Sheriff Respeto in a cele-bratory press conference. In recent times, Sheriff Respeto had appeared mostly to explain mass shootings and mob scenes, so she was effusive with the media in discussing the happy result of finding Barry alive and only slightly damaged. "Lars will get my vote for the National Sheriff Association's Medal of Merit. And my hope is Reggie is not promoted into some regional FBI office. We need her tenacity right here in our part of California."

Once the TV cameras were gone, her mood turned more serious with Reggie and Lars. "The Guv sends his thanks and a request. This cannot turn into a cold case. We don't want the criminals to thrive by kidnapping Valley billionaires and millionaires. We don't want to become like Haiti, Central America, and certainly not Turkey, which leads the world in kidnappings per capita. We have to find the perps—and quickly."

She turned to Reggie and said, "I would like for the two of us to present at various local corporate headquarters and events on best practices in executive security. Many are too casual. Some of them are outright reckless, like Barry was."

Reggie, in turn, texted Patrick. "Thanks so much for your help this week. If you are around the area next week, we may need to pick your brain as we round up our suspects."

Patrick responded, "I saw you on TV. Glad the Sheriff was generous to you and Lars. We are staying in the area for the next week. I plan to show Maya some of my old haunts and your beautiful scenery."

■ ■ ■

The door opened and two people walked in. A woman asked the guard to please step outside. Barry raised his eyebrows in inquiry. They approached the bed and she extended her hand. "Regina Williams, FBI, and you may call me Reggie. We met earlier today, but I don't expect you to remember."

The man followed her lead and also reached over to shake Barry's hand. "I'm Lars Jensen, senior detective for the San Mateo Sheriff's Department."

Reggie said, "We've talked with your doctors and they tell us that you're well enough for a chat. How do you feel?"

Barry replied, "Firstly, I feel extremely lucky to be alive. Thank you for all your help in saving my life. I do feel a lot better than when you brought me out of the cell. I was struggling to breathe, but it was the fear I was going to die that really got to me. I never felt so alone. I was really terrified. On the whole, I feel a lot better than I deserve. Nothing broken, and the bruises are healing. The asthma attack wasn't as bad as it could have been, and they're treating my symptoms. My throat is still sore but taking sips of water helps. I've eaten, so I'm not hungry. I know you're here to ask some questions and I also have a lot of questions for you. So yes, I'm definitely ready for this session."

Reggie and Lars pulled up chairs and sat beside the bed. Reggie reminded Barry: "Well, you're safe now. Besides the guard near your bed, there is a considerable police presence outside your door."

Barry looked at them and asked, "Before you start, I have some questions. No one has told me what happened to Phillippe."

There was a silence. Then Reggie responded, "I'm sorry to tell you that Phillippe is dead. It was discovered at the autopsy that he didn't die in the accident but that someone broke his neck. As far as we can tell, it happened at the same time as you were taken away. The security company has been a big support for his wife and family. Elizabeth has

223

visited Phillippe's wife and promised all kinds of support in the future."

Barry sat straight up in bed. "Those fucking bastards! All the time I was kept locked up, I asked what happened to Phillippe, and they refused to give me any information. Just said they didn't know. Like hell they didn't know. When I get out of here, I'll go and see his wife."

Barry then asked, "And what about Elizabeth and the kids—how are they handling things?"

At that moment, they decided not to tell him that Elizabeth had been considered a suspect in his killing, in the early part of the investigation. He was bound to find out, but now they wanted his cooperation and that disclosure would not generate any goodwill toward them. They could easily justify why they considered her a suspect but they didn't think he would be likely to hear that. They would handle his outrage later on.

■ ■ ■

Reggie said, "Elizabeth had Theresa and Emily supporting her, right from the time it was clear you were missing. Since then, she has had Patrick and Maya staying at the house. The children have been kept out of school, instead playing unlimited amounts of video games, spending hours in the pool with Max, playing tennis with anyone who is available, and generally being spoiled by everyone at the house. Elizabeth also arranged for a therapist to come and spend time with them. They were kept busy so they didn't have hours to watch the news and all the crazy stories that were making

224

the rounds. So they're okay. I hear it's party time at the house now that you've been found. They have had to be restrained from coming right over to see you. They know you've had an asthma attack but are doing well. You can expect to see them later. Barry, your family is fine. "

"Now tell me about Polestar and what happened to the stock price when I went missing. The kidnappers told me the company lost 50 percent of its value. Tell me what's going on."

Reggie said, "Look, when it was announced that your car had been found, your driver was dead, and you were missing, things got a little crazy. You do realize you are the 'star' in Polestar, so the stock just dived. Everyone in your company, from my understanding, bought all the shares they could with any spare cash they had. Some even got loans. They all appear to have great confidence in the company and its future. I have to tell you I really admired the faith they all have in the company, with or without your presence. How about that?!"

Lars added, "There were many theories as to what happened to you. You have to understand there was no ransom note and it started to look like you may have been killed. Also, the crazies came out in strength and you were sighted in all parts of the world, which fed the idea you'd gone rogue. The stock has been going up and down like an elevator all week. After a few days, when things settled a little, Elizabeth tells me that some large investors poured in, convinced the stock price was a steal. For now, the stock seems to have stabilized at 30 percent less than when you went missing. As you can imagine, the SEC has been watching these events carefully to make sure there's no funny business. Now I think you can expect the price to go up further on Monday, with the news you are back, safe and sound. It was truly awesome to see your employees have so much confidence in the company."

. . .

Maya and Elizabeth discussed how unfair it was that Patrick could not have been thanked during the press conference. Maya blurted out, "Because we have NDAs with them! The outside world doesn't need to know we work with them."

Tucker had also seen the press conference and sent out an all-company email congratulating Patrick for his unrecognized assistance in finding Barry. He warned that, "Due to NDAs, we have to be careful talking about our work with clients."

Oxford's marketing director, Angela Levine, saw an opportunity. She called a blogger friend and said, "At the right time, we can give you some information, in deep background, and you could use your imagination and potentially turn it into a great story."

. . .

Reggie turned more official. "This is a formal interview, so I will be recording. Do you have any problems with this?"

"No," said Barry.

"Okay, let's get started with you going over what happened after you left the house on Sunday."

Barry took a few sips of water and began. "We left the house late evening. I remember finishing a call with India where it was Monday morning. Phillippe had picked out the

Lexus sportscar for us to drive. I was on my way over to Tiffany's."

Lars said, "The fact that Phillippe was driving led to speculation you had convinced him to drop you off somewhere and you had skipped the country. We had sightings of you reported from Belize to China to Zanzibar."

Barry continued, "Suddenly, all the electronics in the car died. Just died. Nothing. Phillippe struggled to keep the car on the road when some kind of a sedan pulled alongside on the driver side, and as Phillippe was trying to avoid it we smashed through the guard rail. Time just seemed to stand still, and I remember we rolled down the ravine. The car came to a resting place and all was silent. I was kind of groggy and I remember two men pulling me out of the car. I kind of registered that I hadn't broken any bones. I didn't have time to see what happened to Phillippe. I have no idea what these men looked like. They were masked. They seemed big and strong. They never spoke. Suddenly I felt pain all over. Horrible pain. I heard myself scream. I think maybe they tased me. The last thing I remember is someone putting what felt like an injection in my arm and then I woke up in that cell where you found me."

Reggie asked, "Even if you didn't see their faces, do you know how many were there in total?" "No, it was dark." Barry replied.

"Can you give a better description of the sedan which forced you off the road?"

"No, although the windows looked blacked out. It just all happened so fast. We had no control of the Lexus. The panel was dead. In the cell, it didn't take long for me to figure out someone had deliberately killed the electronics, which is why Phillippe couldn't steer the car. That car was in top-notch condition and it couldn't have happened by accident."

Reggie confirmed this. "Yes, we've pulled the car out of the ravine and, as you say, found the electronics dead. We believe someone used an electronic communications disrupter. We think it was possibly military grade and not something you can just go out and buy at your local Walmart.

"To continue, when you woke up you found yourself in a cell, and then what happened?"

"Well, when I awoke," Barry answered, "I found every part of my body felt like it was in its own kind of pain. I had a splitting headache, my arms hurt, my stomach was sick, and my back felt the worst. When I stood up, I felt dizzy but I didn't feel any broken bones. When I examined myself, I found I was covered in bruises. They had changed my clothes and I was wearing a very baggy olive drab T-shirt and camouflage pants.

"I just knew I was in trouble. Big trouble. I yelled out and immediately two men appeared. The shorter one called himself Athos and the taller D'Artagnan, from *The Three Musketeers*. I told them I felt awful and they said I had a concussion. Apparently, I had been seen by their doctor. Also, I was still feeling the effects of some drugs they'd given me. They never told me how long I had been out. They allowed me to have a shower, a new change of clothes, and some food—and then the questions started. I told them I had kidnap and ransom insurance, and they said I was a guest of the US government and nobody was interested. I demanded to see a lawyer, and Athos said, 'We know you're a spy, and as a spy you aren't entitled to a lawyer.' A spy! I was shocked. And then I saw my

18-carat-gold Rolex on D'Artagnan's wrist. He just laughed and said, 'You don't need it now.'"

Lars asked, "Were you kept in that cell the whole time?"

"Yes, it had a shower, sink, toilet, and a plastic pad for me to sleep on. I hated that windowless cell, with its bare concrete walls and metal bars. They interviewed me through the bars. No natural light came into the room. There were LED light fixtures across the ceiling and I had no idea of time. The lights were left on the entire time I was there."

Lars asked, "Did you ever meet more than those two?"

"No."

Reggie, leaning in, asked, "Can you tell us a little more about them?"

"One was about 5'6" and the other 5'10"," Barry said. "They were really kind of nondescript. Caucasian, with mirrored glasses. Both wore baseball hats and were heavily bearded. They were both muscular, wore business casual with long trousers, decent shirts, and medical gloves. They always wore those gloves. The taller spoke with a definite New York accent and the other seemed to come from the South. They shared no personal information with me. Sometimes I could judge the change in days by their change in clothes, but I know that is not a very reliable way to keep track of time."

Reggie said, "We are sending a forensic sketch artist to you and let's try and get a good sketch of these two. Also, a description of the clothes they wore would be very helpful. So, let's continue. They told you that you were being held by the US government and you were considered a spy."

Barry said, "Yes, and they kept reminding me that I was in a holding facility that was soundproofed so no one would hear me. They just kept repeating, 'We know you're a spy,' and insisting that I was using Polestar to send restricted customer data to China. They wanted to know my contacts and what the Chinese were doing with the data. They were particularly interested in what data was being sent that related to the US government.

"One day when I was feeling sleep-deprived and hungry, I said to them that the Three Musketeers were the good guys, and not two scumbags like them. They just laughed and continued with the questioning. I seriously thought I was going mad."

Reggie asked, "Did they tell you what evidence they had you were a spy or that Polestar equipment was being used to deliver this classified information?"

"They asked me to tell them about Chongqing in Western China," Barry replied. "I was very annoyed and taunted them by asking if they meant 'Cheech and Chong.' They mentioned that they knew Polestar had some connections there. I told them our R&D chief has some smallish outsourcing contracts in China, and she may have an inkling, but I'd never met those folks. Of course, I also remembered that Tina, my new CTO, had told me about a contact called Ming in Chongqing. I'd never met Ming. But I wasn't about to make it easy for these assholes by sharing this information. Nothing I said made any difference. I told them if they looked, they'd see we make very little money in China. Believe me, these two guys were very convincing in that while I knew I was not a spy, it did make me wonder if there was a spy in the company sending restricted data to the Chinese. I certainly planned, if I ever got out, to go looking myself and have the FBI and all my high-level contacts in Washington quietly look into the matter for me.

"I, of course, threatened them that I had the money and contacts to find them and to ruin them, but they just laughed. On the last day I saw them, they were wearing white Hazmat suits and sanitized the place. They said they were giving me a break because the smoke gave them a headache. I knew they were cleaning their traces. When you guys came through the door with K2, I thought a different crew had come to finish the job, just like a different team had done the kidnapping. The smoke made it hard to breathe, but I really believed it wouldn't be the smoke that finished me off."

There was a knock on the door. The police officer announced the forensic sketch artist was there and asked if he could come in. Reggie and Lars got up and moved the chairs back. Barry looked at them and said, "That just about covers it. They believed I was a spy and Polestar was being used to send restricted data to China. Same questions, day after day. How I kept my sanity I don't know. Thank you so much for rescuing me."

Reggie said, "Well, that's a long story for another time. But just know you owe a big debt of gratitude to Patrick. Also, for the moment, could you please not mention to anyone that your kidnappers claimed they were working for the US government? I would like to keep that out of the newspapers. It would really create a firestorm."

Barry nodded.

"Okay, let's have the sketch artist come in."

The artist spent the best part of 90 minutes with Barry, who'd expected it would be a pen-and-paper process but it was actually a digital forensic sketch. Fascinating to watch, and of course it took longer because there were two men to describe. Two men who probably were clean-shaven by now and likely had gone to someone like Alejandro and got a fancy haircut.

■ ■ ■

When the sketch artist finally left, Barry started to go back over the past few days and then found himself reviewing his relationships with Elizabeth and Tiffany. While imprisoned, he had found himself obsessing over his children and wife, praying he would get to see them again.

Had he thought of Tiffany? Yes, he had. But it was different. Somehow, he knew they were finished. In fact, he had started to strongly regret the affair.

Barry knew that it was his close brush with death that was causing him to seriously assess his relationship with Elizabeth. He'd recalled the therapy sessions he had after his first and second affairs. He felt he finally could see what the psychologists were talking about in their assessments, which he truthfully had not taken very seriously at the time. He did have a problem with external validation. He did want people to admire him—and more than that, to envy him. He had flaunted his wealth and what he perceived as his power, his genius ideas, and his sexuality. He loved to be unpredictable and couldn't bear to be considered ordinary. He tried to play out Coldplay's words, "I used to rule the world . . . seas would rise when I gave the word." In short, he spent his life trying to prove he was better than everyone else. He still

232

didn't know why he wanted others to envy him, but he knew that drive was unhealthy.

Now that he had survived the kidnapping and incarceration, he was committed to making major changes in his life. He wanted to go back home, but knew he had seriously hurt Elizabeth, Jennifer, and Julian. Could Elizabeth forgive him? Could his kids?

Barry saw clearly that Tiffany had no place in his life anymore. He hoped very much that she was not going to be difficult, and pledged he would take care of her financially. He would have his lawyers put together a parting gift for her, and hoped that it would be enough to keep her from being a problem. It would be highly embarrassing if any breakup drama were played out in public. He knew he was a coward for not calling her, but was grateful to her for making it so easy. That part of his life was over.

But what was he going to do to repair the damage with his wife and children? When he thought of what they'd been through while he was living a bachelor life with Tiffany, he felt ashamed. *My poor kids. They're so wonderful, and I could tell this was putting them through hell.*

He knew he was lucky to be married to such a beautiful woman and thought of the last fundraiser when she had looked ravishing in that cream evening dress. He saw her take the stage with him and remembered how proud he felt that they raised such enormous amounts for charity. But in thinking about the event, a recurrent thought popped—It just wasn't diverse enough! Silicon Valley had changed so much in the last couple of decades. Now there were Apple millionaires and others from Google, Nvidia, Meta, Salesforce, Workday, etc.

So many Indian, Chinese, and Eastern European entrepreneurs. A new generation of VCs. A majority of their annual attendees represented generational wealth, California style, going back to the mining days of the 1800s. He decided they would talk to the event managers and raise the bar—to double the collections next year, and then double that again the year after. To make the guest list younger and more diverse. He wanted Sharon, Polestar's HR head, to tease him: "This is Barry's version of DEI!" Barry started to laugh at himself, when he realized that once again, he wanted people to admire him. With these thoughts, he fell fast asleep.

Sometime later he awoke to hear his bodyguard say, "Mrs. Roman! So happy to see you." Elizabeth pulled open the curtain and the guard closed the door on his way out of the room.

"Thank you for coming," Barry said.

His expression was a mixture of surprise and relief. The room was quiet, creating an intimate space for their conversation. Elizabeth approached Barry with feelings of apprehension. After almost a year of tumultuous estrangement, her very presence comforted Barry, and reminded him of the life they had built together.

"I was told you were wearing some odd clothes and had no phone so Alisha rushed around and got you a new phone," Elizabeth said, handing Barry an iPhone along with a piece of paper which listed his new number. "Alisha has switched over your contacts, emails, and photos. The FBI is monitoring your old phone number. Also, I've brought a small case with some clothes and your toiletries."

"Thank you for helping to stabilize Polestar's stock prices," Barry said. "Reggie told me it made a huge difference in what I hear was a very rough week."

There was silence. Their conversation was tentative at first, tiptoeing around the brutality of his kidnapping and the wreckage of their relationship. Elizabeth talked about the children and conveyed their messages of love to him.

Barry opened up. "This ... situation, it's made me realize just how much I've hurt you and the kids. How much I've missed out on."

Elizabeth moved closer, "Talk to me, Barry. No more lies, or pretending. Really talk to me."

"Tiffany is history," Barry said. "I'll never see her again. All I want is you, our kids, and our life together."

Elizabeth took a deep breath. "I want to believe you, Barry. But it's not just about ending things with Tiffany. Look, I put up with your affairs for years. And, somehow, we made it through until it came to Tiffany. I now realize I wasn't respecting myself, and it was a terrible example for the kids. I also admit I allowed you to disrespect me. This ends right now. I don't know if we can find a way through this but I was really scared at how much rage I had inside and that I actually wanted you to die. Right until you went missing."

Barry reached for Elizabeth's hand, his touch tentative. "Betsey, I deserved that. I want to make things right and this time I'll do whatever it takes."

Elizabeth's eyes filled with unshed tears as she considered his words. "Barry, I still love you. But love isn't enough on its own. We need to understand why, to ensure this never happens again. It will require individual therapy for us both as well as marriage counseling. A marriage is about two people and I think the 'why' is going to be painful for you, and maybe for me."

Then Elizabeth called Julian, and asked him to put the phone on speaker so Jennifer could join in the call. Barry poured out his love for his children, and told them he would be fine and home in a few days. "I hope you'll come see me tomorrow," he said, and they assured him they would.

As Elizabeth left the hospital room, there was a fragile thread of happiness that hadn't been there before.

That evening, the security guard was Desmond Russel. He had known Phillippe, so Barry spent some time talking with him about Phillippe and how much he was going to be missed. He was having trouble falling asleep and Desmond found a book for him that was lying around. It was about a US Air Force fighter pilot, Joshua Reams, who was shot down over North Vietnam in 1967. After ejecting from his aircraft, he was captured and endured six years of brutal treatment. Reading this, Barry kept thinking, *"I am so freaking lucky. Not sure I could survive even a month, forget six years."* A nurse came and insisted he take a sleeping pill, which he did. He was soon asleep.

■ ■ ■

All week, Tiffany had followed any news she could find on the different networks. Her eyes felt burnt to the sockets and her sleep was terrible. She slowly became convinced Barry was dead and felt absolutely awful about all the horrible things she had said about him. Ashley and other friends had taken time to be with her, and she was very thankful for the company. When she heard the news conference stating that Barry Roman had survived kidnapping and false imprisonment and was expected to be released from the hospital within a few days, she was over the moon. She cried with relief.

Ashley waited with her as she hoped she might hear from Barry or someone would call on his behalf. The hours slowly ticked away. Ashley tried to console her, "Perhaps in all the excitement you were overlooked."

"No, I know it's over," Tiffany said. "Before this happened, I could sense a change. Maybe something happened when he stayed overnight with Elizabeth. I've also never forgotten how truly happy he looked when he stood beside Elizabeth at the fundraiser. I'm not going down to the hospital. It's obvious that Barry does not want to see me. I have some pride and I'm not going to grovel.

"As you know, I don't have a plan B. I thought we would work out. I'm going to wait a couple of weeks to see what Barry does. I feel Barry will look after me and if he doesn't then I will hire a lawyer," she said sadly. "You were all right when you said it would not have a happy ending for me."

Ashley sympathized, and then said, "Enough! This has been one long, depressing week. Let's go and get a drink."

■ ■ ■

At night, the mood at Elizabeth's was jubilant. As everyone was getting nicely inebriated, Theresa reminded Maya she would still like to see her Florida real estate presentation. Maya hesitated at bringing attention to a relatively mundane manner at this moment of such celebration and relief, but she offered to show a shortened version, sans graphs and spreadsheets, and so the group went back to the AV Room.

Maya started by contrasting older US migrations—generally westward—to current trends within the US. She said now we are seeing a wave of people moving from California, the Northeast, and the Midwest to states in the South, especially Texas and Florida. Many of those on the move are seeking not so much better opportunities as an improved quality of life—less crime and homelessness, lower taxes, more affordable housing, and more.

"Our CEO, Tucker, who's long bristled about 'Taxachussets' and complained about how tough it's become to recruit for our Boston location, asked Patrick to conduct a Florida office feasibility study. Patrick had too many things on his plate, so Tucker reassigned the project to me.

"Patrick had asked Barry—who was raised on the east coast of Florida—for advice. Barry said we would get far better deals and quality of life on the state's west coast. And so, I was open to this idea of being on the 'West Coast on the East Coast.' But honestly, I was mostly nervous about what I had heard about 'MAGA-land.' As a liberal Brown alum, I thought it might be a poor fit politically and culturally.

"Our firm helps clients make disciplined, quantitatively sound technology decisions, so I used a similar format of weights and scores to evaluate four potential West Florida locations, and St. Petersburg won handily—over Tampa, Sarasota, and Fort Myers.

"But I needed convincing that Florida could be a good fit. To make this brief, I'll focus on three people who endeared

Florida to me. Maya pulled up three photos, and said "Meet three salt-of-the-earth souls who offered to me, in different ways, a vision of Florida.

"First is Charlene, a real estate agent who showed me around Tampa, but had started out in Silicon Valley at a tech startup. She opened my eyes to the vast range of technology to be found in Florida, in all directions—there's Kennedy Space Center and space and aviation entrepreneurs; south in Miami, NOAA tracks hurricanes with satellites, supercomputers, sensors, drones, and more; Gainesville has STEM education and research galore. The state is teeming with technology—logistics firms redefining supply chains with robotics and satellites, fintech, oceanography, agritech, animation, gaming, medical cities, and so much more. As Charlene said, Silicon Valley has no right to snootily look down on this STEM 'backwater.'

"Next is Julie, the supreme cat woman, who has a rescue-and-rehab center on her farm near Gainesville where she takes care of 250 felines, all awaiting adoption. She also cares for a wide assortment of other species—horses, hogs, chickens, everything. All on a nonprofit's shoestring budget. I was so touched by Julie's warmth and love of animals that I drove to a nearby ATM and took out $200 that I gave to her. I also told her we may have Kat, my mother-in-law's pet, join her community if they move to Florida.

"Finally, here's James, an elderly gent who I met at the Ringling Museum in Sarasota, which features a famous miniature circus exhibit. James said he'd been in the circus as a teenager, and he thought it was a damn shame that kids now don't get to see exotic animals they used to bring to town, or people who had all kinds of unusual skills. The circus was truly a family while they traveled around the country, he said. I found him a glorious specimen of Americana at its best, and of a vanishing world.

"Those three were so different and yet they all touched me. By the end of the trip, I was gushing to Patrick that it's actually more like 'Maya Land' down there than MAGA-land.

"So Theresa, I encourage you to keep an open mind and talk to plenty of locals when you do your search."

■ ■ ■

At the same time that Barry found himself recovering in the hospital, two nondescript but clean-shaven men who knew a lot about Barry's kidnapping entered an interior meeting room at their employer's headquarters, and locked the door behind them. The flag outside the door changed to "Occupied." Already seated at the small conference table were three other men. Only one of the three men was known to them. He was their immediate boss, and when they introduced themselves, the other two men said nothing.

Their boss started by saying he had their report but would like to walk through the whole episode with them. The two men shared a look and the older and possibly more senior man started to explain what happened during their time with the captive man.

"When the first team brought Mr. Roman to the cell, he was unconscious. In the handover, we were told he had been in a car accident and the car had fallen 50 feet into a ravine. No limbs were broken but he was badly bruised. They said he was coherent after the accident and they gave him drugs to knock him out. He was the passenger and the driver had been taken care of. Our doctor did see him and believed he had concussion, as well as still being affected by the meds they had given him at the time of the kidnapping. He was out for about eight hours and he was never informed how long he had been unconscious or what drugs he'd received.

"When he came to, he had soiled himself so he was allowed to shower and change his clothes. He was also fed. We called ourselves Athos and D'Artagnan, from *The Three Musketeers*. He starting screaming about the right to call a lawyer and we told him he was being held in a holding facility, courtesy of the US government."

This information did not seem to bother the three men behind the desk, who just nodded.

"He asked about his security guard who had driven the vehicle and we denied any knowledge. And then we began our questioning. Told him we knew he was a spy and that he and his company Polestar were sending his customers' restricted data to China and we wanted to know his contacts. He told us we were crazy. He claimed that if we looked, we would see the company made only a little money in China and besides he was 'a fucking patriotic American.' He said that any idiot knows they would compete and commoditize his business in a couple of years and so what would he gain?

"We asked him about Chongqing in Western China. He could not even pronounce the name and called it 'Cheech and Chong.' We even told him that Polestar's stock had dropped 50 percent since he had been reported missing, and that if he wanted to save his company he needed to tell us what we wanted and then he would be free to show his face and restore confidence. He got really mad about the damage his company was undergoing due to the kidnapping but it yielded no new information. We used all our training and experience to pry details out of him but no matter what angle we used he never contradicted himself. Threats and sleep deprivation didn't yield any new facts. We passed on any information we obtained and we heard the results were disappointing. As we put in the report, we believed he was telling the truth.

"The air quality of the unit was rapidly deteriorating as the increasing smoke from the ongoing wildfire had over-whelmed the HVAC system. Mr. Roman told us he had a history of asthma and our doctor got him an inhaler. We gave it to him but as the smoke continued to get worse, he started to cough quite badly, and it became less effective. As instructed, we terminated the interrogation and sanitized the place."

There was a pause and their boss asked them: "Do you know the FBI has found Mr. Roman? Did you know the FBI also found the Airbnb you stayed at? We had an extraction team *en route* to Mr. Roman when the alarms were triggered. They observed the FBI SWAT team extracting Mr. Roman from the building. Luckily for us, the FBI arrived at the Airbnb just after the cleaning crew had done their work. They know nothing and the booking is untraceable. Hopefully, you also did a good enough job of cleaning the house as well, and that we are not dependent on the Airbnb cleaners.

"Now, your report does not mention any unusual activity around the house or the holding cell. Would you care to add something to your report? It appears to be a matter of luck that because the decision was made to end the interrogation

242

early, you were not found with Mr. Roman. It was another matter of luck that our extraction team was not found at work by the FBI. That is just too much dependence on 'luck' for my taste. Would you care to explain how the FBI has managed to find both sites?"

The two men looked anxiously at each other. They truly didn't know how it had happened. They were skilled professionals and they noticed nothing to alarm them. They had varied their routes, paid cash for everything, used a variety of restaurants, kept to themselves at the house, and never noticed anyone showing any interest in them. They had good instincts for when they are being observed. Nothing. What could have happened? In their minds, as they went over the past few days, they both had the same thought at the same time . . . the watch!? They knew it should have been destroyed but one of them wore it for a few days and it had been worn when moving between the two sites. They shivered and thought surely if there was a GPS on the watch, Mr. Roman would have been found days ago. No, it couldn't be the watch. There had been a massive row about keeping it, but in the end they had left the watch with Mr. Roman. Better to say nothing about their carelessness. They reassured their boss that they had followed all protocols.

As they were leaving, their boss cautioned them: "We have contacts within the FBI and I hope, for your sake, that Mr. Roman being found had nothing to do with you. We will also find out what they know about you two. In the meantime, we have arranged for you both to fly to two different countries. Here are your itineraries and please use your current passports."

Section C
Law & Order

15

Safest Place to Be?

Barry was free, but the case was not solved. Reggie was discreetly reaching out to her superiors in Washington. In the meantime, Lars and Reggie ranked their list of suspects and the search continued for Paulie and his friend.

They decided to touch base with Barry and continue their debriefing. Dr. Sinclair, who was in charge of Barry's care, said, "Barry is doing great. Much better than expected. He's longing to get home and wants to be discharged today. We'd feel more comfortable if he could stay until tomorrow. It's good that he feels able to talk about his experience and appears to be handling it well, but please remember he is very traumatized by the past week, even if that is not always apparent. So go easy in your questioning and be sensitive to his responses. His asthma is responding well to treatment and can be managed at home. We will strongly recommend that when he is home he starts seeing a therapist who specializes in trauma."

They were surprised to see that Barry had changed into his own clothes. Noticing their surprise, Barry said, "I couldn't take the hospital gowns any longer." The drip was gone and he had only the nasal canula left. The guard left the room and Lars and Reggie sat on either side of Barry.

Reggie said, "Thanks for giving us a good likeness of the two men that you knew as Athos and D'Artagnan. The sketch artist said you were easy to work with and very clear in your description with their glasses and headgear."

Barry replied, "I ought to be able to describe them as I looked at them for days. I described them with their beards. They could be clean-shaven by now.

"I don't mind admitting I was never so scared in my life. I'm glad to have the guard by the bed and the police outside. I've always taken safety for granted, but not anymore. From now on, Clive is going to have no difficulty in plying me with security."

Reggie took out the recorder and reminded Barry he was being recorded. "We'd like to ask you some more questions if you feel up to the job."

Barry said, "Absolutely. It's a huge relief to be able to talk about my experiences and not keep it bottled up. I also want you to find the bastards."

"You mentioned they claimed they worked for the US government and thought you were a spy," Reggie said. "Did they give you any information on what section of the government they worked for?"

Barry replied, "They claimed they were funded by 'M' account funds, via subcontracts under subcontracts. They talked of Expired Appropriations Accounts. Funds are given to specific programs for a specific time frame. Every program asks for more than they need, just in case. Whatever's not spent in time gets swept up into these accounts. They claimed it was a bunch of accounting tricks, and that the unspent money gets moved around into other programs that Congress doesn't know about. And that some agency then uses that money to issue a classified contract to some firm. And that firm issues several classified subcontracts. And some of those subcontractors give classified subcontracts to Black Ops firms to do something that no one knows about. In the end, they insisted they were on official US government business, as I was classified as a spy. Basically, they were telling me I had no hope in hell of finding out who they worked for."

Reggie asked, "Do you have enemies in any foreign governments? How about US politicians or bureaucrats in DC?"

"None that I know of. We have contracts with many agencies in DC. The interrogators appeared to know some of the officials there. They were careful not to name names. They just kept taunting me that they were the good guys, on contract to the US government and conducting official business. Conducting official business? Can you believe that's what they said?

"I threatened them with my wealth, connections, and decades of campaign donations, to let them know that when I got out I'd have Congress convene an investigation into the funding of their firm and all the other Black Ops firms. They just laughed. They found the notion of 'Barrygate' very funny. Anyway, they also told me that even if I could draw an accurate picture of them, and someone identified them, they are employees of a firm that is contracted by the feds, to do exactly what they were doing. They claimed their firm could provide documentation they were in Prague or Paris that week and I would look insane.

"In the end, I came to believe that whomever they worked for was honestly convinced I was a spy and that it was either a rogue DC or foreign black ops job. Look, I didn't know Phillippe was dead. They just said they didn't know what happened to him. I assumed they just left him behind and I hoped he hadn't broken any bones. I also knew there would be a search for us and I hoped he would not be in the ravine for long. I knew he would be able to tell everyone what happened to us and how the accident occurred.

"So, while I was in pain from the bruises, driven insane by all the questions, I never really thought I would be killed. It's true the lights were left on but when they were not there, I took off my shirt and covered my eyes and got some sleep. They fed me some cheap food, plenty of protein bars, and lots of water. They even got me an inhaler when I told them about my asthma. I took this as a good sign. There were times when the questioning seemed to go for hours but at other times I actually got a lot of sleep. And perhaps I had too much time to think about things. If I was not the spy and they were convinced there was a spy, then who was the spy?"

Barry came to a halt, for a moment, then resumed, "Well, enough of that. Can you explain to me how the hell you found me? This looked like a very professional operation and I believed them when they said the building was soundproof and someone would have to know where to find me if there was any hope of me getting out."

Lars said, "You owe it all to your friend Patrick and your watch. Patrick decoded your distortion of the GPS coordinates. We found you and also the house your interrogators used. It seems someone wore the watch when moving between the cell and the house."

"Oh my God! When I first woke up after being tased and drugged, I saw D'Artagnan wearing my watch. I got really mad and thought I would never wear it again.

"I overheard a nasty argument on the last day where D'Artagnan had wanted to keep the watch and Athos told him not to be a fool, that it wasn't a safe thing to do. Anyway, they did return the watch, and then they left me with food and water. So it is thanks to D'Artagnan's greed that I got out? Athos had been uncomfortable all the time D'Artagnan wore it and insisted it should have been destroyed, along with my clothes and phone. Boy, was I lucky!"

Reggie said, "Look, I know you want to shout from the rooftop that you were held by people claiming to be government employees and perhaps are considering getting in touch with your many contacts in Washington, but please keep that quiet for now. Give us a chance to delve into this mess and see what shows up. We also have a list of other suspects and we are exploring these avenues as well. Please give us time and we promise to keep you informed when we have any concrete news."

Reluctantly, Barry nodded.

There was a knock on the door and a nurse entered to take Barry's vital signs. Reggie and Lars took that as a signal to leave. They again reminded him to limit the amount of information shared, and promised to keep him informed of any new developments.

■ ■ ■

The next visitor was a complete surprise. The security guard was given a business card which he passed to Barry: James Bradshaw, Esq., from the law office of Bradshaw, Homes & Fellows, based in Washington, DC. "Send him in," Barry said.

A very well-dressed gentleman, around 6'0" in height, middle-aged, and exuding an air of assurance, walked into the room. He walked over to Barry and held out his hand. "Good morning, Mr. Roman. I am James Bradshaw and I practice law in Washington. I would like to discuss a business deal and I wonder if you could ask your guard to please step out of the room for a few moments." Barry nodded his head and the guard pulled a chair over to the bed, then left the room. Mr. Bradshaw reached into an inner pocket and pulled out a slim device that had a small antenna. "I'd like to keep our conversation private so excuse me while I check for any hidden devices." He moved the device gently around the room, appeared satisfied, and put it away. He next sat down.

"Mr. Roman, I am here on behalf of a client who was sorry to hear of your kidnapping and imprisonment. They would like to be of assistance and help your company make a rapid recovery from its recent financial woes. They wonder if you might be interested in competing for a few lucrative defense contracts?"

Barry was speechless. His first instinct was to call security and have this sweet-talking man thrown out. He could not believe the gall. One minute they wanted to kill him and in the next minute they claimed to want to do business with him?

Mr. Bradshaw, sensing Barry's turmoil, continued, "I'm very sorry to hear of your distressing experience but I know nothing about your kidnapping. My specialty is to broker deals between interested parties. My client is well aware of your innovative technology and they would be inclined to look favorably on any competitive bids you present. In fact, it is surprising that Polestar has not been more involved with defense contracts. Would this be of interest to you?"

Barry looked directly at Mr. Bradshaw. "You sons of bitches—military contracts for my silence? You know I intended to shake the Washington tree and use my contacts to find out who was responsible for my kidnapping. Obviously, I could've made a lot of noise, could've been an embarrassment for the government, but I doubt I would've gotten to the truth. My FBI contact has asked me to be quiet for the moment and let her handle it. However, I want you to know that I'm morally outraged that I was literally lifted out of my life and imprisoned. But I suspect I will never get to the truth, and my company needs as much support as it can get at the moment, so I'm prepared to listen to what you propose."

Mr. Bradshaw smiled and said, "Thank you. I will pass on your interest and you will be given information on the contracts that might be of interest to you." He got up and said, while shaking hands with Barry, "I'm personally very pleased to see you looking so well. I trust you will soon be out of the hospital and back at the helm. Good day."

Barry already knew no one would have gone to jail, or even been fired, for what they did to him. While his anger demanded otherwise, he might as well help his company and do business with these devils!

Barry got up and cleaned up. It was nice to use his familiar toiletries after a week. It promised to be a busy day with lots of visitors. Elizabeth had called and would be there soon, with the kids.

As promised, Elizabeth, Jennifer, and Julian arrived in force. For Barry, it was wonderful to see their faces and just know all was well. "I'm coming home and there will be no divorce," he told them. Elizabeth and he sat holding hands. "I'm very sorry for all the pain I caused," Barry said to his children. "I know it has been difficult for you, both at home and at school, with the divorce being played out in the papers. Your mom and I are going to do therapy to help us reach the next level in our relationship." Tears were shed, many things were said, some very painful to hear, but he felt it was good to know what his family had to say about the past year. He felt incredibly lucky to be given a second chance.

■ ■ ■

Clive had been kept updated on Barry's recovery and decided he would go visit in person. He spoke with Elizabeth, who told him Barry was bored and impatient to get out of the hospital. She said Barry would welcome a visit and probably thank him for his work during the week to help stabilize the company.

Once he was admitted into Barry's room, Clive was delighted to see how well he looked after all that had happened. The guard stepped out to buy them coffees at the hospital café. Reggie had kept Clive informed about the details of the successful rescue and Barry's transfer to the hospital.

"I have to tell you that Alisha sends her love and you can expect to see her later today," Clive said. "With great difficulty, she has been restrained from bursting in here and hurling herself on your chest at your safe delivery. You might want to apologize to her for all the worry you caused. That girl has been in a bad way all week."

Clive grabbed a chair and the two men sat in a friendly silence, all disagreements forgotten. Eventually, Clive asked about Barry's health and Barry happily said he was really doing well, all things considered. Shifting subjects, Barry said, "You know, Clive, I didn't know at the time what happened to Phillippe but when they cleaned up the place with Hazmat suits, I felt sure I was a goner. You may not know it but when the good guys arrived, I thought it was a team coming to kill me.

"As Reggie no doubt told you, they were convinced I was a spy and using Polestar to send customer data to China. Well, the FBI is involved now, so I expect them to look into this allegation and see if Polestar is involved in any such illegal activity. I know I'm not a spy, but what if there is someone in the company using our data for illegal purposes? It could even include a partner so it's going to be a big wide search.

"These same bastards told me the stock had dipped 50 percent and they just taunted me about the company going down. Reggie tells me the stock has been going up and down like a roller coaster and had ended the week about 30 percent lower."

Clive said, "Yes, it just went crazy when the car was found, with the driver dead and you missing. Then, when there was no ransom note and it looked like you were dead, it got really bad. I have to tell you, Elizabeth and her family immediately threw everything they had into buying stock. We had a meeting to reassure everyone that the company was solid, even without you. Tina did a great job in presenting all the innovative technology we have coming online and all the plans for the future. There was a series of Zoom calls with all our partners. In the end, it appears most of the employees bought stock because they considered it a great buy."

"I also spoke with several of our large institutional investors and reminded them that Polestar is now a multinational company, not a startup dependent on the brilliance of just one man. I showed them that we have five- and 10-year plans, and were quite capable of running the company without you. Once they settled down and looked at our plans, they invested fairly heavily. Charles Morgan at Sheldon was one of the first to put out a Buy rating and others followed. But I won't deny it was a mess for a couple of days. Now that you're back, and hale and hearty, the stock price today is starting to climb."

"Clive, thank you for all you did this week. I also want you to know how grateful I am for all your efforts to keep me safe, and I'm sorry I made it so difficult for you. You always kept reminding me that perception is so important with Wall Street and not to do anything to shake their confidence. I know I really was pushing it when I pulled these stunts and couldn't be reached for hours at a time and people ended up covering for me. My last two trips to Alaska and Hawaii come to mind. Going forward, I will always make sure the company knows where I am and that I have enough security with me. I don't know if it would've made a difference in this case, but I promise to have a driver and security guard in the future. I can't help but wonder if there would've been a different outcome if Phillippe could've used his gun if he had been in the passenger seat, when the sedan first sideswiped us. I have had my 'Come to Jesus moment,' and I intend to profit from it."

Clive chuckled. "We'll discuss your expenses very soon as you seem to be in a very penitent mood. I should take advantage of this new Barry."

. . .

Alisha arrived a couple of hours after Clive's visit. While she did not throw herself on his chest, she certainly expressed great delight in seeing how well he looked. All was forgiven, when she heard him say, "Alisha, I'm so sorry for all this worry I caused you, and I promise to be a good boy in the future." Barry talked of going home with Elizabeth and there was no mention of Tiffany. Alisha followed his lead and also did not mention her.

She made herself comfortable in the chair across from Barry, and both enjoyed cups of tea provided by the guard. Alisha said, "I was so shocked when I heard that Phillippe had been murdered. The funeral is to be this coming Friday at Simpson's Funeral Home. They have family coming from out of town and a brother flying in from London."

"Be sure to give me the details and I will attend. When I get out of here, I plan on visiting his wife and expressing my deepest regrets for what happened to Phillippe. I'm sure it has occurred to her that it was incredibly bad luck that he happened to be driving me. It could have been any one of the others. Of course, I intend to make sure she and his children are financially set."

Alisha told Barry: "I'm sure you don't care, but I'm letting you know that while the Lexus is badly damaged, our mechanic has examined it and he thinks it possibly could be fixed. Yes, it probably would cost a fortune, but I wonder if you want to do anything with it at all."

"Absolutely not. Phillippe loved that car and he died in it. I almost died. When I thought back on the accident, I did wonder how badly damaged the car was. I knew I was very lucky to walk away with nothing broken. I also wondered about Phillippe and if he suffered much before they murdered him. What I want is to never see it again. I also want to know that no part of it is ever on the road again. So, when the police are finished with the car, tell Fred that he is to arrange for it to be crushed into scrap. Tell him to oversee the job himself, so no one gets the idea of using any of the parts."

"Barry, it is so nice to have you back!" Alisha said. "You won't believe how worried people like Alejandro and Tommy Chu were. They must have called every day. And of course, I had a parade of our employees every day checking in."

Barry brushed his hair with his hands and said, "I missed my trim last week—tell Alejandro I'm ready for him! And tell

Tommy that I think I've lost 10 pounds and need some new clothes.

"And thank you, Alisha, for holding down the fort. You continue to amaze me," and he asked for a tight hug.

■ ■ ■

Patrick was the next visitor. "I'm finally allowed to come and see you," he said. "Elizabeth and Maya put me low down on the visitor list and I needed multiple permissions before being allowed to enter your room."

Barry laughed. "Thank you for all you've done. The FBI tells me I owe my life to your sleuthing, and the watch. That was amazing how you decoded the distortion of the GPS coordinates. Going forward, I don't intend to keep that watch. It has too many memories attached to the kidnapping and one of the kidnappers had actually worn it for several days. I hear that is how you were able to track me. Thank you, thank you. I intend to get a new watch and make sure the GPS coordinates reflect where I am—no distortions. There will be no more secrets. Clive is not going to have any more problems with me.

"I hear it's been a very rocky week, and it must've been hard for Elizabeth and the kids. Thank Maya for coming to stay at the house. Elizabeth mentioned how much effort you both have put into helping to keep her distracted. I saw Jennifer and Julian today and they both look great but I realize it must have been tough. I'm finished with Tiffany. Elizabeth and I intend to work at our marriage. I've made her and myself a promise, and it will involve a lot of therapy."

Patrick looked at Barry, and asked, "Do you know that at the beginning of your disappearance, Elizabeth was considered a possible suspect? When the FBI considered the serious possibility that you might be dead, they got together a list of suspects, and she was on it. Now don't get mad; you know why she made the list. She's been very outspoken about her rage at you for parading Tiffany around town and upset that your children were dealing with spiteful comments at school. The divorce proceedings have dragged on for months and it was no secret that the two of you were fighting over every stick of furniture you owned. While staying with Elizabeth, I've clearly seen that she still loves you."

Patrick smiled at Barry, then said, "I just love it when things work out in the end." They laughed.

"The other thing that kind of muddied the waters," Patrick said, "is that a number of loonies started to call in, swearing they'd seen you in all kinds of places. Pick a point on the map and I bet someone was calling from there. As there was no ransom note, one possibility being considered was that you had gone rogue. The FBI's list of top fugitives includes many from our sector running away from their cybercrimes. I seriously argued against that possibility. But it did add to the workload as each sighting had to be examined. They even considered the possibility Tommy Chu may have hidden you in his garment truck, taken you to his factory in San Diego, and from there ferried you across the border!"

Barry then asked Patrick about Sherlock. "I imagine it helped in the investigation, but which version were you using?" Patrick smiled and said, "The base product our labs developed and we licensed to Polestar. I am sure you have evolved the tool, but somehow I doubt it has a GPS fudge factor feature." They both chuckled and Barry said, "Thank God for brilliant friends. Even more for loyal ones." and also asked him for a hug.

16

The China Connection

Reggie called Maria to ask if Polestar's own internal investigation had revealed anything that could help her and Lars.

Maria agreed to meet with them if they consented to the stipulation that Polestar was not opening its kimono to its commercial and customer data. Reggie and Lars checked with federal and state attorneys, who agreed on the condition that the stipulation "would not cover information publicly shared or already known to us"—in order to not compromise any IRS, SEC, or other federal, state, and local investigations of Polestar already in progress.

Maria also insisted any meeting take place at the Polestar campus. Lars snarked to Reggie that they should add their own stipulation—"Only if they guarantee a pot of hot black coffee at all times. No Americano crap and not the witches brew Patrick drinks."

When the meeting convened, Maria also had invited Tina Chang and Polestar's CIO—Vijay Mehta. Vijay looked Indian but spoke like a natural-born US citizen. He elaborated that as CIO he had been asked to investigate a complaint of a breach of data from a pushy CEO named Bob Lonigan at a partner firm. He had called in a menacing tone and said that his customers were threatening lawsuits and that Polestar would have to be part of the defense because it was their hosted GPU as-a-service infrastructure his company used which had allowed the breach.

Lars asked Vijay to repeat Bob's name and, upon hearing it again, looked at Reggie with raised brows, to indicate that this was the same guy Patrick had on his suspect list.

"We started our investigation and it looked like the breach originated in Western China," Vijay explained. "Tina uses an outsourcing vendor there, KoalaSoft in Chongqing."

It was Reggie's turn to give a meaningful look at Lars.

Tina jumped in and said the Chinese pronounce it "Chaan-Ching." She then presented what she knew. "Vijay asked me for the names of key people at our outsourcing firm there, and his staff did forensics around their access to our systems. I know the owner, Ming Yueng, as a straight-up guy from the time I first met him at the large HP plant there. That's before he started KoalaSoft. Back then, in his broken English and with my basic Chinese—and plenty of hand motions—he communicated how grateful he was to both HP and the Chinese government for their roles in developing that part of the country. Historically, China's industrial development was in the eastern part of the country. Lots of his friends and neighbors would migrate east for work, come home for short holidays, and then tell him of their loneliness and isolation. He was one of the lucky ones to find a reasonably local job at the plant.

"He asked to start an email relationship with me—to improve his English—and I always liked his optimistic tone. He would describe how Chongqing was blossoming into a major logistics hub as China transformed Marco Polo's Silk Road into a modern-day network of rail and air cargo connections to Europe. He hoped to travel one day on today's version of the Oriental Express.

"He still occasionally sends me proud updates on his city. But his relationship now is much more formal, and it's with Vijay's group—which suits me fine. The mood in the US these days is suspicious of anything or anybody Chinese. Even though I'm not from the mainland and my parents left Hong Kong when I was very young, I told myself to stay away from this hot potato. I have a long but casual relationship with Ming, and I figured at the right time I could discreetly ask Ming to do his own review.

"With Barry's disappearance, I had another session with Vijay, who said it looked like the breach had downloaded data from the partner's banking applications. His team's investigation was pointing to someone in Ming's firm but they weren't sure if that employee had his credentials compromised.

"I knew if I asked Vijay for permission to call Ming he would refuse. So I decided to ask for forgiveness instead, if it was needed. I called Ming and cut to the chase. I told him,

'Your firm is under a cloud. Can you discreetly ask your IT to review who has been accessing Polestar servers?'

"Ming said 'Absolutely!' He has a strong IT team going back to his HP days and they defended his company from some of the world's best hackers who were his neighbors in China. Not surprisingly, his IT team jumped in with both feet.

"Ming called me back in a couple of days, and said, 'Three of our employees registered for one of Polestar's webinars. They all reported strange phishing emails soon after. We're continuing to investigate but you may want to have your IT check on how your marketing team protects event and registration data. I have emailed you the webinar details.'

"I passed it on to Vijay, asking him how we protect webinar registration data. I told him I'd received a complaint that someone in our marketing group may be selling their email and other information."

Vijay then took the floor. "We have a group responsible for data privacy and they followed up with Tina, who passed on information about the specific webinar. The marketing team confirmed they had a temp who had helped administer the webinar, but he was long gone.

"Our security team checked on this temp's credentials. His name is Josh Hemsley. Somebody had extended his access to Polestar systems long after the webinar. He had logged on a couple of times. So had one of Ming's employees or someone with their credentials. They had signed on for extended sessions.

"We checked on Hemsley's details in our vendor master. Further investigation showed that Hemsley has a history as an Initial Access Broker, an IAB, on the dark web. IABs know how to gain access to corporate environments and then sell that access on dark-web alleys. Polestar had hired him on the recommendation of the previous CMO—Chad Rogers."

Lars looked at Reggie again, as if to say, "*Another* name on Patrick's suspect list!"

Maria took over. "I'll let you guys connect the dots, but Chad called our law firm and told them he had proof Barry was downloading GPUMagic's banking data. GPUMagic is Bob Lonigan's company and they do business with several NYC banks."

Maria had specifically told her team not to mention that Sheldon Freres data was involved in the breach. She thought it was more of a commercial issue and had nothing to do with the Barry matter. If they had mentioned Sheldon Freres, Reggie and Lars would have also gotten a bead on Tony, another name Patrick had mentioned.

As CIO, Vijay had briefed Clive, Maria, and Bill. Vijay said, "A flurry of audit trails have led to the sickening realization that Polestar's own language models had ingested data that belonged to a few banks without their explicit permission. The only tiny bit of good news is that the data had been anonymized. The bad news is the banking GenAI use cases were the showpiece of Barry's recent presentation at Analyst Day."

Vijay said that his team was leading an investigation on how someone like Josh could cut across different firewalls they had for their hosting business, suppliers, and marketing employees.

17

Just Rewards

Reggie and Lars debriefed with Patrick after their visit to Polestar HQ. This time Lars was much more friendly and volunteered what they had learned so far.

Patrick listened and then said, "Paulie is somehow connected to Tony. And Chad and Bob also appear to be linked. Start by questioning Paulie and Chad at the same time, though separately of course. I mean one is in California and the other is in Florida, so synch it to reduce chances they may talk if they know each other."

Reggie asked Ramon to round up Paulie and Lars would pick up Chad.

They had found Paulie in New Port Richey, in Pasco County, FL.

"Hello, Paul Carlo Modigliani," announced Ramon when Paulie answered the door.

At first, Paulie denied leaving Florida. "California?! What the fuck are you guys smoking?"

Ramon said they had a video of him flying the drone into the ravine.

Paulie cracked, "Do you motherfuckers track me everywhere?"

When Paulie was brought in for questioning, Ramon shared with his lawyer that they already knew plenty about Paulie's UPC and QR code tampering scams. "We know that Paulie knows his way around print technology," Ramon said, "courtesy of an internship at the Hillsborough Tax Collector's office. They issue driver's licenses, vehicle tags, fishing and hunting permits, auto titles, and other title certificates. They print on polycarbonate, specialized plastic and paper and use a wide variety of printers. They also outsource large-scale copying tasks. Paulie knows how to work with the firmware to control the printer speed to optimally heat car license tag stickers. He learned about various fonts and inks and holograms that citizens received on their documents. He observed the UV imaging, microprinting, raised characters, and laser perforations on plastics and other security techniques that various agencies were trying out. He learned from the outsourcing contractor about high-speed mass copying and printing.

"One of Paulie's earliest scams was that he would print UPC and QR codes at home with a jury-rigged printer. His bros would walk into stores and stick them on top of the authentic codes on the packaging of electronics and digital toys. That way they would pay $34.99 for an item priced at $199.99, or $21.99 for a $99.99 item. Then they'd sell the packages under assumed names on eBay at 20 percent below list and still rake in a solid margin.

"Some of his bros were not very careful in their practices. One had been caught on surveillance tapes at a couple of Targets, affixing the fake codes. Another had used a self-checkout counter at Home Depot and they had a crisp photo of him paying a fraction of the cost for a cordless blower. At Best Buy, the system didn't recognize a fake UPC code, and that gang member ran off in a panic—all of it captured on video.

"Also, Paulie had gotten greedy. He'd print fake debit and credit cards with data from the dark web, and then his gang was using them to pay for even the base $21.99 and $34.99 purchases.

"Clearly, Paulie has moved on to bigger things, including drone technology. You can make it easy for both of us and tell us what he was doing with drones in California in the first place."

■ ■ ■

In the meantime, Lars had caught up with Chad, who initially tried to humor his way out. He also did more of the talking than his lawyer did.

"Chad, we know a lot about your marketing skills. I am a simple guy. All I want to hear is why you felt comfortable calling Polestar's law firm and saying Barry was helping himself to customer data."

"Because I heard that from Bob Lonigan," Chad replied.

"Start from the beginning. Who is Bob and why would you believe him?"

Chad then ran off at the mouth, until Lars finally interrupted him.

"How do you know Josh Hemsley?"

"Who?"

"Polestar tells us Josh was a contractor you brought in when you were there?"

"My team hired hundreds of employees."

"Chad, this one may have you in deep trouble. He managed to abuse Polestar webinar access credentials then used them to download data using a Chinese IP address."

"Who? What?"

"Chad, I think we should stop right now and reconvene when you hire a different lawyer or let this one do more of the talking."

∎ ∎ ∎

Meanwhile, Paulie's lawyer was explaining to Ramon about Jimmy, Paulie's "uncle." "Jimmy took Paulie under his wing from when he was little. Paulie was always good with gadgets. Jimmy would buy him Lego sets when he was young and continued to give him mechanical sets, robots, drones, and 3D printers as he grew up. You know all about his wizardry with printers. You guys nailed him for that. Jimmy owns several rental properties and Paulie is Jimmy's IT manager. He also likes to work with drones."

"So, what does that have to do with Paulie being in California?" Ramon asked.

"Jimmy suggested Paulie open a technology startup and get on the *Barracuda* TV show to raise some money. Next, he said there's a company called Polestar which does something similar for investments, just not on TV. Go to California and see if you can get into the second stage where you get to meet the CEO, Barry. The first round is a slide presentation.

"Paulie went well prepared with his slides about a fictional startup which had a security solution for the various scams in the verticals Polestar focused on. They were sure Paulie would get a follow-up, one-on-one meeting. What he didn't realize was the presentation format was the real challenge."

Ramon asked Paulie to elaborate.

"Each fucking presentation was limited to five minutes and HAD to go through all 20 slides. Presenting for only 15 seconds a slide is way tougher than you would think. Why the stingy time? The tagline was, 'Mrs. Generous will gladly spend more time with you if you need more time,' which was a swipe at one of the judges on the TV show. If you met the rules and Barry liked what he heard, he would invite you back for a longer presentation. I fucked it up royally and then I tried to make small talk with Barry, but security asked me to leave."

"Barry, the CEO? And why did you specifically want to meet Barry?" Ramon quizzed.

"Because Jimmy had a message for Barry that he wanted me to deliver."

And the message was?

"Can't you go easy on Tony in New York? He's struggling with the costs of caring for his disabled child."

"Who's Tony?"

"I don't know," Paulie claimed. "Jimmy just told me to memorize that line and said Barry would understand. I was to make it sound like an offer Barry would be unwise to refuse. But I couldn't deliver the message. I had one job, and then I tried to unfuck it on my own. I had to deliver that message. I needed a car and somebody hooked me up with Juan."

"Is that the guy with the tattooed head?" Ramon asked. "How do you know him?"

"We don't—other than he is a vicious motherfucker. You're lucky you escaped alive. Worse, the car was stolen and you're on tape with it. Don't ever bother going back to California. If Juan doesn't get you, California's finest will," Ramon counseled him.

■ ■ ■

When Lars reconvened the interview, Chad finally let his lawyer take over. "Look we want to make a plea deal and in return Chad can provide information that would help you nail Bob as the one behind the kidnapping."

Lars called Reggie. "Chad is such a flake—could we trust him? However, we need more information to incriminate Bob in the actual kidnapping. I'm loath to discuss a plea deal with this 'fearless leader' but we need to have as much information as possible before questioning Bob."

Reggie agreed. "Okay, let's go for it."

Once again, the interview continued. Chad said, "Look, it's well-known that I hate Barry for what he did to me and so when Bob called me and ranted and raged about Barry stealing his data and selling it to the Chinese, I happily joined in and we bashed Barry. We talked about how Barry was literally a spy and deserved to be properly interrogated. We fantasized about him being kidnapped. We even talked about how easy it would be as Barry is famous for his light security. Bob felt it was unfair that the worst Barry would suffer is a fine.

"As usual, Bob was drunk and I want to make it clear that it was just a 'bash Barry' session and I never thought that Bob might do anything. However, as soon as I heard about Barry going missing, I immediately thought of Bob. He'd told me he had connections in DC to make it happen. Look, I didn't know for sure it was Bob but I hate Barry and I decided to say nothing. As far as I was concerned, after talking to Bob I believed Barry was selling information and he deserved to be punished. He ruined my life and I had no sympathy for him."

Lars asked, "Did Bob talk about the ravine at all?"

"Yes, as I said we talked of a fictional kidnapping and the ravine was considered a good spot."

Lars thought this information fitted with what Barry called a "professional hit job." He said, "I want to remind you that you are still on the hook for your guy hacking the Polestar system. It all sounds suspicious." He also thought that Chad was a piece of shit but that at least this would be very helpful in questioning Bob.

• • •

Ramon next interviewed Jimmy. Figuring Jimmy wouldn't be the cakewalk that Paulie turned out to be, Ramon went in loaded with facts. "We know you sent Paulie to deliver a threatening message to Barry about Tony. We know that from a video featuring Paulie and his drone and his phone call to you, plus Paulie has spilled his guts. We know you're Paulie's godfather and you've been extremely generous to him. But we want to hear about Tony."

They had expected Jimmy to be feisty, but he was surprisingly reasonable.

"This is all my doing. Tony specifically told me not to intervene and I still did. Tony and I go way back to when we were young punks. He went the clean route, into corporate life. I went into real estate. Tony has a disabled son, and I'm the kid's godfather. I'm as generous to him as I am to Paulie. Tony and I meet two or three times a year. We both love the Yankees and we love steaks. The Yankees' and Rays' stadiums, Lugers and Berns, the steakhouses, are big parts of our lives."

Ramon interjected, "Look, we all have a love/hate relationship with the Yankees, especially in Tampa. The Big Apple vs. the Big Guava rivalry. But what does Tony have to do with Barry's kidnapping?"

"That I don't know. Paulie swears he didn't get close to Barry during his presentation. Then he stupidly tried to follow Barry's car and somehow deliver my message. And he happened to see Barry's car dive into the hole in the ground. And even more stupidly, he tried to use his drone to check on Barry. You know, I used to think Paulie was off the charts on

274

smarts. Now I'm pretty sure he's a dumbass. Sure, a bright guy in some ways, but for common sense—nada."

"So, you're saying Paulie just happened to be at the wrong place at the wrong time?"

"Yeah, that's the scoop."

. . .

To interview Bob, who had lawyered up with a power-house attorney, Reggie and Lars tag-teamed.

First, Bob attacked Chad. "You know he had a humiliating exit from Polestar. He's the one you guys should be focused on. His boy wormed his way into several Polestar systems and made it look like Chinese intelligence was involved. That fooled me too."

From then on, Bob's legal strategy was to "deny, deny, deny."

In the end, it was the SEC which nailed Bob. As a Polestar partner, over the years he had accumulated a sizeable chunk of PLST stock. He had sold some Polestar shares on the morning following Barry's kidnapping, hoping they were small enough bundles to fly under the SEC's radar—but in total, they amounted to over $9 million, definitely enough for the SEC to notice.

His lawyers argued the sell trades were timed to be just ahead of the earnings call that day, nothing to do with the kidnapping. Then they argued he was not an "insider" and that the SEC was merely on a fishing expedition to help out the FBI investigation. Neither strategy worked.

Bob settled with the SEC, agreeing to turn over the profits from the Polestar stock sales and paying a fine of $1 million. Barry was furious Bob got no jail time and made sure Polestar decertified Bob's firm GPUMagic as a partner, which got Bob fired as CEO.

. . .

Reggie got the big guns from the FBI's Manhattan office involved. In turn, Tony was even more lawyered up. His interview was the first testimony in this investigation where everyone was wearing a jacket and tie.

Tony's position was pretty straightforward. "Let me just say, Jimmy overreached. He tried to have the kid Paulie do my work? I have never met Paulie and I warned Jimmy to stay out of my business. Jimmy's well-meaning but he has zero idea how corporate negotiations work. Lots of expensive talent screaming and cussing, but no physical violence. For the sake of my son, I would hope you can go easy on him."

"What about Bob?"

Tony replied, "Is he involved in the kidnapping? His company has access to some of our bank's data and I know Polestar allowed a breach of our data. We are in legal negotiations with them. Again, all very corporate, no physical violence."

. . .

Reggie and Lars spent many hours over the next week looking at all the notes, reading the transcribed interviews, and confirming the connections they found.

They still did not know who exactly had kidnapped Barry. Chad indicated that Bob had used his connections in DC, but nothing could be verified. Bob denied everything and it was thanks to the SEC that they had a conviction. The two investigators were also surprised that Barry stopped threatening to call all his contacts in Washington and try to find out more about the kidnappers. When asked, Barry told them that he was now convinced that he would never find out the truth and it was better to use his contacts to help with his business needs. His company's stock price was still down.

■ ■ ■

It took a while for all of the indictments to be pulled together. In the meantime, the rumor mill took off.

One tabloid managed to get a hazy picture of the four ladies in swimsuits at Elizabeth's. They ran a column titled, "Partying while Barry was burning." Other rumors flew about Bob, Tony, Tina, and Maya. While the technology sector likes to think of itself as analytical and "science based," it can be as gossipy as Hollywood.

Someone even started a rumor that Elizabeth and Patrick had been in cahoots and organized Barry's kidnapping. That rumor particularly irked Tucker. Not only did Patrick not get any of the credit for his help in the investigation, but he was also getting the blame? Noticing Tucker's irritation, his marketing chief, Angela, called her blogger friend and said, "the time is right."

The blogger ran a story about how Oxford labs had a long history of working with law enforcement and that Patrick had been embedded in the Barry kidnapping investigation. Oxford refused to comment for the story.

The blogger next turned to tweeting: *"If frigging bee-keepers can have movies made about them and become part of FBI folklore, then why not technology analysts?!"*

He had links to his article in the tweet, and created a groundswell of interest, especially in technology and intelligence circles. After hearing about it, Reggie called Patrick to remind him of the NDAs Oxford had with the Feds, and Patrick apologized and said he would get to the bottom of it.

Tucker shared with Patrick that with all the publicity, plus renewed market interest in Polestar, the phone was ringing nonstop at Oxford headquarters. New business was flowing in, and Oxford's IPO was likely to happen sooner than planned.

■ ■ ■

Shortly after the SEC made known their findings, Bob was found dead on the streets of San Francisco. An eyewitness claimed two disheveled men had knifed and robbed Bob. A description of the men was given to the police but the perpetrators were never found.

When Barry was informed of Bob's brutal murder, he showed little surprise. He merely quipped that overused phrase, "Karma is a bitch."

■ ■ ■

The investigators later found out that Sheldon Freres informed Tony that due to the publicity from the FBI investigation, they were severing ties with him. However, they gave him a $5 million exit package for negotiating a $100 million settlement with Polestar for the data breach. That enabled Tony to set up a healthy-sized trust fund for the care of his disabled son. He was also advised by his attorney to not have any connection with Jimmy going forward.

In fact, Tony came through the whole process better than unscathed. With some of the exit package from Sheldon Freres, he started a consulting practice to help companies monetize their data assets. The firm was named TOUOS Partners. They would tell everyone it stood for a Japanese alphabet or a take-off on the French word for "everyone," but in reality, it was an acronym for "The Oil Under Our Sand."

Tony and his new partners invited many of his procurement executive clients and prospects to TOUOS's first meeting with this manifesto, "We are brothers in arms. For too long, technology vendors have kicked us around and gotten away with obscene margins and poor service levels. We will help you renegotiate your contracts. We will help you lobby for "right to repair" laws so you are not dependent for life on vendors you buy technology from. Even better, we will help you monetize your data assets. You deserve the status of a salesperson with a proprietary asset, not just a powerless, back office executive."

■ ■ ■

Chad was sentenced to 18 months in prison. Rumors circulated that he was welcomed there to chants of "All Hail, Chad Caesar," and that he fit in remarkably well.

■ ■ ■

The contractor, Josh Hemsley, was nowhere to be found other than on the FBI list of fugitives under the "Cyber" category.

■ ■ ■

Jimmy was fined $250,000 and instructed to disassociate himself from Paulie. He was to be closely monitored by digital surveillance going forward. But he was also told not to worry about Tony's son—he was well taken care of.

■ ■ ■

Paulie was sentenced to a year of community service helping libraries and schools with their tech support. In the end, Oxford Research hired him for their labs team in St. Petersburg. He became an excellent "white hat" ethical security hacker.

■ ■ ■

Tiffany was surprised and delighted by the generosity of the offer Barry's lawyer presented to her attorney. She thought *"I'm taking it as a sign that some part of him still loves me."* She signed all the papers and didn't object to the nondisclosure.

Once she cashed the check, she treated all her friends to a meal at the famous French Laundry in Yountville, CA. Her lawyer screamed at her, "I hope your guests didn't order the Miyazaki Wagyu and Regiis Ova Caviar Tasting Menu!" He insisted she visit a financial advisor he knew. "Let me remind you that you owe taxes on the settlement I helped negotiate on your behalf. Also, Barry will never be your sugar daddy again. You'll need serious help stretching out the money."

■ ■ ■

The FBI never did find the shadowy men known as Athos and D'Artagnan.

■ ■ ■

To the surprise of many, Polestar started to win several lucrative Department of Defense contracts. No one had previously considered them serious contenders but now they needed to be watched in all future bids. Additionally, the Sherlock tool was getting a lot of interest from law enforcement agencies around the world. The stock had recovered nicely with the promise of these new revenue streams—helped by Charles Morgan upgrading them to a "Strong Buy." Many Polestar employees facing retirement and navigating divorce settlements were greatly relieved.

■ ■ ■

The caller with the 'Don Corleone accent,' who had threatened Maya, was never found. Upon their return from California, Patrick and Maya found the Oxford staff in

Cambridge more relaxed as Tucker had assured them that no one would be forced to relocate to Florida. Maya shook her head and said to Patrick: "We obviously did not do a good job selling Florida with its low taxes or St. Pete and its pier, the Dali, and the James."

18

West Coast on the East Coast

Maya excitedly chattered with Elizabeth about the Romans' upcoming Florida trip.

"We're going to put you and the kids in suites at the historic Vinoy on the St. Petersburg waterfront. It's a book-end to a mile-long stretch which ends at the Dali Museum and has a private airport you can fly into. There are several other museums, a grand Pier, banyan trees, the Yacht club, plus all kinds of cafes and restaurants on that stroll. And our new office."

Elizabeth said, "Maya, I can't wait to go to the Dali and the James museums in particular and the kids would love all the stuff on the pier. Barry has already checked out the flight path into Albert Whitted Airport. Thanks so much for helping with the logistics."

"I'll plan your week and we'll join you as often as you want," Maya said, "and my boss, Tucker, may fly in for a day. Barry knows him. Tell the kids I have some unusual games and beach time planned for them. And a visit to a miniature circus they will talk about for a long time."

■ ■ ■

"Life is good," Barry said, lines crinkling around his eyes and a broad smile across his face. Patrick could not recall a time when he'd seen Barry so relaxed and genuinely happy. "I don't think I've told you yet. You wouldn't believe how many phone calls I get every day from people wanting to tell my story!" Barry said.

"We saw the *People* magazine article," Maya said. "They did a great job. And I loved the photographs."

"Me too!" Elizabeth agreed. "In fact, I ordered a 30-by-40-inch canvas print of the family portrait for our house. Not sure where I'm going to hang it yet."

"In my Polestar office, Betsey," Barry said. "To remind me who I'm working for."

Barry continued, "But really, you'd be shocked by all the media attention I've gotten. Everyone is fascinated by the story of my kidnapping. All of the big Hollywood studios." He counted them out on his fingers: "20th Century, Warner Brothers, Paramount, Columbia, and Universal. They all want the movie rights. And I'm sure given our tech connections we can entice Netflix and Amazon."

"Aha," Patrick thought. *"Now here's the Barry I recognize. He's gotten plenty of placements for Polestar products in movies. Why not himself?"*

Barry added, "I've told them all, 'First studio that can get Henry Cavill to agree to play me, that's the offer I'll listen to.'"

Maya thought, *"Barry only wishes he looked like Henry Cavill,"* but refrained from saying that aloud. She asked, "What do you think of that, Elizabeth? Is a movie a good thing, or an invasion of your privacy?" Maya herself was pleased that due to Oxford's NDAs, *"Patrick and my role would never catch the attention of Hollywood. And I am especially glad to stay away from Bollywood."*

Elizabeth replied, "If, and this is important, they can get Henry Cavill to play Barry in the film, then it's fine by me. As long as I get to hang around the set and ogle him." She laughed.

"And they need to get Blake Lively to play you, Betsey. She looks just like you," Barry said, and meant it.

■ ■ ■

Barry asked Patrick to take a walk with him. Not surprisingly, they ended up at the James Museum where Barry opened up to Patrick. "Grisham encouraged me to take this sabbatical. I'm spending quality time with Elizabeth, Julian, and Jennifer. You know how we technology vendors guilt our customers about 'technical debt' when they don't keep up with our speed of upgrades. My body reminds me every day I owe it a technical debt of sleep. After decades of only sleeping four hours, lately I've been sleeping a good six hours each night.

"Honestly, I think Grisham doesn't want me back. And I can't really blame him. But Elizabeth and I are still the biggest shareholders, and I want us to do a proper CEO search. It could end up being Grisham or Swanson or even someone from outside. I would like that outsider to be Patrick Brennan."

Patrick was startled. "I'm an analyst, not an operational executive."

"Don't kid yourself. You helped me launch our most successful division," Barry said.

"I'm flattered, but I've promised Tucker that I'll help him take Oxford public."

"Patrick, Maya is better at numbers than you are. Talk it over with her. I lost you once because I was too cheap. I won't fuck up again, I promise."

Patrick stayed silent but thought to himself: *This was the second such pledge he had made in the wake of his kidnapping. Could he stay true to his promises to both Elizabeth and to Patrick?*

■ ■ ■

The week flew by. They went to the Dali Museum. Patrick gave them a tour of the James.

Tucker flew down for a couple of days and invited Barry to present at the office. Henry from the labs division and the analysts in the office were particularly pleased to meet this giant in the automation sector. At lunch in the Yacht Club, Tucker and Barry discussed the flight into KSPG. Barry sheepishly admitted, "My chairman doesn't let me fly myself anymore, and I always have to fly with a bodyguard or two. So, we flew on a bigger plane than you probably did. Good news—we could fly nonstop. Bad news—the landing was a bit scary at this tiny airport. But man, isn't it great for you to fly in and just walk to your new digs?!"

There were plenty of nice meals. Patrick invited Ramon to join them for one.

Maya took them to the Ringling Museum in Sarasota. They dropped the kids off at the miniature circus and the adults went to admire Rubens' monumental canvases from the *Triumph of the Eucharist* series. They also took a tour of the opulent Ringling Mansion on the campus. Maya joked, "This was considered a 'billionaire's smart home' in the 1920s."

While Barry and Elizabeth lounged at a cabana at the Vinoy pool, "Aunty" Maya took the two kids to St. Pete beach with its soft white sand for parasailing and wave runners. They hit Uncle Andy's ice cream parlor at the Don CeSar coming and going.

Julian came back and pleaded with his parents—"Can we check out of here and spend a couple of nights at the Don? I want to go parasailing and jet skiing with Dad."

And so they did. Elizabeth and Jennifer spent quality time together at the spa and in the pool at the "Pink Palace." The kids were, of course, over the moon to have so much together time with their mom and dad.

Epilogue

Salt of the Earth—and the Ocean

The Romans were flying back home. Their plane trajectory had given them a last look at the waterfront where they had done so much in the past week.

Patrick suggested to Maya they go for a sunset sail under the Sunshine Skyway Bridge and farther into the Bay to the remnants of the old Skyway Bridge.

Patrick sailed from the North to the South Pier. Several fishermen waved at them. The piers were open 24-7 and the lights attracted fish at night.

He told Maya: "Look at the people waving at us. Each one of them has a similar story to the three you mentioned in your presentation at the Romans' place—the cat lady, the circus veteran, and the real estate agent. They pay a few bucks to be able to fish for a couple of hours and feed their families. People in our sector look down on these common folks. But I was really proud when you chose to describe those three 'salt-of-the-earth' Floridians."

The sun was dipping in the west, and Patrick said, "Hey, relocation wizard, why don't you find us a place where we can enjoy this view every evening?"

Maya responded, "Hey, hotshot detective, when you take us IPO."

Patrick considered telling Maya about Barry mentioning the possible Polestar CEO opportunity. He thought about telling her Tucker was going to file for IPO much earlier than anticipated.

Instead, he just hugged Miss Maya in the salty spray of the Gulf to the sound of countless pelicans. There would be plenty of time to discuss those opportunities—if they came to pass.

Acknowledgments

Vinnie Mirchandani

I am a storyteller. I have written countless case studies about corporate strategies, breakout products, and high-tech events in my technology innovation books.

This book required an intense focus on human emotion in terrifying, joyful, and humorous situations. For that I thank my wife, Margaret Newman. She always does a readability review of my business books and she dramatically shrunk here my usual analysis of technology speeds, feeds, and economics. She is also an astute observer of people and she forced us to dwell longer in many scenes and bring out emotional reactions from each character.

I want to thank my coauthor, Kimberly, for her persistence. We first discussed writing this book over 20 years ago. A lot has changed in the fast-moving tech sector, but unbelievably the major characters have survived somewhat intact since our earliest drafts. Along with Margaret, she also gets credit for fleshing out many of the strong female characters in the book. I have worked with many of them over my career and I am glad our book reflects their contributions to the technology world.

Writing a thriller was a whole new experience. Margaret convinced me to write more like John Grisham, and to be less wordy than Tom Clancy and James Michener, all authors I deeply respect. We also benefited from generous input from Tom Waite and Keith Raffel, both successful serial novelists. Mark Baven, my long-time editor, adjusted his style and brought a lot more humor into the book. In her usual professional manner, Michele DeFilippo and her creative team at 1106 Design polished the look and feel.

Of course, both California and Florida, the two main settings for the book have changed dramatically in those two decades since the first draft, as have the AI and automation sectors. There are even more changes in the technology analyst landscape. I have learned plenty on these topics from Malcolm Frank, Jujhar Singh, John Wookey, Oliver Marks, Bruce Rogow, Duncan Chapple, Brian Sommer, Kay and Rusty Sanborn, Emilio and Beth Malave, Lydia and Tom Chimera, Russ Wiener, and many others.

I am grateful for the front-row view of the technology sector I have enjoyed for four decades. There are so many who have been consistent and reliable sources of counsel and inspiration including Ray Lane, Hasso Plattner, Marc Benioff, Aneel Bhusri, and Sridhar Vembu. I have learned plenty from execs such as Sandra Lo, John Taschek, Angela Barbato, and Stacey Fish who keep evolving the Analyst Relations craft and from colleagues including Dennis Howlett, Paul Greenberg, Frank Scavo, Ray Wang, and Erik Keller. I should apologize for not naming countless others who have influenced me along the way.

The technology analyst world does not get much publicity. We quite like it that way, but I am glad we could shine a light on this influential corner of the technology sector.

As Kimberly mentions, in spite of all this coaching and support, we likely got a few things wrong. No one to blame for that but us.

Kimberly McDonald Baker

I would like to acknowledge and thank the following people:

Dr. Sofia Merajver, who was the inspiration for the character Dr. Sofia Sapientiais. Dr. Merajver is an expert in breast cancer, and serves as the Scientific Director of the Breast Cancer Program and Medical Director of the Breast and Ovarian Cancer Risk Evaluation Program at the University of Michigan Rogel Cancer Center. Learn more about her life-changing research at https://merajver.lab .medicine.umich.edu/

Chuck Story, retired FBI Supervisory Senior Resident Agent, for helping us understand how the FBI works, and telling us exciting real-world stories. If we got it wrong in our book, it's not Chuck's fault!

Vinnie Mirchandani, my coauthor and writing mentor. Theresa Clark, whose insight from a career as trusted assistant to technology CEOs helped imbue plausibility into our fiction. Randy Egger, who kickstarted my Silicon Valley career and mentored me for decades. John Wookey, who set positive examples at Oracle that I carried with me throughout my career. My husband, Brinton E. Baker, whose encouragement is unwavering. My cousins Fred Bibik, Elizabeth Williams, and Alishia Terrill, for their insight and inspiration. And Zeta Tau Alpha sorority and my Zeta sisters, who taught me to always Seek the Noblest.

About the Authors

Vinnie Mirchandani is a leading technology analyst with a four-decade career at PwC, Gartner, and a firm he founded, Deal Architect. He has consulted with clients around the world and has worked, lived, and traveled in 75 countries. He has written nine books, countless blogs, and records a video channel on technology-enabled innovation.

He has been happily married for 35 years to Margaret Newman. She is no slouch either when it comes to global travel. They live in Florida and have two grown kids, Rita and Thomas, who have inherited their nomadic gene and spend very little time in Florida. Neighborhood pets have gladly taken their place.

Vinnie can be reached via https://www.linkedin.com /in/vinniemirchandani/

Kimberly McDonald Baker is a former Senior Product Director for the Oracle project management suite of enterprise applications, and former vice president of marketing and advisor for firms in the Oracle and Amazon Web Services ecosystems. After writing tens of thousands of pages of product and marketing content, this is Kimberly's first venture into fiction. She's been blessed with two decades of marriage to Brinton E. Baker, also a Silicon Valley veteran, with whom she shares a blended family of four daughters and three granddaughters.

Kimberly lives in Michigan and can be reached via https://www.linkedin.com/in/kimberlymcdonaldbaker/

Made in the USA
Columbia, SC
27 January 2025

52490457R00183